Windblown

www.facebook.com/fernfmusselwhite.author
fernfmusselwhite@gmail.com

ISBN: 978-0-9995419-3-7
Library of Congress Control Number: 2019945372

Cover Design and Artwork: Raghu Consbruck
www.eighteyes.com

Published in the United States by Inword Publishers
Interior Design: Bhakti-rasa
www.inwordpublishers.com

Genre: Fiction / Women / Grief / Love

Windblown

A Novel

Fern F. Musselwhite

Dedication

To my brother Phil, who never worried where the wind would take him.

And, of course, to my husband, Bob. My greatest love and support. I'm forever grateful to the northern gales that brought me to you.

Prologue

Maya

2013

Maya watches the wake disappear as she guides her boat through the channel. It's 6:51 a.m. The sun already glistens on the water, leaves a string of jewels behind the stern, sparkling and fleeting. Water. Heat. Wind. She feels each element on her skin. Feels the salt seep into her soul.

Every morning this moment calls her. The warm petals of the first rays of sun. The last few breaths of night. The cackle of a seagull; the movement of the tides. The simplicity of her presence. The beauty of her absence.

These are her days, a long way from the sandy streets of small-town Seaport, Massachusetts. Some afternoons when Maya stands on the boat platform, poling through the mangroves, she thinks about the improbability of her situation. The incongruity of a slight, quiet tomboy, who never really liked to swim, spending her days and earning her living on the water.

Maya likes the feel of the Keys, particularly Islamorada, which she calls home because it's where her mail comes and her boat sleeps. But she isn't sure if she has settled in Islamorada or settled for it. She isn't sure if her feet are firmly planted here or shifting with the sand. She isn't sure of a lot of things.

One

Charlie

1996

"WHERE WE HEADED TONIGHT?" Maya asked her dad as she climbed into bed, ready for her favorite ritual, their Saturday night Raymond Adventure.

"You said last week you wanted someplace more adventurous. Under that directive, we're going to Everest." Charlie sat on the edge of the bed, tucked the comforter around his eleven-year-old. She grinned and settled into her pillows.

He launched into the lengthy trip. A week trekking to Base Camp. Waiting as the body adjusted. Khumbu Icefall. Lhotse Face. The retreats to lower elevation to refuel, recover. Finally, the push from Camp 4.

"The last night before we summit, Mom crawls into the tent while you and I are catching a few extra minutes of sleep. She whispers to us, 'Naptime's over. Time to venture out into the cold, beautiful world.' She shimmies between us and unzips our sleeping bags, kisses each of us on the cheek.

"You, of course, whine about wanting a snooze button."

Maya nudged her dad. "No I don't! And I'm so sure you just jump out of your sleeping bag."

"*Ha, ha.* This is my story, so yes, I do. And, yes, you whine." He nudged her back. "Anyway, by this point it's almost eleven thirty. We need to be on the move by midnight. We add some layers, set our headlamps in place, eat a quick meal. Peanut butter and oatmeal," he said, before his daughter could ask. "Your mom, the consummate planner, hands me a hunk of cheese and some beef jerky to add to the protein bars and almonds in my pack. She loads up our oxygen canisters, checks our clothing."

Maya nodded, closed her eyes, pictured them finishing final chores as they prepared to leave.

"Wind whips across camp as the lights of our headlamps dance through the tent city. Above us a team is already beginning the climb. Your mom attaches our lines to the rope and leads us into the night. You pace a few steps behind. I keep you both in front, marvel at your tenacity. I watch your heads bow into the gusts. Check your feet as you trudge up the glacier. Make sure you stay on track.

"It's a slow, wrenching climb. Sometimes, as the snow blows across our path, it's a struggle to take just one step. Our breathing labors as we follow the line of climbers up the mountain. We can't see each other's faces behind the oxygen masks and goggles. After hours of straining, we clear the Hillary Step and reach the summit. The sky opens up, the world spreads far and wide below us. You and Mom rip off your masks and hats." He pictured their faces. Sierra's smile bright as the sunny morning. "Then you scream like crazy people. *Woohoo!*" Charlie jumped off the bed, hopped around the room. "We did it! We made it!"

Maya opened her eyes, laughed at her father. She reached up a tired hand to offer a high-five. He held her hand. "Then I gather you up and lift you higher still into the sky." He paused. "I can see your mom, her hands in the air, fists clenched. Head tilted back with joy." He swallowed the lump in his throat. "She would have been on top of the world."

He gently placed his daughter's hand under the comforter as her eyelids fluttered.

"The story can't end there," she said, sleep cradling her voice. "You talked about the trip up, but you skipped the trek down. What about getting back to the South Col? Base Camp? Back to Kathmandu and coming home?" She stretched an arm into the air and yawned.

He smiled, shook his head. "You barely stayed awake for the summit. Why don't we finish this one over pancakes in the morning?"

She rolled over and hugged her pillow. "Chocolate chip."

"You got it." He kissed her cheek and crossed the room.

I wonder what she would have loved more, he thought as he switched off the light. Summiting Everest, or a Saturday night bedtime story with us.

Two

1997

SUNLIGHT CREPT OVER WINDOWSILLS in the mornings. Evening nudged it out after a long day. Charlie shuttered windows and closed doors, hoping that by swaddling this growing child he could shield her from whatever else the world would try to take from her.

A house can be a prison or a refuge. A place of pain or comfort. Whatever the image, the feeling evoked, it is home. For Maya, the walls surrounding her in childhood provided shelter, stability, and by age twelve, moments of suffocation.

Maya was still feeling the contours of the world around her when Charlie moved them from the apartment over his parents' garage to a small house a few blocks from the ocean. It was a midcentury home that needed a little work, but he liked its quirks, liked the light and air that filled the rooms.

A few weeks after they moved in, Charlie brought a crew from his family's company, Raymond Construction, to the house to begin remodeling. He helped them unload their saws and drills, lumber and tile. As they worked around him, he thought about the last few years. How he became a single father, waking each day wondering if he was doing it right. If Sierra would be happy with how he was raising their daughter.

"Charlie, where do you want us to set up the tile saw, backyard?"

Startled, Charlie turned to his superintendent.

"Uh, yeah, Teddy, that's good, thanks."

"You okay, boss?"

"Yeah, fine, thanks. Backyard is good. I've got to get back to the office. Call if you have any questions."

Charlie walked out of the kitchen, letting the screen door slam as he headed to his truck. That will be the new sound in our life here, he thought. Maya will come home from school or a friend's house and swing that door open. She'll throw her book bag on a chair in the kitchen, and I'll have to tell her to put it in her room before she goes to the fridge for a snack.

He climbed into the truck and closed the door. Leaned back in his seat and stared at the house. That'll be our new normal, he thought, but will it ever be normal enough? He ran his fingers through his hair and rested his hands on the bottom of the steering wheel. It has to be, he thought. He sat for a moment, listened to the still of the truck. The empty street. He released a deep breath and started the engine.

As he drove to work, threads of last night's dreams floated across his windshield. Sierra standing in the doorway. The room dark, her face lit by the moon, a light that faded as she backed away. He called to her, but she turned toward the window and was gone. Waking with a start, he'd ripped the covers from the bed and jumped to the floor. The panting, the sweating. The hoping Maya hadn't heard.

He dried his palms on his jeans as he pulled into the office parking lot.

Over the next few weeks, Charlie's crew updated the kitchen and bathrooms, covered the surfaces in new flooring and paint. Other than these few changes, the settled nature of the place suited Charlie. He liked to sit at the kitchen table in the evening after Maya was in bed, the window open, and listen to the delicate notes of the wind chimes as the breeze carried away the remnants of another day. He hoped the change would be a fresh start. That's what his daughter needed, he told himself. What he needed. Maybe here he could stop waiting for his life to begin again. Maybe here he'd feel the cold floor under his bare feet in winter. He'd smell the grass when he cut the lawn on a summer evening. The world would come back to him.

Charlie chose this place for these and other reasons, but it was the other reasons he shared with those who asked. The business was doing better, so he could afford to move them out of the apartment. Maya was in middle school now. Time for her to have her own home, one she'd return to during college breaks and remember fondly as an adult. She should have her own yard, he'd said. She should have a dog.

Those were the reasons he shared with his family and friends when they asked about his house hunting. He didn't talk about the waiting, the dreams, the need for change. He didn't talk about anything that mattered.

Maya liked her new home, its shapes and sounds and smells, but not long after they moved in, wanderlust blew in with the ocean breeze. She took walks to the beach after school, sat in the sand to watch a bird dive into the surf, sometimes emerging with a fish that hadn't quite finished its last swim.

Other afternoons she walked down to the marina to watch

the commercial fishermen return with the day's haul. They smiled and waved, asked about her dad, encouraged her to get home before dark. Everyone knew each other around here, knew each other's stories. They looked out for each other. For Maya.

One night after the renovation was complete, she came home from school to find her dad in the kitchen unpacking groceries. "You're home early. What's up?" she asked, letting the screen door slam. Charlie looked up and grinned.

"I thought it would be nice to cook dinner together. We've been eating out of pizza boxes and at your grandparents' houses long enough. Figured we could use a new-home-cooked meal."

They stood at the counter, peeling carrots and potatoes and seasoning chicken, the smell of curry enveloping the kitchen. Charlie asked Maya about her day. She rattled off the results of a vocabulary quiz and the description of a reading assignment. Then she quieted into the work.

He stirred the sauce and thought of the old place, of the years he'd spent nurturing the toddler. Of how the training wheels seemed to come off in so many ways every day.

"Dad," she said slowly. "I love our new house. But do you ever feel like we left something behind at the apartment?"

"What do you mean?"

"I don't know, like, Mom?"

Maya looked at her dad and then away. At the cabinets, the floor, anywhere except at her father. She was afraid she'd hurt him, that just mentioning her mother would reignite whatever fire scorched his skin. Whatever pain he kept inside that made him scream at night.

Charlie turned down the flame on the stove and set the spoon on the counter. He stood for a moment looking at Maya, trying to remember the last time they'd talked about Sierra outside of a made-up bedtime story. He couldn't recall. It was easy to spin fairytales, wisps of pink and blue cotton candy, the sweetness melting on the tongue. The real memories carried the weight of sadness, the salty brine parching the throat as the words tumbled out.

"Do you think about Mom a lot?" he asked.

She didn't answer right away. She'd been stirring noodles, but his question drained the motion from her body. Maya held the spoon over the pot, a few inches above the heat, and stared into the vast space the kitchen had become. Charlie took the spoon from her hand, placed it on the counter, led her to the table. He sat her in a chair and pulled one out for himself. Looked at her face.

"Maya?"

"Yeah, I mean, I don't know. What's 'a lot?'" she asked, wondering if already she was failing her mother's memory. She thought of her mom but didn't live for her the way he did. Maya was aware she had her own life. She wasn't sure her father felt the same for himself.

He considered his daughter's question. How the lines between "a lot" and "enough" and "too much" blurred. Did you fill the void by never forgetting, or by giving yourself permission to think of something else?

There was no easy answer, at least none he could offer a twelve-year-old. A child needed to go to school and play outside and figure out the person she would become. An adult, well, his course was set. He could live amidst his grief, wrap himself in it, cover his ears and face against the wind and cold the sadness brought. But a child needed to be free, needed to shed those layers in hopes the frost would melt beneath a spring sun.

"I don't know, honey, everyone's different. But you have to live your life. Do your homework, see your friends, play with your cousins. Trick-or-treat, blow out your birthday candles. And if you think about Mom from time to time, if you wish she was with you, that's okay. But you don't have to think about her all the time. You need to live your life for you. Not for me, not for Mom. Understand?"

Maya nodded, afraid to ask her father whether he took his own advice. She rose from her chair and climbed into his lap, rested her cheek against his shoulder. He wrapped his arms around her, their breathing finding a common rhythm, the spices from the curry simmering into the evening air as the screen door tugged against the breeze.

"Dad," she said quietly, "I love our Saturday night stories. How you make up all these wild adventures about you and me and Mom traveling the world together, like she's still here. But you never really talk about her. What was it like when it was the three of us? Before she died?"

Charlie raised his daughter off his lap and motioned her to her chair. He gathered plates and utensils and placed their dinner on the table.

"The beginning was a challenge. We were so young when we had you. Your mom thought since we were newly married and you were a baby, she needed to focus on learning how to be a wife and mother before becoming a college student. So she put off her education. Your grandparents offered us the garage apartment, so we moved in there. After you turned one, Mom started taking classes." He paused, smiled. "She was excited to be back in school."

He sat down and continued between bites. "She was taking English and psychology. I think she was planning on becoming a therapist, or at least heading in that direction. And your Grammy Carolyn started taking care of you when Mom was in class."

He hesitated, chewed a fork full of curry.

"Then she got sick." Charlie looked off into the distance, down the hall, out the front door, up the block to the edge of the ocean. He looked into the far reaches of everything he knew, and he saw her. He saw her everywhere.

"She got sick, Maya," he said, standing to take their plates. "You were too young to remember. It all happened so fast." He stopped, unable to find any other words. "She got sick."

Maya stared at her lap as her father cleared the table. She heard the clatter, the silverware falling aimlessly into the sink. She turned to look at him, to watch his head fall below his shoulders. She saw him inhale, straighten, turn to face her.

"It's okay," she told him. "I have homework anyway."

She stood to leave, pushed in her chair. I don't need to know, she thought. I don't need to know why he hurts so much. I just need to watch out for him, make sure he's okay. She walked down the hall into her room and sat on her bed. Hugged her arms around her. The walls seemed close. Tomorrow, she thought, maybe I'll walk down to the ocean and watch the waves.

When the screen door closed behind her the following afternoon, Maya Raymond took the first steps that would lead her away from home.

Three

OVER THE YEARS CHARLIE took Maya on local trips. A week in the summer with his sister Karen and her family at a beach house. A few days camping in the mountains in the fall. With the construction company's success, he decided it was time for a real vacation.

He thought a kid her age deserved a trip to Disney World. He planned a week in Orlando at a high-end resort and spoiled his daughter with fancy dinners and t-shirts. They park hopped and laughed their way through rides and shows and parades. Yet from time to time, each drifted away in private thoughts of Sierra, quickly looking back to check on the other when the mind wandered too long. Neither wanted to admit that the trip felt incomplete. Having included Sierra in so many bedtime stories, each felt her absence. Home was a place for two. Travel meant three. After all these years of life as a pair, the father and daughter each grieved the loss of their imaginary travel companion.

Without discussion, they returned to the familiar comfort of local vacations, surrounded by family and the distractions of the large group. They made memories over campfires and hot dogs and plastic wine glasses the adults left beside Adirondack chairs to chase errant frisbees and footballs. They read books and watched movies and soaked in the love and frenzy, and on Saturday nights they wandered down to the beach, sat in the sand, and shared a story with Sierra.

From time to time Charlie drove his daughter into Boston. Holding her hand through the stalls of Faneuil Hall, stopping for giant slices of pizza dripping with gooey cheese. Strolling down Hanover Street to Mike's Pastry for luscious cannoli so big she'd squeal each time they approached the counter. Small journeys away from home into the wonder of the city and its sweet delights. And each year, on the third Monday in April, he took her to Boylston Street. They'd line up across from the library, eating bagels and drinking hot chocolate, and they'd cheer for the runners, screaming out bib numbers. When a runner heard them, gave them a thumbs up, they'd high-five each other. Celebrating the Boston Marathon became a special tradition that belonged to them. To father and daughter together.

On occasion, they'd rise early on a Saturday morning and drive north or west. New Hampshire, Vermont, western Massachusetts. Anywhere he found a trail head. A dirt path that led up and up through the trees until the forest of oaks dwindled, then spruce. The climb through open clearings, past the tree line and the last few scattered shrubs that shivered in the cool winds of craggy elevation. Winds that blew a harsh chill through the mountains even in summer. They would walk silently up the trail, deep in thought, over roots and rocks until they reached the top. Until they couldn't get any closer to heaven. To her.

Father and daughter learned to talk without speaking, to touch without feeling. They understood this silent language to be one of survival, the unspoken words charging the air like a thunderhead rolling in off the ocean. The low hum buzzed just behind the ear, just out of reach. The undercurrent like the ache of a dull pain.

As Maya entered adolescence, she learned more of the language of loss from watching her father. She learned stoicism, and that movement kept a mind busy, kept it from further breaking a fractured heart. She learned that sometimes it was easier to avoid than to face, easier to leave than to stay.

Raymond Construction continued to grow. Charlie's work days lengthened. He stayed later at the office, took work home. The stresses of the business kept other thoughts away. Contracts and deadlines dominated his dreams. Sierra appeared on occasion, but the space between her visits allowed Charlie to move along, if not on.

Maya took on more responsibility, cooking meals on her own. She never complained, handling her chores in quiet solitude. Without the presence of her mother, the sunlight faded into a deeper shade of night in the Raymond home, nudging Maya into adulthood.

By the time she entered ninth grade, Maya found comfort in the simple tasks of chopping, stirring, seasoning. They became routine, a function of her life. Cooking taught her to be self-sufficient and gave her time to think. Charlie watched as his daughter began to run the house. Time for a reward.

She was marinating steaks when the front door opened.

"Hey, Dad," she yelled. Before he could reply, she heard the rush of small feet. She turned to see a puppy skidding across the kitchen floor.

"Oh my God! He's adorable! Wait, is it a he or she?"

"It's a he," Charlie said, laughing. "Straight from the pound. I thought about taking you, but I knew you wouldn't be able to pick just one. This way, all you have to do is name him."

"Does he have a name yet? We don't want to confuse him." She knelt to pet the dog.

"They called him Archie. He came in with a brother, who they named Jughead. Jughead's already been adopted, so we have this one. He's some kind of mutt. I think he has some lab in him, but I don't know what else. So, Archie?"

"Archie's perfect."

"Then Archie it is. You'll have to walk him in the morning and after school and feed him. He's your responsibility."

"Dad, please, I've totally got this," she said, ignoring her father and picking up the puppy. He turned his scruffy head, looked at her sideways out of one big, brown eye and licked her cheek. Awesome, she thought.

Maya kept her promise. When Archie woke before her or her father and pattered down the hall, she was the one who leapt from bed and grabbed his leash. After a few weeks, the dog learned to come to her bedside when he needed to go out. He'd circle the room, wag his tail and pant, and if that didn't wake her he'd put his front paws by her pillow. Maya might be in the middle of a dream when the heat of doggy breath roused her, but she loved it. She'd rub his head and grab a jacket and flip flops, boots if it was winter. She gave him a treat before she left for school and dinner following his afternoon walk.

Before long she was teaching him to sit and shake. He sat by her chair while she studied and by the kitchen table while she cooked. Bits and pieces of love she couldn't give to her father or friends and family she gave to this dog. Archie swallowed them whole and gave them right back. Archie loved Charlie, but he adored Maya.

Quiet by nature, Maya's introspectiveness followed her through high school. She had close friends and made good grades, but she didn't stand out, didn't perform in school plays or earn varsity letters. For release, she laced up a pair of running shoes and jogged along the beach. Sometimes she brought Archie. Other days she craved the space of being alone. When she needed to think, she ran south to the lighthouse. When she felt like racing her shadow, north toward the pier. Stride after stride, breath in, breath out, with an occasional nod toward the ocean.

After a run one afternoon, she walked along the shore to cool down. Piles of seaweed dotted the beach. Seagulls skittered along the wet sand, dodging the last bubbles of receding waves. She wiped the sweat off her forehead and stopped to look at the horizon. It seemed endless, as did the possibilities. Out there, she thought. Out there is a life.

One Saturday night Maya returned from a movie. She'd been out with friends, including one in particular. She came in the front door and dropped her keys on the table in the hall, strolled into the family room and plopped down on the couch next to her dad. Archie came over for a head scratch. Charlie turned to look at his daughter, raised his eyebrows.

She'd changed over the couple of years since starting high school. Besides running, she was doing push-ups and sit-ups in her room. Her arms and legs were stronger, though still right for her five-foot four-inch frame. And she'd let her hair grow out. She wore a blond ponytail the way her mother had. Sticking out from under a baseball cap.

On this particular evening, her hair was loose, flowing. She had a glow about her.

"What?" she asked, looking at him. "You look weird. What are you doing?"

"Nothing, it's just that even though I always see your mother in you, tonight there's something else. It's like I see her spirit."

"Geez, Dad, how many have you had?"

"Hey, don't get lippy. Seriously, though, you look different. It's like your guard is down." He hesitated, turned back to the TV and popped a chip in his mouth from the bowl in his lap. "Must have been a good movie."

"It was. The company was good," she said smiling.

"*Ah*, I see. Curt?"

"Yeah, and some other people. It was nice. He and I have been spending time together over the last few weeks. It's been, I don't know, comforting, I guess is the best way to describe it. Nice to hang out before he leaves."

"Leaves?"

"His family is moving to New York. His mom got a new job in the city, and his dad is looking for something. But they've decided it's best for them all to go together while he looks. They used to live there before 9/11, and that's where their families are from. He says after the attack his mom needed to get away, but they miss their families so much they want to go back. They leave at the end of the school year."

"Well that's a bummer."

"Oh, it's fine with me. I mean, I like him, but I think I more like the fact that he likes me. He's sweet, but he wouldn't last five minutes in a Raymond Adventure." She dipped her hand into her dad's chip bowl. Raymond Adventures were what they called their Saturday night story sessions, the journeys into the unknown they shared with her mom.

Charlie looked back at the screen but kept stealing glances at his daughter. She was becoming more like Sierra. More adventuresome. Something was brewing. He ate another chip.

"So, 9/11. We haven't talked about it in a while. Do you think about it much?"

"I don't know. I guess I do. I mean, I still feel bad about the things that happened, all the people that died. Curt says his mom worked with some of those people. She had a doctor's appointment that morning. Otherwise she might have been in one of the towers. I think that's why they left New York, and it still freaks him out knowing she's going back to the city again."

"Do you kids talk about it? Outside of class?"

"Sometimes. A couple of guys in my class are thinking about joining the Marines after high school. We were sitting around at lunch one day and they were talking about it. They say they want to defend our country and go find the people who did this and kill them."

"Wow. That's a lot for kids your age."

"I know. I mean, it's great these guys want to protect us, but I wish I knew why people hated us so much. I guess I'd rather figure out how to get them to stop hating us instead of just blowing them all up."

Maya thought about 9/11 quite a bit, but rather than worry her father she kept her thoughts to herself. Hatred existed. She understood it. There were times, when she thought about God, that she felt the outer edges of hate. Why would He take her mother away from her when they were both so young? She hated God for that, or thought she did. Other times she recognized her emotions as misplaced anger and sadness. She had no place else to put them.

But these strangers, these monsters, who murdered thousands of people, she couldn't make sense of that. Before 9/11 she'd believed most people were good. Now, she wasn't sure.

Some nights she'd lie awake thinking not of those who died, but of those who remained behind. She'd wonder about the kids who lost parents. About the mothers going into labor in the days and weeks afterward with babies who would never meet their fathers. In those moments her hatred subsided, but her doubt grew. She felt the world's sadness creep into her heart. On those nights, a lullaby of grief rocked her to sleep.

An hour later, ready for bed, Maya roused her sleeping father from the couch.

"Come on, Dad. Got a story for you." Since freshman year, she'd shared the storytelling. To Charlie the change was bittersweet. More evidence she was growing up.

She lifted the chip bowl from her father's lap and took it to the kitchen. Rinsed the dish and placed it in the dishwasher before coming back to the family room. She grabbed her dad's hand and leaned back, pulled his rumpled body up and toward her.

"Okay, okay, I'm coming," he groused.

They went into her room. Maya climbed into bed. Charlie sat on the edge and waited for her to begin.

"So it's early on a Saturday morning. We're all in the truck. You and Mom are in the front and I'm in the back. It's Labor Day weekend. The air is still warm from summer. There's no traffic. We make it to Logan in less than an hour."

Charlie sat back against the headboard. He closed his eyes and listened.

"We pull into departures and up to the curb. You jump out and grab my bags out of the bed of the ..."

"Wait a minute, you're going without us?" Charlie sat up. "We don't do that."

"We haven't. You're right. But it's time."

Charlie shook his head as the puzzle pieces locked into place. He turned toward his daughter.

"We're not talking about a story anymore, are we?"

Maya sat up and folded the comforter back. She straightened the edges and flattened the navy blue cotton against her lap. She peeked over at her father.

"No, not exactly."

Charlie looked at Maya's dresser, at the trinkets that no longer belonged. An old purple barrette. A charm bracelet. A music box whose ballerina twirled in circles but never managed to escape. He scratched his evening whiskers, glanced at his little girl. He couldn't bring himself to ask why she needed to leave. The answer floated in the silence between them.

"I haven't figured it all out yet. But I'm going away next year."

He hesitated. "Let's talk about it tomorrow, okay?"

"Sure." She pecked his cheek and slid under the covers. He touched her arm, stood and turned out the light.

She rolled over on her back and faced the ceiling as he closed the door.

"You can do this," she whispered. "You need to get out of Seaport. He'll understand."

Charlie wandered into the kitchen. He sat in the darkness, listened to the wind blow restless leaves across the yard. The screen door rattled. He sat until the night turned over. Until he no longer heard the tick of the clock.

Sunday passed. He was out of sorts most of the day. Maya watched him, gave him space, waited. She did her homework, a little cleaning. At the end of the day she began pulling vegetables out of the fridge. They stood at the counter together making a salad. Maya dumped lettuce into the bowl while Charlie chopped carrots, cucumbers, and tomatoes. She reached over him to grab a towel and dry her hands.

"So," he said to the cutting board. "Where to?"

"Not sure. Somewhere warmer than Seaport. I'll narrow it down over the next year. I'm thinking I need to wander a little bit." She paused.

"I don't know what I want to do. And it's stupid for me to go to UMass or somewhere expensive and waste your money while I keg party my way through random classes. I can take a few classes at a community college and get a job. Credits are cheap. It'll give me time to figure out my future."

Charlie sighed. "You've been thinking about this for a while?"

"Yeah. But I didn't know how to tell you."

The things you didn't know how to tell someone, Charlie thought. "It's okay," he said, his smile a cloak for his grief. "I'll be okay."

~

Maya finished her junior year and found a job working at the marina for the summer. She cleaned the office and answered the phone. When the fishermen came in with their catch, she grabbed their lines and watched them unload their haul. On her days off, some of the old-timers took her offshore and let her help with the nets, teaching her the beginnings of a day on the water. Her back and arms thickened and her face tanned. At summer's end, when she stood on a boat she moved with the sea.

Senior year began. Her friends talked about college, nervous about rejections and tuition and the SATs. Maya sat at the lunch table and listened. The sameness of their plans highlighted the divergence of her path. She only had to look to her best friend to question her own choices and the depth of her resolve.

"Have you heard anything from NYU?" she asked Beth one afternoon when they were sitting on the floor of her room doing homework.

"Nothing solid. But I keep telling myself it's too early to get nervous. The admissions officer said it would be a few weeks after the interview so I shouldn't worry. And she said that volleyball and yearbook really do mean something to them, not just my grades. They liked my letters of recommendation, so apparently talking in class actually makes a difference." She sat back against Maya's bed. "I just hope they don't think I want to go to film school because of *Dawson's Creek*. I will literally kill myself if after all this hard work that's what keeps me out."

"You literally won't. Right?"

"Noooo. I'm just being dramatic. And I know the other schools are good, too. But I would love to be in New York."

"Beth, you are like the least dramatic person I know. Which I guess, given what you want to do, is a little odd." She smiled at her friend and elbowed her arm to lighten the mood.

Maya liked being around Beth. Her presence allowed Maya to avoid the spotlight. Beth didn't need to be the center of attention. She stood out by default. In class, other kids might think they knew an answer, but they stayed quiet with self-doubt. Beth was willing to risk being wrong. She enjoyed conversation, whether she was injecting new ideas into a discussion on what Shakespeare was thinking or how a geometry proof could be shortened by three steps.

"Life's already a movie for you, isn't it?" Maya asked her friend.

"What do you mean?"

"Nothing bad, just that you see it in front of you like it's on a screen. You sort of know which way things are going to go, or at least how you want them to. Even if you're not sure, you ride it out to see how the picture ends. Like today in calculus. You go up to the board, and I can tell when you take the chalk from Mr. McKnight that you aren't sure how to solve the problem. You hesitate, put the chalk up to the board, pull it away, and then just go for it.

"If it were me, there would be no way I would have taken that chalk if I wasn't positive of the answer. But you don't mind being up there in front of everyone, giving it a shot. Like you just figure it'll come to you, and if it doesn't, no big deal." Maya shook her head and smiled at her friend. "Frankly, I think it's amazing and I'm totally jealous. I wish I had that kind of confidence."

"Are you kidding? I mean, you're right about me. I don't mind giving it a try. If I don't get it, I know Mr. McKnight will rescue me. And let's face it. There are worse things in the world than being rescued by Mr. McKnight." She put her hand under her chin and batted her eyelashes at Maya. They both laughed.

"But I don't do that unless it's clear no one else knows the answer. If Bobby or one of the other brainiacs is raising their hand, I don't say a word. If no one else has a clue, then I figure what's the harm. If I'm right, great. If not, it's not really embarrassing. At least, not to me."

Maya nodded. Beth didn't want to answer all the questions. She wanted to save the teachers when no one else was willing to try.

"To be honest, though, you're the one who's impressive to me."

"Me? Why?"

"I've been a rule follower and a planner all my life. My brothers and sisters either flunked out of college or if they did make it through, racked up a bunch of loans or worked three jobs to get a degree. So I watched all that and thought, I can do better. I can get a scholarship. So I study hard and get good grades, and for what?"

Beth put her hands over her face and leaned over, her elbows sinking into her lap. She shook her head and pulled her hands away.

"What if I go to NYU and when I get out, instead of making films I want to be a journalist or an accountant or massage therapist?"

Maya moved next to her friend, put her arm around Beth's shoulders and looked her in the eye. "My friend, I can guarantee you won't want to be an accountant. No offense to your mom."

Beth laughed. "I won't tell my mom you said that. But still, here I am trying to plan my whole life, and I'm not even out of high school. It stresses me out. Then I look at you. You're not sure what you want to do, but you know you don't want to waste your dad's money trying to figure it out.

"That's cool, being all responsible. But the best part, the thing that impresses me the most: You're not even worried about it. You'll figure it out when the time comes. I wish I could be like that. If I didn't have a plan, I might lose my mind."

Maya dropped her arm from Beth's shoulders and leaned back against her bed. She pulled her knees to her chest and rested her chin on her knees.

"We are sort of opposites in that way. Maybe that's why we're such good friends." She smiled and stretched her legs out in front of her. "But to be honest, sometimes I wish I knew what I wanted. Sometimes I worry about not having anything to worry about. If you don't have a plan, you can't fail. But you also might not succeed." She grimaced and looked out the window at the tops of the trees.

"And it's not going to be easy leaving my dad."

She slid away from the bed and lay down on the carpet, put her hands behind her head.

Beth hesitated. "What does he say?"

"He doesn't say anything." She paused. "We don't talk about it."

"You're still focused on the community college in Key West?" her guidance counselor asked during a meeting the following week.

"Yup. It's cheap. The weather's warm. And it'll let me see if college is the right fit."

"Maya, your grades are good. You could get into any of the state schools, and plenty of others. I don't know that you're Ivy material, but you wouldn't want that anyway. You could certainly start at a four-year school now. Why don't you consider it? If you want to go south, apply to some four-year schools in Florida. You'll get in."

"It's not about that. Part of it is I don't want to waste my father's money. Part of it is I feel antsy, like I want to work, not study. This way I can take some classes and get a job and see how it feels. Plus, the community college credits are cheaper. If I try something and don't like it, I won't feel as bad about trying something else."

He sat back in his chair. "Will you at least go to the college fair next week? Talk to some schools? There will be a few from the south there, including some with good marine science programs."

"Sure, I'll go." She stood up to leave. "But don't worry about me. I'll sort it out."

~

She went to the college fair and spoke to some recruiters, but she felt like each of them was talking at her rather than with her. She didn't respond well to the sales pitch. Beth, on the other hand, made deliberate stops at certain tables and engaged with each person. Maya watched her friend, her firm hand shake, eye contact. Beth collected materials from a few choice schools. She asked questions she'd prepared based on her research. Maya noticed that the physical stance of the college representatives changed when they spoke to Beth. Like they were talking to a peer. They weren't selling like they were with Maya, or fishing as she liked to think of it. They were engaged, interested. Maybe that was part of the sales job, Maya thought, part of fishing for different types of students. For me, good grades, but not interested, they just throw a bunch of chum in the water and see what swims up to the boat. For someone like Beth, they bait the hook. She's the catch of the day.

Four

2003

EARLY APRIL, THE FOLLOWING SPRING. Maya and Charlie finished dinner. They sat on the couch with the TV on, the anchor describing an accident on Route 128. The three northbound lanes were closed. Plastic and metal dotted the highway. An ambulance sped away. But the weather tomorrow would be sunny. Warm and dry.

Maya watched the screen as her mind wandered around the room. How to break news that would shatter a heart, she thought. After graduation, she would leave for Florida.

Charlie stared past the television into the memories of the day. He'd walked into her room that afternoon while she was in the kitchen, a pile of clean laundry in his arms. He'd stopped when he saw the palm trees on her laptop screen. The logo of Florida Keys Community College in Key West. Charlie had wandered out of the room. He was down the hall before he realized he was still holding her clothing.

Maybe she was just web surfing. Maybe she hadn't applied. He shook his head. Their conversation from the year before nagged at him.

He thought of Thanksgiving when they were preparing the meal. She'd seemed far away as she stared out the kitchen window. He'd started to reach for her and stopped. He was afraid she wasn't there. That she was already gone.

He'd seen flashes again in early spring, after she'd returned to work at the marina. He drove by one afternoon and saw her standing at the seawall, looking out over the ocean. Something was coming over that horizon to take her away.

But now, whatever was threatening had crept into the house. It lived in her room. Hovered in the kitchen. It lay down on the rug in front of the television, deciding not what they would watch, but what they would see.

Beer bottles began to consume more space in the fridge. Maya turned away when Charlie's speech slurred. He was decompressing from work, she told herself. The recycling bin overflowed with Charlie's self-medication.

He sat up as an ad for Miller Lite flashed across the screen.

"You want to go for a ride?" he asked.

"What, now?" Maya looked at her watch. "It's almost nine thirty. And you've had a few. I don't think you should be driving."

"You can drive. I just need some air. What do you say? Quick trip around town?"

She opened her mouth to speak but hesitated. He seemed to need something from her. "Sure. I'll get the keys."

They drove past the town hall and the high school, up the hill to the new shopping center. The Target sign blazed red in the night.

"I don't think there's a moon tonight," he said, sticking his head out the window. "Pretty dark. Getting warmer, though. Summer's coming."

He looked over at his daughter, wistful. He searched for the right words, but they escaped him, fluttered out into the night. They drove for a while in the quiet.

"Let's go to the marina," he said.

"Why? The gate's locked. And I don't have a key."

"I know. I just want to be down by the water," he said as they passed a CVS. "Away from all this."

Maya nodded. She and her dad shared the trait, the need to be away from ordinary life. Errands and obligations. The stuff that made each day look like the last. No indication the next would be any different.

"Okay. Let's go listen to the ocean."

When they arrived at the marina, Maya pulled up to the front gate and turned off the engine. They sat listening to the waves meet the shore. A salty breeze blew in through the open windows.

Charlie sat for a moment, inhaling the air before opening his door. "I'm going in."

"What? Dad, you can't. It's all locked up. And if you try to get in they'll lock you up."

"I don't care. I'm going in. It'll be fun. An actual Raymond Adventure. Walking around the marina at night with no one around." He smiled. For a moment, she saw a glimpse of what her mother must have seen twenty years earlier. The fun Charlie. Reckless. The one everyone loved.

Before she could stop him, he was out of the truck standing barefoot on the hood. She watched as he hoisted himself over the fence. Wow, she thought. Didn't think he'd make it over. Pretty good for an old man.

"Dad, come on. I don't want Mr. Hughes to be mad."

"Don't worry. I'll be in and out in no time. I just want to walk through in the dark."

He landed on the other side. "You stay there. I'll be back in a few."

"This is not a good idea," Maya said to the windshield. She opened her door and stepped down.

"Dad, wait, I'm coming."

"No! Stay in the truck. I'll be right back."

Charlie took another step. Then he saw the boat ahead of him light up. First with headlights, then with flashing lights. Red and blue.

"Move away from the fence, and put your hands on the truck where we can see them." An officer with a flashlight climbed out of the passenger's seat of the cruiser.

Shit, Maya thought. I do not need this right now.

"What do you think you're doing?" the other officer asked as Charlie climbed back over the fence. He peered at the trespassers.

"For crying out loud. Charlie? Maya?"

Nicky Malone was a friend of Charlie's from high school. He was the driver of the police car and a sergeant in the Seaport police department. His partner was younger, a few years older than Maya.

"You know these people, Sergeant?" the younger officer asked.

"Charlie, what the hell are you doing?"

"Nothing, Nicky. Just being an idiot. It was a mistake." He looked down at his hands.

Nicky stared at him for a moment and then looked at Maya. "Don't you work here?"

"Yes, sir."

"So did you lose your key or something?" he asked her, lowering his chin and raising his eyebrows.

"I don't," she started to say as he slowly shook his head. "I mean yeah, I must have left it at home. Stupid, right?"

"Yeah, next time just go home and get your key instead of making your old man hop the fence, okay?"

"Yes, sir, I will. Sorry."

Nicky nodded and turned to Charlie. "Business good? Your folks?"

"Yeah, Nick, everyone's good. You? How's Lisa?"

"She's great. I'll tell her you asked. You guys get home safe." He and Charlie looked at each other for a moment.

"Thanks, Nicky. Appreciate it."

Nicky nodded and headed to the patrol car with the young officer. Maya and Charlie climbed back into the truck. They sat in the dark as the car pulled away.

"You okay, Dad?"

"Yeah, I'm good. I just needed a little air." He sighed. "Let's go home."

Maya fired up the truck and headed toward the house. Before the last turn she held the wheel straight.

"What's up, sweetheart?"

"Let's drive. Let's talk."

Maya guided the truck along the coast. She cruised through dark inlets and told her father about Key West. College majors. An apartment. Roommates. Charlie watched her hands as she spoke. In her excitement, they bobbed through the air as if on a current, kites soaring and diving in the breeze. Like her mom.

When he couldn't mask his sadness, he looked out at the ocean hiding behind the night.

On the outskirts of Ipswich, she pulled into the parking lot of a diner. Inside they ordered chocolate cream pie. When the waitress took their menus, they looked at each other again.

"So, are you okay?" Maya asked. She looked at the creases lining his forehead, worried about the thoughts cascading behind them.

"Honey, I'll be fine. I am fine. I'm not gonna lie. I wish you were staying closer to home. But you need to do what makes you happy. Besides, you're only a plane ride away. Right?"

"Right, of course. And I'll be home for Christmas. Though maybe not Thanksgiving."

Before Charlie could protest she added, "But I promise to reserve every Saturday night for a Raymond Adventure."

The server set their dishes on the table. The chocolate pudding and whipped cream paused their conversation as the sweetness settled on their tongues. Maya waited until her father seemed relaxed.

"I've already picked out a few classes for the fall. And I found a marina in Key West and set up an interview. Down there I can work all year round." She grinned at her father as she scraped the last of the whipped cream from her plate. "That was so good. I'll miss their pie."

Charlie nodded, smiled. He wanted to be supportive, to encourage her to travel, to take chances. To do all the things that neither he nor Sierra had been able to do. He put down his fork as he swallowed the truth. Once Maya left home, she'd be gone for good.

Five

"KNOCK, KNOCK," Maya said, poking her head in her dad's office.

Charlie looked up from his desk, sat back in his chair. "Hey, honey, what's up?"

"Just wondering what you were up to. You're usually finished with work by the afternoon on Saturdays. Thought we'd be able to go out and do something. Unless you're avoiding me."

"I'm not avoiding you," Charlie said. He sighed, threw his pencil on the desk. "I'm avoiding what's coming."

"That's not going to keep me from leaving. I only have a few more days."

"I know." He paused, looked out the window into the backyard. At the table on the patio where they ate dinner on warm summer evenings. Where in a few weeks he would sit alone and watch autumn leaves tumble across the yard. Where the wind would blow through him on its way some place else.

Maya followed his gaze into the yard. She wondered whether sadness had entered the room, had taken his hand and led him away.

Charlie turned toward his daughter, smiled, chased the grey from the windowsill. "Let's do something, anything you want. How about we drive up to Maine and get some lobster?"

"Nah. I'd rather just take Archie for a walk down to the beach."

He pushed his chair back. "Okay, let's go."

Maya called the dog and took the leash from the hook in the front hall. The three ambled down the street, the dog pausing their outing in spots to investigate new smells along the sidewalk. An ocean breeze rustled their hair, grazed their skin.

Not yet, Charlie thought, squinting into the wind. Please, not yet.

At the beach they found a spot on the seawall, a place for Archie to lie in the sand. The water stretched before them, the waves shimmering in the late summer sun.

"You said we could do anything I wanted today, right?" she asked.

"Yeah, but you wanted to come here. Do you want to go somewhere else?"

"No, just here. But I want you to do something else for me." She turned to face her father. "I want you to tell me about Mom. How you met. How she got sick. How we were as a family."

Charlie stared at his daughter, then turned toward the water. He dropped his chin to his chest, released a long breath. "It's hard to talk about. You know?"

She nodded. "I know. Maybe just a little bit. How you fell in love?"

He smiled, his cheeks flushed. "Okay. We'll start with that."

He thought about his earliest memories with Sierra. He was surprised how quickly, how clearly, his past came back to him.

Six

CHARLIE

1981

THE AIR CHANGED. Sometime after the first of August, the winds began to rustle through the maples of Massachusetts as the soft green leaves of summer crisped to red. Charlie Raymond felt the chill on his skin. He'd be running on the track in the evenings after working for his dad, sprinting until the walls of his lungs clamored for reprieve, and he'd feel a thread of the coming cold break the heat. The hint of a northern gale borne somewhere off the Maine coast. A breeze carrying the promise of fall and school and football. The promise of the beginning of something.

Charlie jogged to the edge of the grass and grabbed a towel from his gym bag. He mopped his face and gazed at the football field as the scene played out in his mind.

The teams lined up. The ref placed the ball and backed away, whistling for the start of play. Seaport had possession. Lynnfield's defense scrambled, trying to match up their speed to

Seaport's. They didn't know Charlie yet. He was new to the varsity.

The quarterback looked to his left and right, called the numbers that would send them on their various routes. The center set the play in motion. Charlie faked left and sprinted past the cornerback down the right sideline, long strides that took him ten yards from scrimmage before the defender turned and tore after his man. Twenty, thirty, forty yards. Charlie looked up over his shoulder as the ball descended, falling into his hands and leading him into the end zone.

"There goes Raymond!" he yelled to the empty bleachers, dropped his towel, and sprinted across the grass toward the goal posts. "He's at the thirty! He's at the twenty! He's at the ten! Touchdown!" he shrieked, tumbling into the grass. He rolled onto his back, knees bent, chest heaving. He closed his eyes and listened for the sound of the crowd. The whole town would be there, calling his name. And the girls, the girls. Charlie Raymond would be a legend in this town. It was his only chance.

"Charlie, bring your laundry down after you shower," his mom, Carolyn, told him as he walked in the back door. "Your dinner's in the oven. We already ate."

"Thanks, Ma." He leaned down to kiss her cheek.

"Did you go through those estimates this afternoon?" his dad, Pete, asked, looking up from his newspaper as Charlie passed through the den.

"Yeah, got them all filed. I think I found a mistake in the concrete calculation for the school bid. I'll show you after I shower."

"Good, I was wondering about that. Nice work," he said, folding his paper. "How was the workout?"

"Great. I scored a touchdown." He flashed his dad a smile and headed up the stairs.

Charlie wiped the steam from the mirror as he combed his damp hair. He looked at his reflection, examining the changes that seemed to be coming whenever he wasn't paying attention. The square jaw, the faint stubble. He was close to six feet, putting on some muscle. He had a good chance of making varsity if he kept working hard. He released a long breath.

Football was great, he thought. But it wouldn't change anything. His course was set.

Pete was Raymond Construction's second generation. Charlie's grandfather had started the company, and Pete and his brother Rick joined construction crews in their teens. They followed their dad's work ethic. The family rule for all Raymond children was once you were old enough, you contributed. Sweep an office, empty trash cans, haul materials. By the time the Commonwealth of Massachusetts allowed a child to legally work, a Raymond kid had a résumé.

Charlie wrapped a towel around his waist and headed down the hall to his bedroom, thinking about his future. He and his cousin Todd were the third generation. By thirteen Charlie had spent Saturday mornings cleaning the office, and by fourteen he'd been on jobsites. Now he was old enough to sit with his father in the evenings as Pete prepared estimates, the son learning the business from his father.

He pulled on sweatpants and a t-shirt as he considered the months to come. His friends thought school was an annoyance to be endured until they could break out of Seaport, an ocean to be crossed to reach the lands of adventure that waited. Charlie swam slowly across that sea, drinking in the drops of salty water. He knew the lands he would find on the other side. They could wait while he dove into the deep blue of the next three years of high school. He sauntered down the hallway with sweaty clothes in hand.

"Here's what I've got," Charlie said, settling in next to his father at the dining room table and spreading out the paperwork after handing his laundry to his mother and thanking her again. "You see this calculation?" He pointed to the third column on the first page. "In the school bid, we used a larger factor to figure the amount of concrete. We just got that information a week ago, so I don't know why we'd be using a different number. Do you?"

Pete shifted his reading glasses and compared the sheet Charlie handed him with the one on the table from the school bid.

"I see what you mean. Looks like we used the number from an old bid rather than what they gave us last week. Probably just human error, most likely mine. Good catch. I see why the boys call you Mit." He smiled at his son, who blushed at his father's compliment.

Charlie loved football, but he wasn't above tackling a complex math problem. He complained to his buddies that his dad was always on his back, but he looked forward to these quiet evenings with his father. Still, at this point in his young life, Charlie approached the world around him with the negligence of youth, running through at full speed and moving on to the next thing, the next stop, the next piece of the puzzle of adolescence. He ran and ran because change was coming.

Notwithstanding the nickname his buddies had given him, Mit, or MIT, short for Massachusetts Institute of Technology, Charlie knew his collegiate career would be limited to an associate's degree in accounting from a local community college and full-time work for his old man. MIT was a world away. Nothing more than a nickname that would fade with his varsity letters.

He'd accepted the path ahead. Football. Seaport. Raymond Construction. A life he could live, he told himself. Love.

Maya stood from the seawall to stretch her legs. "Geez, Dad, you must have been quite the football player," she said, smiling. "Or were you just a player?"

He shook his head, blushed. "You have no idea. I wasn't exactly what you would call boyfriend material." He glanced up at his daughter, patted the spot next to him for her to sit. Squinted out at the horizon. "Until your mother came to town."

Seven

Sierra

"SIERRA, YOU READY TO GO?" her father, Jim, asked as he walked into the empty bedroom.

"Yeah, just taking a last look around." Sierra traced the faint line on the wall where the yellow paint had faded. She hadn't noticed the passage of time until she'd peeled off her pictures.

"Seems bigger without all those magazine pages covering every inch of space," he said, nudging a smile out of his daughter. "You've been a little quiet the last couple of days. You okay? Sad to be leaving your friends?"

"I am, but we have a visit planned so it's not so bad."

"Nervous about school? Being the new kid?"

"I guess a little, but I haven't thought about it too much." She hesitated. "I'm a little sad for Nonna and Poppie."

"Honey, you'll see them soon. They're coming up in a few weeks."

"Oh, I know. It's not me. I mean, yeah, of course I'll be sad not seeing them all the time, but I'm sad for them. They're going to miss me and you and Mom so much."

Jim wrapped his arms around his daughter. "Sisi, they'll be fine. Sometimes I think you spend too much time worrying about everyone. You don't always have to be taking care of someone else. You're a teenager. Just look out for yourself, okay?"

Sierra pulled away from her father, returning his sad smile with a puzzled grin. He's always telling me to be myself, she thought, not to worry what other people think. But how can I be myself and not care for the people I love?

Eight

CHARLIE HEARD RUMORS OVER THE SUMMER about the new girl. Friends saw her at the supermarket with her mother or running along the beach in the early evenings. He thought little of a freshman new to town, preferring to focus on his second year of high school. Team depth charts. Senior girls. His mind whirled as he lifted weights, preparing for football practice to begin. On the first day of school he saw her.

"You look lost." She was standing next to a wall of lockers, looking back and forth between the numbers and the crumpled hallway map in her hand.

"Yeah, uh, I guess I am lost." She glanced around, not at him. Charlie watched her chin move toward and away from him. He saw an eyelash resting on her cheek and resisted the urge to brush it away.

"I'm Charlie, Charlie Raymond. You're new here?"

"Yeah, moved here over the summer from Providence. My name's Sierra Marini." She eyed him closely, not yet trusting the intentions of the young men in her new town. "What's your story? Are you some kind of welcoming committee or something?"

"Only for the pretty girls." He grinned and turned away as his face reddened.

"Uh huh. Well, sorry to disappoint you. Anyway, I need to go find my locker."

"You're in luck. Lockers are my specialty. Give me the number and I'll help you look." He motioned for her to show him the map. She hesitated then shrugged her shoulders and handed him the paper with her information.

"You're in the next wing, near me. Come on." He turned to head up the hallway. "So, Sierra, huh?"

"Yeah, my parents met on a group hiking trip in California in the sixties. I think they were hippies. They always tell me it could have been worse. They could have met at Woodstock." She smiled at Charlie as they walked to the east wing.

"I do believe my little brother is in love," Karen said as she entered Charlie's bedroom. She plopped down on his bed, fluffed his pillow as she placed it between her head and the headboard. "You're a smitten kitten." She laughed at her brother's scowl.

"Knock it off, Karen." Charlie pushed his chair back from his desk and turned to face her. "You don't know what you're talking about."

"Oh, my little brother, I most certainly do. I know you've spent the last few weeks joined at the hip of this new girl Sierra. What's up? Are you going to bring her around or what?"

"Yeah, I will at some point. I just, I don't want to screw this up."

"Wow, you really like this girl." She watched her brother look away. "Okay, I'll be nice." She sat up. "Seriously, I've never seen you like this before. Why this girl?"

Charlie leaned back in his chair, shifted his weight until the front legs lifted off the carpet. He put his hands behind his head and looked up at the light fixture.

"I don't know. I mean, I know, but it's not just one thing. She's cute, of course. But she's just so different from everyone else. She doesn't worry about clothes or makeup or jewelry. It doesn't matter where we are or what we're doing, she's just happy to be there and wants to make sure everyone else is okay. She makes you feel like you're the only person in the world. The only one that matters."

Charlie couldn't describe what made Sierra different. Her presence, her kindness, her essence, each had a calming effect on those around her. She had a quiet way of watching a person, young or old, frail or strong, and finding a way to offer them strength without their knowing. This gentleness, this elegant benevolence, it floated in through open windows in cool fall evenings. It wrapped around the shoulder of a friend preparing for a final exam. It preceded her. It followed her. It emanated from her.

Nine

FOOTBALL CAME AND WENT, as did classes and dances and all the other shiny objects reserved for lucky boys from small towns. With the passing of weeks and months, Charlie Raymond forgot about senior girls and last week's touchdowns. He fell in love. With Sierra Marini, with his life. With love itself.

Over time Sierra learned Charlie was not like other guys his age.

"You know, Mit, you're not normal." They were driving to a movie.

"What do you mean? I'm normal. I shower. I don't talk to myself in public all that often. And I try my best to keep my mouth closed when I'm chewing my food. But let's face it, if Larry Bird hits a winning shot against the Lakers with no time left on the clock, food is bound to fall out of my mouth. You can't hold me accountable for that."

"I'm not talking about that, you idiot. I mean you're smart and cute and funny, and you don't let it go to your head. You're nice to me and your parents and sister. And you could be a jerk if you wanted to. Look at your friends. Most of those morons barely know how to tie their own shoes."

"It's true, they are morons. And I am cute." He put his arm around her as they walked into the theater. The next day he scaled the Seaport water tower and painted the evidence of his love. That stunt cost him several weeks pay. But he didn't care. He wanted to marry her.

He didn't count on having to.

~

"I'm pregnant."

Charlie released the last bit of air he thought his lungs might ever hold. He looked at Sierra, at the familiar wrinkle above her nose. This was the face he would know for the rest of time. It would lie next to him on pillows that would lose their heft. It would greet him after long days and smile at him over eggnog and birthday cakes and summer nights at the Dairy Barn. It would be the face of their child. This was what he had wanted.

Charlie was in his first year of community college, Sierra her last year of high school. She'd been accepted to UCLA and was deciding whether to go. Her pregnancy would change everything.

"Jesus, okay. Uh, are you sure? Never mind. That was stupid. Are you all right?"

"I don't know what I am right now." Her eyes welled.

Charlie took her hand. "It's okay. We'll figure it out. It won't be easy. But we're in this together. We'll tell your parents together.

"It'll be okay. It'll all be okay."

"What the hell were you thinking? Or, obviously, not thinking? Jesus, Charlie, didn't we raise you better than this? We're not even going to talk about the fact that you were having sex. God knows we can't stop that." Pete turned to watch Carolyn leave the den.

"But for the love of God, did we not teach you to be smart? To realize your actions have consequences? You've ruined Sierra's life and your own. And you broke your mother's heart."

Charlie sat frozen on the couch. Pete paced around the room.

"What do you want me to say? I fucked up, okay? I know it. But I'm a man now. It's my responsibility. I'll figure it out."

"You think it's that simple?" Pete stopped to stare at his son. "You think you can raise a kid at your age?"

"Well, I guess we're going to find out aren't we?" Charlie yelled, rising. "What the hell do you want from me? I'm a fucking idiot, okay? Does it make you feel better to hear me say it?" He put his face in his hands and sobbed.

Pete sighed. "Come on now, don't do this." He crossed the room, wrapped his arms around his son, and let him cry. He hadn't held him like this in a long time. When did he get this tall? He is a man, Pete thought.

Charlie pulled away and sat down, wiped his eyes and nose with his sleeve. His father sat beside him.

"I'm sorry, Dad. I'm sorry I did this to Sierra and to her

family and to you and mom and our family. I know you're disappointed in me. I am, too."

Pete put a hand on his knee. "Has Sierra decided what she wants to do?"

"Not yet. But whatever she decides I'll support her. It was my mistake. It's her decision."

"You don't have to keep the baby you know."

They were sitting on the floor of her bedroom a week later when she told Charlie. He took her hand and said she could change her mind, hoping as the words left his lips that she wouldn't. "I know you're a good Catholic girl, but this is your future."

She looked at him and shook her head. "You make it sound so simple. It's more complicated than that. Sure, religion is important to me, but my gut tells me I don't want to end this pregnancy or give away this baby. Maybe I won't always feel that way. But right now, this is all I know." She looked away. "I understand if you don't want to be a part of it. I'm not asking you to."

Charlie brushed the side of her cheek and turned her chin toward him. He thought of the day they'd met, how he'd wanted to touch her skin right away. He thought of all the moments they'd had together over the last few years. How he'd reach over to feel the softness of that cheek or her hair or the spot on her wrist where she hid a birth mark under her watch strap. He thought of how he loved his family and he'd liked girls before, but how he never considered he could love someone as much as he loved this girl sitting beside him. This girl who gave so much to so many. This girl was everything.

He shook his head and smiled. "I'm not going anywhere. Did I want a baby right now? No, not really. But if this had to happen with anyone, it could only be with you. I always knew we'd end up together. We're just starting that part of our life together a little early." He'd known Sierra would never give up a child. He paused. "What about college? Have you thought about it?"

"Have I thought about it?" Her voice rose with a twinge of resentment. "Yes, Charlie, I've thought about it. I've thought about it almost nonstop since you pulled your clothes on that night. After it happened."

She looked up at his brown eyes. At the scar above his left eyebrow from a kindergarten tumble. At the worry that betrayed his words. She sighed, released the anger, and drew in the resignation with her next breath. "Yes. I've thought about how upset I've made my parents. How scary it's going to be to go to school when I'm showing. And to answer your question, how college is going to have to wait. I've thought about all of it." She paused, looked away. "It doesn't matter anymore."

Charlie nodded. He couldn't argue, couldn't offer anything but his compliance.

Sierra sat quietly, face drawn, hands in her lap. After a few minutes, she turned to him.

"Do you ever think about what this will be like? I mean actually think about it? I don't mean diapers and bottles and how to afford it, but the bigger picture. The life we have ahead?"

"Not like you describe it. But I don't think about life that way. I mostly focus on what's next. College, work, maybe a new truck. I don't plan that much detail." He paused, considered her. They were different in so many ways. She'd had plans for her life. He'd stolen them. "But you probably do."

Sierra's face crinkled as her brain leapt from one thought to another. "I don't mean the planning so much as what it will feel like." She hesitated. "I'm not explaining this right."

She gathered her thoughts, turned to face him. "I know what it feels like to be a senior in high school in a small town in Massachusetts. To have summers off, to work part-time bagging groceries. I know what it feels like to apply to college and dream about my future. And now I know what it feels like to be pregnant. Like I'm in someone else's body. But it's more than that." She looked away and back at him, considered each word. "I know what it feels like to sit on the beach at night and stare up at the sky, stars twinkling, my hair blowing all around in the wind. You're sitting next to me."

She stopped, leaned back against the side of her bed, closed her eyes and smiled.

"You're holding my hand, and my other hand digs into the sand. It's damp and gritty. I know what that feels like, because I've lived it and it has left me happy and sad and wondering about what's next." She opened her eyes to look at him, then away. "I sound crazy. Never mind. Must be the hormones talking."

"No, no. I get it. I feel those things, too. I feel it when we're out driving around, not going anywhere special. The windows are down. It's a sunny day, and the seat in the truck is just warm enough that you have to keep moving around so you don't stick to the vinyl. And you smell the salt air and you see one of your buddies and he beeps as he drives by. In this picture I'm holding your hand, too, like this." He picked up her hand. "And you smile at me. There's this happiness, this rush, this feeling that life can't get any better and I want to hold onto it forever. I know how that feels." He stopped for a moment. "But it's also how I know it doesn't matter what the future will feel like. It's okay, because this is so good right now."

Charlie looked down at his lap, let go of her hand. He folded and unfolded his hands, wringing the excess energy from his racing heart. He looked up at Sierra and took her hand again.

"I know we're young and this is not going to be easy. I get all that. But I love you now. I have no reason to believe I won't love you forever. And anything that comes with that is going to feel really, really good."

She shook her head. "I love that you have this image of us as this happy little family, but I ..." she let go of his hand and bowed her head, started to cry. "I don't see it." Her body shook as she sobbed.

He moved closer and put his arm around her shoulder, held her until her tears slowed and she pulled away.

"I'm scared," she said. "Really scared."

He pulled her in and kissed the side of her head. "I know. I am, too."

~

The weekend after Sierra's graduation, she and Charlie married at the beach. Their immediate families and a few friends came. Sierra wore flowers in her hair and a white dress that flowed gently over her belly. After the wedding they moved into the apartment over Charlie's parents' garage. Three months later, Sierra gave birth to a baby girl.

The young parents spent hours narrowing a list of names and finally settled on Maya.

"You don't think it will jinx her that she was inspired by photos of ruins? I mean you could interpret that to mean she's destined for a ruined life," Sierra said.

"Not at all. They represent a beautiful, magical place, one that we hope to see one day as we travel the world on our family adventures." He kissed Sierra's cheek. "She's a Raymond. The world is waiting for her."

Archie stood, turned in a circle, settled into the same spot. Maya reached down to rub his belly. He rolled over on his back, paws elevated, in willing surrender.

"So, my name," she said. "And all that talk of travel. Were you surprised when I told you I was leaving for Florida? Or did you always expect me to go somewhere far away?"

"I was surprised. But only because I refused to recognize the signs. I have a habit of living in denial." He paused, thought of what he was ready to tell her. What he wasn't. He nudged the memories back into the murky crevices of his mind, forced a smile past the melancholy. Put an arm around his daughter. "But once you came along, it was a wild ride."

Ten

"CHARLIE!"

Charlie threw the covers off and raced down the hall. Maya's door was closed. He backtracked to the bathroom and looked inside to see Sierra pulling herself out of the toilet.

"I'm going to kill you," she hissed at him. He rubbed his head and stifled a laugh.

"Sorry." Second time this week. He knew he should do better, but you'd think at some point she'd look first, right?

"It's not my job to make sure the toilet seat is down." She washed her hands and pushed past him. "It's your job." She stopped to poke him in the chest. "Get it?"

"Yeah, yeah, got it." He laughed once and she turned to glare at him. He shrugged his shoulders. "Sorry."

They climbed back into bed, she turned away from him. He rested a hand on her shoulder. "I'm sorry."

She rolled over to face him. "I know. But I'm so tired. I can't have you fucking up. I need more help. I know you have school and work and you're learning the business, but I'm here all the time with her, mostly by myself. And," she started to cry. "I have no idea what I'm doing. I don't know if I'm doing it right or wrong. She's almost a year old, and I feel like I know less now than when she was born."

"Hey, hey, come on, you're doing great. You're the best mom. I didn't realize you were having such a hard time. I'll try to help more, okay?"

"Okay," Sierra sniffled. "Let's get some sleep."

At dinner the next night, Charlie apologized again.

"What can I do to help more?" he asked, spooning something brown and mysterious onto his plate. Sierra's cooking had not improved with her mothering, but Charlie learned to eat whatever she made. Eventually Charlie learned to cook, remembering that sometimes the best defense is a good offense.

"Well, I feel like I need to get back in school. I've been thinking about signing up for a class or two in January." She looked up from her plate. "What do you think?"

"I think it's a great idea," he said, hoping the first one would be a cooking class. "My mom can probably take Maya part of the time. She's not doing much at the office anymore."

Raymond Construction had experienced a growth spurt, and Charlie's dad and uncle were busier than ever. Charlie and his cousin Todd, two years his senior, were taking on more responsibility. Charlie's mom, Carolyn, had handled the bookkeeping part-time over the years, but their records were becoming more complicated with the work they were doing and the equipment purchases. The brothers decided to hire a full-time bookkeeper, and Carolyn was happy to relinquish the duties. She told Charlie she would gladly provide babysitting services. Sierra's return to school fit with her new availability.

One night, a few weeks after Maya's third birthday, Sierra put Maya to sleep and crawled into bed. "I can't believe I still have to write that paper tomorrow. I was having so much fun baking cookies with Maya this afternoon I couldn't even think of school. This psych class is kicking my butt."

"But you like it, right?" Charlie reached up and turned off the light.

"I do. It's been more work than I thought, but it's the first class that has made me think. Like I may actually want to do this for a living."

"Wow, that's great! You haven't said anything 'til now."

"I wanted to give it some time, but, yeah, I think there may be a future with this. It's cool, you know? For the first time since high school I'm thinking about a career. We'll see. Right now I'm just tired."

"Too tired?"

"Yup, too tired." She touched the scruff of his cheek, pulled the covers up, closed her eyes. Charlie's forefinger traced the side of her face, following the curve down her neck.

He felt a bump. "Si, what's that?"

She opened her eyes into slits and touched his wrist. "What's what?" she murmured, halfway to sleep.

"That bump." He turned on the light.

Sierra sat up and felt along the side of her neck. "I don't

know. Never noticed it before. Probably nothing. Maybe a swollen gland or something."

"Do you feel sick?"

"No, I feel fine. Haven't had a cold in months. Maybe I ate something and I'm having an allergic reaction. I'll make an appointment to see the doctor."

Sierra saw the family doctor the following day, and the doctor sent her for blood tests. Then came more appointments and a biopsy and right before Christmas, surgery. They were hopeful. She was young and healthy, and as the doctors told her over and over during the first few rounds of tests, if you're going to have cancer, thyroid cancer is the best one to have. Generally slow-growing, in most cases the cancer doesn't spread past the thyroid tissue.

As Charlie had learned in the years he'd spent with this woman, she did not fit into the mold of most cases. Sierra's thyroid cancer was a rarer form. It had spread to her lymph nodes, then to her lungs. By the time the doctors found the end of the disease's travels, her chances of cure were slim.

It happened quickly to the young family whirling in motion. Relatives and friends surrounded them like a caravan of wagons, cooking meals, running errands, tending to Maya. As the buds sprouted on the trees along their street and the last scattered bits of snow melted from the lawn, Sierra grew weaker. When she could no longer climb the steps to the garage apartment, they moved into her parents' spare rooms. By the time the green blades of spring tulips pierced the ground, she could barely leave her bed.

Maya spent less time with her mother, as Sierra didn't want her daughter's memories to be of a failing spirit. She felt her little girl should remember the days of laughter and hugs and warm chocolate chip cookies. The doctor spoke to Charlie and the family about the coming days. One afternoon Sierra asked Charlie to bring their daughter to her.

"I want to say goodbye in my own way. Before she realizes what's happening. I'm only going to get worse, and I don't want her to see me then. At the end."

Charlie leaned down and kissed her forehead, wiping a tear from his cheek as he stood. He went to the living room and lifted his daughter from his father-in-law's lap.

"Come on, sweetie. We're going to see Mommy for a minute."

Maya leaned against her father's chest, thumb in mouth. She pulled her head back to look at him as he turned for the hallway. She touched his damp cheek.

"It's okay, honey." He adjusted her on his hip and kissed her nose. "I'm okay." He smiled as he placed her on the floor outside the bedroom.

Maya held her father's pants leg as she entered her mother's room. She craned her neck to check if Sierra was awake. When Sierra motioned for her, she climbed on the bed.

"Are you okay, Mommy?"

"Yes, sweetie, just resting. I'm a little tired."

Maya lay down beside Sierra and let her mother stroke her back. Her breathing slowed in rhythm with her mother's.

"You're going to have a little sleepover with Grammy Carolyn and Grampy Pete, okay? Mommy won't see you for a little while. You be a good girl for Grammy and Grampy, and for Daddy, okay?"

Maya raised her head and stared at her mother. Her face tightened, but she was afraid to speak up, to ask questions. She nodded and kissed her mother's cheek, brushed a strand of

Sierra's hair out of her face. They looked at each other. For a moment the world stopped spinning.

Two nights later, Charlie watched Sierra slipping away. She motioned him to her.

"There are things I want to say," she told him, taking a breath. Her words were slow, heavy. "I love you. You are my best friend, a great dad, and you're going to take great care of our little girl. Please take care of yourself. Find someone else to love."

Charlie's face glistened. "Please stop." His tears fell onto the blanket crumpled across her bed. He couldn't imagine life without her, let alone with anyone else. He sat up and dried his eyes, stared at the Red Sox logo pulled up beneath her chin. He remembered the day she gave him the blanket. She was still in high school. He'd finished his first semester at college and come home with all As. She'd been so proud she spent a week's pay on it. Now the blanket covered her thin body.

Charlie fell asleep in the chair beside the bed. In the morning he woke to see Sierra staring at him. Her eyes were distant, clouded. She was moving away from him. He sat on the edge of her bed, took her hand, pressed his lips to the back of her fingers. What to say, he thought.

"I love you. I'll love you for the rest of my life." He wiped his eyes. His words felt hollow, lacking. "By the way, you didn't disappoint me."

She looked at him, her forehead wrinkled with confusion.

"The day we met." Charlie's voice broke. He cleared his throat, tried to smile. "You accused me of being the welcoming committee. And I told you it was only for the pretty girls, so you said you were sorry to disappoint me." He shook his head.

"I've loved you since that first day. And you did not disappoint me. Not then. Not ever."

Sierra closed her eyes and drifted into sleep. She slept on and off over the next couple of days. Charlie rarely left her side, taking short breaks for meals or to visit with friends who'd stopped by to offer love and sorrow to Charlie, to Sierra, to her parents.

Late one afternoon Sierra woke from a long nap. Sunlight filtered through the curtains. She smiled at Charlie. He moved his chair close to the bed, watched her smile fade to a thin line. She shuddered once, and in the midst of a dream reached out and touched his arm. She held on for a few seconds before her grip relaxed. He checked for breath or a pulse. She was gone.

Charlie leaned over her and sobbed into the blanket. His body seized as he buried his head next to hers, soaked in the last of her warmth. He rose and called her parents. They came to the doorway, pausing before crossing the threshold into the room. Her mother, Pat, entered first and knelt by the bed. She brushed back Sierra's hair and kissed her goodbye. Her tears dropped on the pillowcase.

Charlie stood in the corner of the room, his arms wrapped around himself, shaking as he sobbed. Jim grabbed him, held the young man until the shuddering calmed, until the body slackened, as he surrendered to the pain of loss. To the sear, the fury. After he quieted, Charlie pulled away, dropped to his knees, and picked up Sierra's left hand. He put the back of her hand to his mouth and wept silently, smelled her skin. He slipped her wedding ring from her finger and put it in his pocket.

"Some day I'll give her ring to Maya. When she's old enough." He looked at Sierra's parents, at the shadows standing where his in-laws used to be.

Jim nodded. Pat murmured a quiet acknowledgment and turned to pick up the phone. There were things to be done.

In the days and weeks that followed, Charlie managed. He managed to endure the funeral, to shake hands and accept hugs and tears and plates of food. He managed to be a father of sorts, whenever Carolyn or Pat would remind him with a touch on the arm that Maya missed his smile, his presence. The Charlie that was gone.

Eleven

"YOU STILL INTERESTED IN THIS OLD STORY?" Charlie asked Maya, clearing his throat, digging a boot into the sand. "It's a lot to hear all at once."

"I know," she said, her voice barely above a whisper. "But I'm leaving soon. I want to have it with me while I'm gone."

He nodded. "I understand." He sighed, took her hand. "Well kiddo, after she died, it was just you and me."

Charlie and Maya moved back to the apartment over his parents' garage a week after the funeral. A few days later Charlie returned to the office. He hoped the routine would help bring normalcy back to him, to his daughter.

Each morning before work he left his little girl with Carolyn or Pat or someone else in town yearning to feel the outer fringes of the Sierra they'd lost. Friends and relatives who knew it took a village, well before anyone coined the term.

Assured his daughter was safe, Charlie turned back toward life. He worked hard at the company and on his course work. He finished his business degree, and between estimating and managing construction projects he became a better cook. Dinner preparation allowed him to put away the day and bring his daughter close. In those moments in the kitchen, when he focused on slicing and stirring, away from words and numbers, he could drift away. He could keep Maya by his side and feel Sierra nearby, while he reached into the pot and pulled out a strand of spaghetti to check that it was ready. That it was right.

His family and friends watched, waited. They came after him from time to time, pushing him to travel outside the four corners of the universe he'd created for himself. One that had high walls and sharp edges, that protected his daughter, or so he thought. They came for him when they saw a chance, an opening, a loosening of a stone that might give way. That if it did, might lead to an utter collapse.

A few months after Sierra died, his mother pulled him aside. "You look tired. You don't need to work this hard, you know. Your dad's just trying to keep you busy to keep your mind off things, but you need your rest. Are you sleeping?"

"I'm fine, Ma." In truth, sleep was an issue. He wasn't adjusting to the empty space beside him. He still woke in the middle of the night and reached across the bed. The cold pillowcase stirred him awake. Night after night the chill reminded him she was gone.

After a few rough nights, Charlie would have a restful sleep. He'd put Maya to bed and crash. When the radio came on in the morning, he'd feel his way across the nightstand to turn it off. Then he'd reach for the warmth next to him, and when he found the cold instead his body curled up to chase away the emptiness. Some days he'd ward it off, jumping out of bed and turning on the light to start the rituals of the day. Other days he'd be overcome. He'd grab her pillow and pull it to his chest. Bury his face and cry into the softness until it had wrung all the water from his heart. As time passed, he adjusted to the cold.

Charlie masked his sorrow when he was with his family, when his appearance mattered. He smiled and joked with them like he used to, and in turn they assumed he was healing in his own way. His parents and in-laws saw a young man devoted to his daughter. Either they believed he was okay, or they hoped.

Whenever they gathered for a meal, Charlie set his mask in place. He leaned back in his chair, observed their play and tussle. He watched them love each other and his little girl, aware they were watching him. He kept his smile loose, made eye contact. Hugged his mother, his grandparents. He did everything he was supposed to do. Then he shut the door behind them and released a long breath.

His sister didn't buy it. Karen was the one person who found a way to watch Charlie when he thought no one noticed. When he stood at the sink to rinse a glass, she saw his shoulders droop a little lower. When Maya reached up for him, in the moment before he lifted her small frame, Karen saw a shadow pass before her brother's eyes. It was like he didn't know how to do this, how to do anything.

One night Karen stopped by her parents' house. After a short visit, she climbed the stairs to Charlie's apartment. Maya had just had her bath and was in her pajamas on the couch. Charlie was sitting down to read her a story when his sister knocked.

"This is a nice surprise," he said as he opened the door. "To what do I owe the honor?" He leaned over to kiss her cheek.

"I had some magazines to drop off for Mom, so I thought I'd pop in and say hi. Just in time for a story?"

"Yeah, you want to handle reading duty while I do the dishes?"

"Sure." She took the tattered copy of *The Cat in the Hat* from Charlie and settled in next to her niece. Maya leaned against her aunt's body and watched the pages turn. Before Charlie turned off the water and dried his hands, his daughter was asleep.

"You must have a more soothing voice than I do," he said when he returned from tucking Maya into bed. "She doesn't usually drop off that quickly for me, but she's out. Thanks for doing that. Can I get you something? Glass of wine?"

"No, thanks. But don't let me keep you, if you want one." She waited to see what he would do. She wasn't sure how much he was drinking.

"I'm good." He sensed she wanted to say something. "How's work?"

Karen looked down the hall. Maya's bedroom door was closed.

"Cut the bullshit, okay? I'm not here to talk about work. I'm here to talk about you, about how you're doing. Come on, you know that. I can't keep anything from you, and you can't keep anything from me. I'm not Mom."

Should have had that glass of wine, Charlie thought. "Jesus, Karen, what makes you think I'm trying to keep anything from you? I'm not trying to do anything more than keep it together and look after my kid. That's about all I've got these days."

"I know. I see you keeping it together, and I wonder how

much longer you're going to keep at it without accepting any help."

"What do you mean? Mom and Dad and Pat and Jim have been great about helping with Maya. I couldn't do it without them."

"That's not what I mean. Yes, they're helping with Maya, which is great. But no one is talking about how you're feeling, how you're holding up. You think if you show up for a family dinner and smile and slap the guys on the back and kiss the women, everyone thinks you're okay? You may have fooled everyone else because they have no idea what to say or do and want so desperately for you to get better. But I see it. I know you're not okay. I know this is all an act.

"Sometimes I look at you and all I see is a house of cards. It's like every day there's another pair of cards, piled on and leaning against each other. If you can just get them to stay up, you make it through the day. Then you go to sleep, and God only knows what you dream about, if you sleep at all."

Charlie looked away. Karen rested a hand on his arm.

"For once in your life, let someone else help you. I mean really help you. You won't talk to me. You won't talk to Mikey."

His head snapped back around.

"That's right, I spoke to him. Damn right I did. The way you're living is not doing you any good. And if you're not smart enough to figure it out on your own, I'm going to tell you: If you're not doing yourself any good, then you're no good for that little girl down the hall."

Charlie flinched.

"I'm sorry." Karen's voice tumbled over the lump in her throat. "I hate to say that to you. Breaks my heart. But I'm afraid that's the only way I'm going to get through to you. You need to talk to a professional. You need some help."

Charlie looked down at his hands. She was right. He needed help. He nodded.

"I'll give it a shot. But if after a couple of sessions I don't feel like it's working, I'm not going to stick with it. All right?"

"Yeah, okay."

She promised to find the name of a therapist through her doctor. Charlie asked for a male, preferably one who practiced a few towns away. He didn't want anyone he knew to see him going for an appointment. And if he had to tell the therapist any of his secrets, he wanted the listener to be someone who didn't know him. He preferred a voice without a face. He didn't want comfort. He wanted release.

Karen gave Charlie the information. He made an appointment for the end of the month.

As he drove to the office for the session, he thought of ways to cancel. He could fake a headache or say they had a crisis at work. Karen was the only person who knew he was going. He could stall for at least a week before she caught on. Then he thought of Maya. She was growing up, asking questions. Sometimes when she looked at him, he felt like he wore a cape. Other times he didn't know if he could run a bath. I need fixing, he thought.

He parked the car and entered the office building. Checked the directory and found the suite at the end of the hall. The small waiting room was empty except for a few chairs and a table with magazines and pamphlets. Charlie paged through a copy of *Time* from last month until the door to the inner office opened.

"I'm Keith," the therapist said as he crossed the waiting room, extending his hand. "Come on in."

Charlie entered the office and sat on the couch. A box of tissues rested on a side table. Posters of fields and flowers decorated the walls. Seemed harmless.

"Tell me about yourself," Keith said. "And if you feel like it, tell me about your wife and daughter." He sat back in his chair, a pad and pen in his lap.

They'd spoken on the phone when Charlie made the appointment. Keith knew why Charlie wanted to see him, but he didn't know much about Sierra and Maya. Charlie settled in and talked about his work, family, how it was to be a young, single dad. How he missed his wife.

He took a deep breath and released the air. Swiped a tissue from the box, tearing it into pieces and piling them on the couch beside him as he talked. His foot tapped against the carpet.

"I didn't realize how hard it would be, you know, afterward," he said. He sat back into the tufts of the couch and folded his hands. "I thought I would cry at the funeral and then be sad for a long time and miss her, but that my life would go back to normal after a while. It's not happening. I cry when I'm alone. A lot." He looked down at his lap. "I feel like there's something wrong with me. Like I'm broken." He reached for the box of tissues.

Keith gave him a moment, waited until Charlie had wiped his eyes and nose and looked back at him. For the first time, he softened his voice as he spoke.

"Crying is a natural part of the healing process. It doesn't mean you're broken. Just means you haven't quite healed yet. Don't get caught up in the amount of time it takes. It's different for everyone, and it doesn't mean there's anything wrong with you, okay?"

Charlie shrugged his shoulders and looked away. He dabbed at his eyes with a tissue.

"You played sports in high school, right?" Keith asked.

"Yeah." He looked back at Keith.

"Did you ever break a bone?"

"Yeah. I broke my arm once."

"And did you wear a cast?"

"Sure. For a few weeks."

"Right. Until your arm healed. If your doctor had removed the cast too soon, your arm would have hurt. Because you weren't healed. Your arm wouldn't have been ready to go back to normal, whatever normal was, playing football or basketball or carrying your books around.

"The crying you're experiencing is part of that same process. It's healing, working the pain out of your body, your mind, your heart. Now, if you can't function, if you're crying all the time, then we need to have a different conversation. But if not, if it's just working its way through you in these moments, then you have to give it time. It doesn't mean there's anything wrong with you. It's perfectly normal. Does that make sense?"

"Yeah, I think so."

The following week Charlie sat down and launched into a story about Maya. Keith smiled and sat back.

"I'm trying to teach her how to throw and catch. It's fun, running around in the yard with her. Takes my mind off work and missing Sierra."

"How's the crying? Getting any better?"

"I think so. I'm kind of thinking about it like a broken bone now, like you said. When it comes, I just let it out. When I'm okay, I figure I'm getting better." He hesitated. "There are times that it's easier to think about her. To remember her. I guess that means something."

He talked about spending time with his family, how they propped him up and helped heal the break. How he looked forward to feeling like himself again.

Keith listened. He watched Charlie's expressions to see if he was getting the whole of the young man. When he heard something, a loose thread, he picked at the stitching to see if it would give way. Some moments Charlie pulled back. Others he let go. Charlie wept when he told a story about Sierra. He beamed when he mentioned his daughter.

Near the end of their fourth session, Keith sensed it was time to press.

"I get the impression there's something you're not telling me," he said as the time wound down. "I know this is difficult, but is there anything else you might want to share with me?"

Charlie held Keith's gaze. The clock ticked. Charlie smiled.

"I don't know what you mean. I've told you all there is to tell. I think I just need more time, like you said. You know how it is. Some days are good, others not so great." He leaned over in his seat and put his face in his hands. Keith waited.

"She was my life," Charlie said, sitting up. "The center of my universe. Then Maya came along, and the two of them were my whole world. Half of that's gone, and I need to adjust. I'm getting there, but I'm not quite there yet.

"Listen, thanks for everything," Charlie said, looking at the clock and rising from the couch. "These last few weeks have helped a lot. But I think I've said everything I need to say. I just need to focus on my daughter and move on. Okay?"

"Of course. You're right," Keith said as he stood.

"Sometimes you need to let things settle down to help the healing process play out. You find there's only so much to talk about. But if you realize in a few weeks or months or years, whatever it is, that you want to talk some more, call me." He walked across the room, opened the door to the empty waiting room, and turned back to Charlie.

"Sometimes we have feelings we're not quite ready to talk about. There's no expiration date on this stuff. You don't get rid of grief like bad milk by pouring it down the drain. I'm here. I'll be here."

Charlie nodded, shook Keith's hand and headed toward the waiting room. He looked back to say something, but he just smiled and nodded again. He closed the door behind him.

Charlie pulled into the driveway one evening as the wind scattered leaves across the backyard. I'll have to rake this weekend, he thought. His mother had placed her annual pumpkins on the front step. Halloween was coming. Maya would need a costume.

He had worked late, leaving his mother to feed his daughter dinner. When he came inside to pick her up, she was sleeping on the couch, her face slack and thoughts miles away in dream.

"Hi, Ma," Charlie said as he came in the kitchen door, pecking her cheek. "How was she today? How was your day?"

Carolyn paused to look at her son. She'd been watching him struggle with the daily battle of grief versus perseverance. She didn't know how he would respond to her latest report.

"She was great, as always, but it was different today." She hesitated. "It was the first day she didn't ask."

Charlie looked away, sighed. "It's okay, Ma. We knew this day would come. It doesn't mean anything," he said, a sound beginning to pierce his ear. Only he would ever hear this sound.

They had talked about this in the days after Sierra's death. Maya had kept asking for her, and it took time and conversations with the priest and pediatrician to figure out how to explain to a little girl that there would be this void, this ache, this unknown part of her life left unknowable. She asked every day, of each of her caregivers. "Where's Mommy?" Each person was instructed to tell the same story: Mommy had been sick and was in heaven.

In the beginning, Maya would ask the questions everyone expected. What's heaven? Where is it? When will she be back? Is God going to make her better? After a while, Maya abandoned illness and geography and asked only one question.

"When is Mommy coming back?"

Every time she asked it of Charlie, the noise returned. Waves crashing the seawall and gulls screeching and sirens blazing and lions roaring, all together in a collage of crescendo. It was all he could do to shake his head, to knock back the shrill. To look at his daughter, swallow hard, and give her the same answer.

"She's not coming back, sweetie."

The first few weeks Maya would cry. She'd stomp her feet or roll on the floor or punch her fists at whoever was closest and offering this unacceptable explanation. Eventually, when she knew both the forthcoming answer and that all the tantrums and cunning of a child couldn't change the response, she did what her father could not. She let go. At least, that's what the adults believed.

So when Charlie came home from work that day and learned Maya hadn't asked for her mother, it was like this reversal. This opposite stage of her development, one that should never happen for someone so small and sweet. The opposite of her first smile, her first "Mama" or "Dada," her first step, first tooth, first everything. The culmination of the worst first. The first death. The first one that mattered.

"It's okay, Ma. It doesn't mean she's forgotten. Just means I have to work harder to make sure she remembers."

The sound inside him quieted. He took a deep breath, released the air and wiped his eyes. He walked to the couch, picked up his sleeping child, and carried her out the door and up the stairs to bed.

Charlie found peace when he settled into a routine. Most days he came home early and created his own way of caring for his daughter. He made dinner, picking up Maya and putting her on the counter before assembling his palette. Some nights it was ramen and applesauce, like a college student rather than a tired father still feeling the effects of his mourning. His mother didn't approve, but he insisted on cooking dinner for his daughter, at least most nights of the week. They had an unspoken understanding, along with Pat, that the grandmothers would make sure the child was well-nourished while under their care. He, effectively, could do no harm.

With time, he resumed the cooking style of the early days of his marriage. He boiled water for spaghetti and browned ground beef with onions and garlic. He poured a jar of sauce in the pan and let the small kitchen simmer with aroma while he tore iceberg lettuce, peeled carrots—always using one to talk like Bugs Bunny to the thrill of his daughter—and chopped tomatoes and green peppers. He taught Maya to eat salad in small doses, working vegetables past her protests until she learned to reach for the carrots on her own.

Twelve

1992

"YOUR GRANDMA MUST NOT BE feeding you very well these days," he said, looking off to the side of his cutting board. Maya was standing next to him, ostensibly to help, but pilfering slices of carrot when he looked away. Biting down on a larger chunk, she muffled a shriek before running for the bathroom.

"Finally getting that loose one out?" he yelled around the corner.

She wandered back into the room, a tissue pushed up against the space in her upper jaw. She'd become adept at the removal, the clean-up, and the payment process.

"Looks like the tooth fairy will be coming tonight," Charlie said. He looked at his second-grader and marveled at how she'd grown, how she knew so many small ways to take care of herself. Then she surprised him.

"Is Mommy coming, too?" she asked.

Charlie's chin dropped. His breath caught, snagged on a

shard buried deep in his chest. He heard a train approaching from far away, chugging up the grade of the small kitchen, its whistle stabbing holes in the quiet as it passed through his heart and out into the dark night. The noise receded but its heaviness remained.

He put down the vegetable peeler and wiped his hands on a kitchen towel. He picked up Maya and sat her on the counter, leaned against the cabinet to study her face.

"Do you think she's coming?"

Maya pulled the tissue out of her mouth, examined the blood as it darkened. She flicked her tongue through the new opening a few times before considering her father.

"Not really. But I thought if the tooth fairy got lost Mommy could show her the way. She'd know where to find us."

He smiled and kissed the end of his daughter's nose. "You're right, honey. Mommy would know exactly where to find us."

It had been a long time since Maya had asked about the return of her mother. Sierra was a part of their lives. She lived on in pictures on the shelf, thick albums, and bedtime stories. On Maya's dresser sat a photo of Sierra at the top of a mountain after a long hike. Her smile filled the frame, eyes twinkling through the glass.

During these years bedtime stories became a special ritual for Charlie. No matter how crazy his day, he could settle in next to his daughter and escape into a fairytale. Sometimes Maya would ask for one of her favorite books. The cat with the striped hat bringing rainy afternoon entertainment. Pooh's paws dripping with honey. But Saturday nights were the special story nights. The tradition started after Maya spent an evening with Carolyn and Pete while Charlie went out for dinner with Mike.

Mike and Charlie had been inseparable since elementary

school. Mike was a bigger kid, and athletic scholarship offers arrived from schools all over New England. He chose Portsmouth State in southern New Hampshire. The school was close enough for him to run home whenever he needed, whether for laundry or lasagna, and it allowed him to play football and study marine science, his two passions. He earned his degree and a conference championship while his best friend endured potty-training and built homes and office buildings.

Mike made sure to come home periodically to drag Charlie out of the house. One Saturday night, the two enjoyed a boys' night out.

"What's up, man?" Charlie asked, looking at the pub menu he could recite from childhood. He barely read a word. He'd be ordering a burger. Menus for these men were props.

"Not much," Mike said, closing his menu. "Grinding through the course work until I can get out on the water." Mike was in a Ph.D. program and would be leaving soon to spend the summer on a research vessel. "I'm pretty psyched to ship out and see what's going on at the bottom of the ocean." He started to explain his current project on cod migration when he noticed he'd lost his audience.

"What's up with you?" he asked. "How's the angel?"

"She's awesome, doing good in school, making lots of friends. She's a blast to be around," Charlie said, smiling as he put the menu down. The waiter came and took their order, brought them each a beer.

"That's great. Good to hear she's making friends." He paused. "How 'bout you? Making any new friends?"

Charlie sipped his beer and set the bottle on the table. He wiped his mouth with the back of his hand. "Nah, man, I've lived in Seaport all my life. I know everyone here."

"That's not what I'm talking about, and you know that." Mike put his beer down and looked closely at his friend. "It's time, Mit. You're a great dad, don't get me wrong, but you live the life of someone decades older than you. A monk. You need to get out there, have some fun, go on a date. Sierra would want that."

Charlie had expected this speech, when his family and friends would beg him to stop the carousel, climb off the horse, steady his feet and move on. To find something else, someone else, to give his attention and love to besides his little girl.

"I gotta take a leak. I'll be right back."

Charlie left the table and walked around the bar to the back hallway. Alone in the men's room, he stood at the sink. He washed his hands, paused for a moment to watch the water curl around the basin and rush down the drain. It all moved so fast. Seemed like just yesterday he was holding her hand.

He sighed and shook his head as he turned off the water and reached for a paper towel. I'm not ready, he thought, looking up at the mirror. I know what they want for me, but I can't give it to them. Maybe someday, but not yet.

He dried his hands and opened the door to the bar. He stopped at the pool table to tease one of his employees about burying the eight ball before heading back to his booth.

"Look, bro, don't get mad, I'm not trying to stir anything up," Mike said when Charlie sat down. He paused. "I just think you owe it to yourself and Maya to start thinking about it. To think about your life without Sierra."

Charlie sat back against the worn vinyl of the booth and sipped his beer. He held the bottle in his hands and began to peel off bits of paper, remembering the old joke about girls picking at beer labels. He laughed and shook his head, looked up at Mike. He thought of his reflection in the bathroom mirror, of the water falling away.

"It's cool, Mikey, I'm not mad. I just, I don't know. Sierra and I talked about all that, and I know I'm young and have my whole life ahead of me and all that crap. But what I don't know is how to get there from here. It's like I have this set of feelings, and I know what they are. I'm happy when I think of Sierra, and I'm sad because I miss her. But she gave me this great gift, and right now, the only person I want to love is my daughter. I don't think I have anything to offer anyone else."

Charlie scraped at the label, leaving the wet paper on the table. He sat for a moment, absentmindedly pushing the pile together until it formed a heart. With his index finger he slashed a jagged line from the top right of the sculpture to the bottom left. He picked up the pieces of the broken heart and dropped them into his empty beer bottle, looked up at Mike with a grin.

"Guess I must be pretty hard up, like the girls in high school, huh?"

"Yeah, man," Mike chuckled. "But don't worry about it. We'll get you out there when you're ready."

They looked at each other a moment longer. Charlie nodded his head once to acknowledge that the subject had been discussed and was done. He cleared his throat.

"This is going to sound stupid, but you're going off to sea and I figure you'll probably get hit over the head by a whale's tail or something and forget I ever said it. So I might as well say it to you since you're my best friend."

The waiter came by and placed their burgers and a second round of beers on the table. Charlie put ketchup on the bun and jammed a few fries in his mouth. He bit into his burger, chewed slowly and swallowed. Sipped his beer before he spoke.

"There was this night when Sierra was pregnant when she started getting all philosophical. Talking about how things feel, and how they made her feel. Like the baby's skin would feel soft, but the experience of touching her skin would bring out all these emotions. I think for her, that was what life was all about. The details. Because ultimately it was the little things that mattered to her."

Charlie pictured Sierra sitting beside him at the beach, digging her hand into the sand the way she'd described, past the powder into the damp grit. The simple pleasure of sitting at the shore, feeling the earth, the water. He saw it now. That the feel of something so fundamental, so whole, could bring joy or pain, laughter or remorse. He thought of his Red Sox blanket. Of how much love and despair he had buried in the soft fibers.

Charlie remembered Sierra's face, how her cheeks had reddened as she'd talked. How she'd looked away, waiting for him to reach for her. To bring her close.

"Anyway, she was always way smarter than me, so I covered. I told her I understood what she meant, but I don't think I did. I think I'm starting to get it now.

"I think she wanted to reach out into the world and touch everything that was coming so she would know what it felt like, and then how it would make her feel. Each moment of whatever was ahead.

"It's like when we were playing basketball in high school. We'd be in a big game against one of our rivals, maybe Gloucester, and I'd be running down the court waiting for Blake or whoever else was playing point to pass me the ball. I'd get past my man or to the zone, and I'd be rubbing my fingers together, waiting for the point guard to pass me the ball. I could already feel the ball hitting my hands, bouncing it to get set and lifting up for the shot. But it doesn't matter whether it goes in or hits the rim or even if I air ball. It's that moment when the leather hits my hands. That's the sensation I'm waiting for. That's when I know I'm living. When the ball hits my hands."

Mike looked at his friend. He watched as Charlie blushed, turned away, glanced across the room at a couple leaving the pub and then down at his plate. He watched Charlie pick up a fry, dip it in ketchup and look at it before he put it in his mouth. Watched him chew, sip his beer.

"I get it, Mit. As much as I love my work, sometimes I feel like I'm moving forward, but I'm still waiting for something." Mike sat up straighter in the booth and looked around the room before looking back at Charlie. "I'm not sure what it is."

"Maybe you're just waiting for someone to pass you the ball."

~

Charlie walked in the door that night as Carolyn was tucking Maya into bed and taking a book off the shelf for a story.

"My two favorite ladies," he said with his usual grin. "Hey, Ma, I'll take care of story time. Thanks for watching her."

"Good night with Michael?" Carolyn asked.

"Yeah, it was good."

After Carolyn left, Charlie returned the book she'd chosen to the shelf.

"Tonight, sweetie, I'm going to tell you a story, not read one. A story about Mommy."

Charlie told his daughter about the day he met her mother. How he woke up late, barely left the house with his teeth and hair brushed, and slipped into homeroom seconds before the late bell. Of course he had to explain to Maya what homeroom and the late bell were, but it made the story that much better. Gave him time to recall the details. What she was wearing. How confused she looked as she checked locker numbers in the east wing of the school. Her small hands, thin fingers. The silver ring on her left hand that later he would turn and turn and turn when they sat together watching movies in the dark.

He ended the story with the finding of the locker. In family lore, this became The Great Locker-Finding story, the start of a family tradition.

On Saturday nights, rather than read a story, Charlie would tell one. Either a part of the true story of his life with Sierra—and Maya depending on the timing—or some adventure Charlie imagined would have happened had Sierra still been with them. Climbing mountains and riding wild horses and looking for buried treasure. He explained that Sierra and he had planned to take Maya to all these fantastical places. He told her stories as if the trips played out in front of him on the bedroom wall. Maya cuddled beneath her blankets, and Charlie wove the threads of love and imagination into magic carpets that carried the threesome around the Earth.

"I'm ready for our story, Daddy," Maya told Charlie a few months later. Saturday nights she was quick to bathe and hop into bed.

"Okay, one day, when you were a baby, your mom and I

decided it was time for an ocean adventure," he said as he swung his feet up on Maya's twin bed. He fluffed a throw pillow behind his head and pulled Maya's comforter over her as she snuggled under his arm.

"It was a summer day, lots of people at the beach and fishing at the pier. We packed up your diaper bag and drove over to the marina. Mr. Hughes, the owner, had just bought a submarine that he was renting out for day trips. So we decided to take it out. There was a rumor around town that someone who rented it the week before had seen a sea monster, so we wanted to see for ourselves.

"We got down to the marina and your mom unpacked our things. We had a cooler of sandwiches and sodas for Mommy and me, and you were eating baby food by then so we had some jars of peas and bananas for you. Mom took all our stuff down to the end of the dock while I went inside to sign the paperwork for Mr. Hughes."

"What were we wearing?"

"Oh, sorry, I forgot. Mandatory details. You had on a yellow onesie with a blue dolphin stitched on the front. I had on some old gym shorts and a Celtics t-shirt and Nike basketball high-tops. Your mom was wearing beige hiking shorts and a red t-shirt. She had her hair pulled back away from her face in a ponytail, but it was a windy day, so by the time we got onboard wisps of her hair had escaped. I had to keep reaching over and tucking them behind her ears so she could see you."

Charlie looked over at Maya. She had closed her eyes as he described the scene.

"No bathing suits?"

"Nope. We were going in the submarine to the bottom of the ocean. If we needed bathing suits we would have been in big trouble."

Maya opened her eyes and smiled, waited for her father to continue.

"So we get onboard and as Mr. Hughes had told me it's an easy machine to operate. There were instructions on the dashboard, but it was basically start her up, push a few levers and off you go. Your mom had you strapped into your car seat, which we buckled into a chair behind us, and then she and I sat down in front. It was a little tight as it was only made for four people, but we squeezed in our cooler and your diaper bag and sealed up the hatch.

"On the inside, there were all sorts of lights and gizmos flashing on the front panel, but Mr. Hughes told me that as long as they all stayed green and blue, all would be well. I read the instructions, revved the engine, and off we went."

"Wait, what color was it?"

"The inside was a light grey, you know, like a space ship. The outside, naturally, was yellow." Charlie smiled at Maya and pinched her nose.

"We started motoring away from the dock while we were still above water so we could run a few tests, and everything checked out so we descended. We puttered around near the marina for a few minutes so I could make sure that all the lights were the right colors, and they looked good so we headed out to deeper water. That's when it got cool.

"It got dark fast so your mom turned on the headlights, and right away we saw all kinds of fish in all sorts of colors. Blue, green, yellow, red, orange. Some had stripes, others were solid colors, and we even saw a few with polka dots on them. Pink with white dots, like your bathing suit from last summer."

"Dad ..."

"No, for real. Anyway, after a while your mom and I decided it was time to go look for the sea monster, so we lowered the submarine down to the ocean floor and put on the high beams. We drove around and saw some sharks and lots of cool plants, and after a while we stopped for a break and had lunch. It was quiet down there, just the three of us, very peaceful."

Charlie took a drink of water from the glass on Maya's nightstand.

"Were you scared? With all the sharks swimming around?"

"Well, the submarine was pretty strong, so I wasn't scared. And then your mom started singing whatever words she remembered from "Yellow Submarine" so I was too busy giggling to be afraid. Then once I started giggling so did you, and before we knew it the three of us were laughing so hard I thought we might use up all the oxygen.

"It was getting near the end of our rental time and we decided we should head back up, figuring we weren't going to find the sea monster. Your mom wanted to drive, so we switched seats and she took over the controls. I was putting our lunch stuff away in the cooler when she gasped. I looked up, and sure enough right in front of the submarine was the sea monster."

"What did it look like?"

"It was big, probably eight feet tall, and it had four legs and a set of tentacles. Its skin shimmered mostly green in the light of the submarine, but it had some blue and orange in it too. It had a long face, like a dog's snout, and when it turned its head to look at us it almost looked like it was smiling. At first it seemed scared, but then it looked right past me and your mom and directly at you. Then it really smiled and gave us a little wave before it swam off into the darkness.

"Wow, so it was friendly?"

"Yup, a friendly old sea monster."

"Did you chase after it?"

"No, that wouldn't have been right. We'd already invaded its home. It was time to go. So we took the submarine up to the surface and went back to the marina."

"Did you get any pictures?"

"No pictures, but maybe tomorrow you and I can draw some, okay?"

"Okay. Of the three of us, on the submarine with the sea monster."

"A drawing of the three of us would be perfect." He leaned over to kiss her cheek and stood to leave. "Night."

"Hey, Dad, can I ask you something?"

"Sure, sweetie." He sat back down, tucked the comforter underneath his daughter's sides.

"Did Mom and me do a lot of stuff together when I was little?"

He smiled. "Yes. You and your mom had lots of special time together, your own adventures. You'd bake cookies. And even though you were little, she'd find tasks for you. Pour the chocolate chips in the bowl. Grease the pan.

"She'd take you to the library about once a week. You'd come home with an armload of books, and she'd spend the next few days reading to you." He paused. "Never took long for you to find a favorite in each stack, and by the third or fourth day she pretty much knew no matter what other story she read you, she'd have to read the new favorite, too. Before long you were turning pages, pointing to the pictures, telling her what was about to happen. She loved how quickly you learned. How much you loved stories.

"But I think her favorite activity was putting you in your stroller and taking you down to the ocean. Even in winter, she'd bundle you up. She'd let you run around, chase seagulls, pick up shells."

He remembered one October afternoon when he'd driven by the beach on his way home from a jobsite. He'd parked his truck in the lot and walked over to where Sierra sat on the seawall. Maya was playing in the sand at her feet. Sierra stared at the water, her face drawn. A sharp gust blew across the shore. He sat beside her, took her hand. She turned to him, offered a half smile. Tears dampened her cheeks. He caught his breath, afraid to ask whether the tears were from the cold wind blowing off the ocean. Or whether they were from sadness, from the loss of what waited beyond the horizon. The loss of what might have been.

~

One Sunday night a few years later, Charlie came in Maya's room to say goodnight. He looked at the shelf for a book.

"It's okay, Dad. I don't really need a story."

Charlie looked at his daughter, nestled in and ready for sleep. He realized the stories over the last couple of years had been her nightly gift to him, not the reverse.

"Oh, honey, of course. You're starting middle school in the fall." He shook his head, smiled at his mistake. He turned to leave and reached for the light switch.

"Hey, Dad?"

Charlie turned back to look at her.

"We can still do the storytelling on Saturday nights, though. I mean, if it's cool with you."

Charlie walked to the bed, kissed his daughter's cheek. "Yeah, honey, it's cool with me."

Thirteen

2003

CHARLIE ROSE FROM THE SEAWALL. They'd been sitting a couple of hours. The sun was setting over the tops of the houses behind them, a breeze crossed the beach. "I loved your mother very much. I miss her everyday. And I'm so grateful for you." He held his hand out to his daughter. "But you're grown now. Time for you to pack your bags and start your own life." He stared down at the sand, the tiny grains. Like the moments of his life, they all blended together and stretched in a blur along the shoreline. An infinity of everything and nothing at all.

Maya took his hand and stood. She thought about her mother as she hugged her father. About how their life would have been had she lived. Maybe this beach would have been their place. Maybe this place would have been enough.

She let her father go. Picked up Archie's leash and led them home.

Maya thought she had a good plan. Move to Key West and room with other kids. Take some classes, get a job in a marina. Some parts worked out.

"Ugh, these girls," she said to her father before their story one Saturday night. "I swear all they want to do is drink."

She'd met her roommates online. Kerry, a young woman from Chicago majoring in nursing, came to Key West in search of a warmer walk to class. Liza escaped boredom in Jacksonville to pursue hospitality. Both girls, Maya soon realized, were more interested in happy hour than study hour.

"Maya, you coming out tonight?" Liza stuck her head in Maya's doorway. "Geez look at all those books. Marine science looks like a ton of work."

"It's not so bad, but I do have some reading I need to do tonight so don't count on me."

"Girl, we don't ever count on you. But we'll be around whenever you're ready. We're not going out until later anyway. Kerry has a shift at the raw bar. So if you change your mind, call me. We'll be at Dylan's for a while." Liza looked around the small room. "I don't know how you put up with this tiny space. I would lose my mind."

"How? It's cheap. I remind myself of that whenever I roll out of bed and bump into the wall." She smiled at Liza, waved her away. "Go. I have to study. I'll call if I want to come out."

"Sure," Liza said, smiling. "Later."

Classes were interesting, but her heart wouldn't connect to the work. She studied, maintained As and Bs. But the sunshine and the marina called her. In class her mind left the lecture and drifted to the wharf.

One Friday afternoon after her shift, she sat down on the dock, slipped off her boat shoes, and dangled her feet in the water. She pulled on the threads hanging from the ends of her painter's pant cutoffs. An old pair of her mother's she'd found in a closet the year before and hacked into shorts. She wore them with her dad's old Patriots t-shirts when she missed home.

Maya's boss, Joe, a wiry transplant from Halifax, spotted her as he left the office.

"Hey, what's going on?"

"Not much. Figured I'd sit here and listen to the commotion while the sun goes down."

The commotion was the nightly sunset celebration on nearby Mallory Square. A juggler tossing pins in the air from atop a weaving unicycle. A mime climbing out of an imaginary box. An old islander sitting at a cart under a canopy, hacking open coconuts with a machete. Tourists strolling along the seawall, sipping coconut milk with pink and purple paper umbrellas, watching the orange sun melt into the edge of the sea.

Some evenings Maya would wander through the crowd. She'd listen to the banter between the audience and street performers, checking for any Boston accents among the visitors. She felt a little homesick when she heard one. More so when she didn't.

Joe sat down on the dock beside Maya. He crossed his legs and faced his young employee. He was in his mid-thirties, a permanent bachelor who lived on a small sailboat in dry dock. Maya reminded him of his younger sister.

"You don't want to walk over? Must be some kids who go for sunset."

"Nah, I'm good. I'd rather be here. I need to go home and study, but I don't feel like it."

"Well, it's Friday, so I understand a lack of motivation."

"Yeah, but that's not it."

On the next dock, a fishing guide stood at a cleaning station and pulled yellowtail out of a cooler. A pelican perched its webbed feet on the boat below him. Another landed steps away and waddled toward the cooler. He shooed them away as a seagull circled overhead.

"I'm just not into marine science, and it was the only subject I thought I might like. So if that's not doing it for me, I don't know what to do." She looked up at Joe and shrugged her shoulders. "Maybe this wasn't the right decision, coming down here. Maybe I should go home."

"Hang on a second." Joe stood and jogged into the office. He returned with half a key lime pie, two forks, and paper towels.

"A friend came over for dinner last night and brought dessert. I think this conversation requires pie."

"Sounds good to me," Maya said. She pulled her feet up, shook off the water, and turned to face Joe. Crossed her legs and picked up a fork.

"So, Boston," he said, taking a bite. "You think that's what you want?"

Maya's mouth puckered as the tang of the key lime danced on her taste buds. She took another bite. The sugary meringue dissolved and broke the tartness.

"Wow, this is good." She put her fork down on the pie plate and wiped graham cracker crumbs from her mouth.

"Do I want to go back? No. But if I'm going to waste time, I can go home and save the rent. Take classes at the community college near my house. Get my old job back."

Joe nodded a few times as he wiped his mouth. "Yup, you can do that. But that's not what you want. Look, I know you're not like your roommates. You're not here to drink rum runners and party with the spring breakers. But you are a wanderer. You may not know what you want to do, but you sure as hell know you don't want to go home. Right?"

Maya crinkled her nose. "Yeah, I guess. But how do you figure out where you belong?"

"Ah, the million-dollar question. Some people never do. They come here for the sun and the salt air and the tequila and think the sound of the breeze through the palm trees will help them find a purpose in life. Most only find the worm at the bottom of the bottle." He took another bite of pie.

"That's what happened to me, but a buddy pulled me out while there was still something to grab onto. Been sober for three years, eight months and . . . twelve days," he said, looking down at his watch. "I don't want to go back to that life. But I also don't want to leave here."

"Don't you miss Halifax?"

"I do. I miss the hills and summers in the public gardens. There's this great park at the end of the peninsula. Point Pleasant Park. Has all these trails that wind through the woods. I used to take my dog there when I was a kid. Just when you think you're lost you turn a corner and there's the water again." He sat for a moment, recalling the gravel paths, the pine forests. The wind pushing him back to the edge of the sea.

A seagull fluttered toward the ground, landed on a mooring post nearby.

"Anyway, I miss it, but not enough. I go up in the summer for a visit, get a little nostalgic. But as soon as I'm back in Key West, I know I'm where I'm supposed to be. Nova Scotia will always feel special, but my life is here. This is my home."

Maya nodded. "I think I feel that way about New England,

too. But it's hard to tell since I haven't been here very long or gone back yet."

She looked over at the next dock. The guide threw a last scrap to the pelican standing beside him. The bird caught the raw fish in his beak. He slurped the morsel into his throat pouch, spread his wings, and flew across the cove. Maya turned back to Joe.

"I don't know if I'm meant to be here for good. But I think I'm meant to be here for now. Guess I just have to give marine science a chance. I promised my dad I'd stay in school."

"Well, you don't have to stick with marine science. If you don't see yourself doing research and going to school forever, take some vocational classes. Learn how to fix engines and run a boat. And if you have some great epiphany someday that you want to be a dentist or write romance novels, you can always go back to school. You know Shep? The guy that fixes engines here at the marina? He teaches engine repair at FKCC. Talk to him."

~

Maya finished the semester in marine science. After talking with Shep, she registered for courses on marine gasoline and diesel engines and fiberglass repair. She added accounting and entrepreneurship, in case she might want to run her own business some day.

One change she hadn't considered was the shift in the student body. In marine science, women filled about half of the seats. Her business classes attracted slightly more men. In marine technology, she often was the only female or one of just a few.

She felt awkward at first. Some of the guys would stare or

question whether she could handle the work. She kept her head down, held her own. Shep helped.

"Don't worry," he told her after her first class. "Most guys will leave you alone. You'll get a few snide comments, but that'll pass. Trust me, most of them will be happy to have you here. Just watch out for the overly friendly ones. They're just looking to get in your pants."

"You're probably right. I just need to work hard. So they see I'm serious."

In the first week of basic seamanship, the teacher asked one of Maya's classmates to pass out reading material. Jeremy was tall and lean with shaggy brown hair. When he placed the pages in front of the blond girl in the Red Sox cap, he pushed the hair out of his eyes and nodded. He blushed as he moved to the next student.

A few classes later, Jeremy found his courage. Maya was leaving class when he appeared by her side.

"Hey, uh, were you in class on Monday?" he asked. "I was out and missed the notes. Could I grab them from you? I'll buy you a coffee." He held the door as they left the classroom.

Maya assessed the invitation. He was cute and a little shy. "Yeah, I was here. Sounds fair." They walked to the café in the student center, each sneaking side glances.

"By the way, I'm Jeremy."

"Maya. Nice to meet you."

"So, what do you think of the class so far?" he asked as they found a table in the café. He pulled out a chair for her and set his backpack on another before taking a seat.

"Thanks," she said, placing her coffee on the table and her bag on the seat beside her. "I like it. I was in marine science last semester. This is pretty different. But I love being on the water so I'm excited. It's just weird being the only female in class. I'm hoping the guys don't notice."

"Trust me, they notice." His cheeks reddened. "I mean 'cause you're hot," he said as the color spread to his forehead. "I should probably just stop talking."

Maya blushed as she sipped her coffee. "Thanks." She shook her head and looked down at the table as his kindness melted into her skin. She felt a warm rush as she reached in her bag for her laptop. She wasn't adept at responding to compliments.

"I guess we should get to the notes?" She hoped her smile would show she liked him. That she wished they could sit awhile longer.

After a few more conversations, he invited her over to study for an exam. He lived in a restored conch house a few blocks off Duval Street. Coconut palms dotted the yard. Their thick green fronds shaded the white clapboards and turquoise shutters.

"What's your story?" she asked. Jeremy was at the stove stirring macaroni and cheese. Maya sat at the table with their books. "This is a pretty nice house for a college student, especially one with no roommates."

"Oh, I couldn't afford this place," he said over his shoulder. "It's my folks'. They come down on weekends and vacation.

"I grew up in Plantation, near Fort Lauderdale. I started at Broward Community College, but I wasted my first year partying. My parents were frustrated. They knew I needed to get out of town. They told me I could come down here as long as I kept my grades up. If I don't, I'm out on my own. They won't even pay tuition."

"You don't think you'll party more down here?"

"Nah, now that I'm away from my boys I'm fine. I miss my friends, don't get me wrong. But I needed to get away. I was partying too much. My grades were all right in high school, but I had no idea what I wanted to do. My folks figured I'd go to a four-year school. But I put off applying so long I missed all the deadlines."

"Wow. Bet that went over well."

He laughed as he placed their bowls on the table. He pulled out a chair next to Maya and sat down.

"Yeah, they were pissed. But I think they saw the writing on the wall. After last year, this seemed like a good compromise. Got me away. Forced me to learn how to live on my own. Plenty of nights of mac and cheese, but I don't mind. I guess I'm finding myself," he said with a chuckle, shaking his head. "And I work as a barback at Capt. Tony's. The money's decent, and the hours keep me out of trouble. At the end of a shift, I'm usually so tired I just go home and crash. What about you?"

"Well, nothing as interesting as that. I just knew I had to leave. My mom died when I was little. My dad's great, but he never got over losing my mom. I needed to get away for a while."

"That must have been tough, not having a mom," Jeremy said, unsure what to say.

"I guess. She died when I was young, so it's all I know."

"Do you have any memories of her?"

Maya pushed the pasta around in her bowl. She picked up an elbow of macaroni and stuck it in her mouth, letting the salt from the cheese dissolve on her tongue. She chewed as she considered his question.

"Yeah, but it's weird. I have some memories I know are real, because I've asked my dad about them. Then I have these dream memories I know didn't happen, but they're so vivid they seem real. I think I've made those up without knowing it."

"Like what? If you don't mind me asking."

"No, no, it's fine." She pushed her chair back and sat cross-legged. "Okay, so a real one. I'm in the kitchen sitting on my little scooter, and my mom and dad are making dinner together. She's cutting up vegetables for a salad, and he's opening a jar of tomato sauce. I'm scooting around them, weaving in and out. He takes the lid off the jar and sticks his finger in the sauce. Then he puts a dot on her nose. She tilts her head back and laughs. This great, big belly laugh, like it's the funniest thing in the world. Like my dad just won *Last Comic Standing* or something." She paused for a moment, smiled.

"Then she wipes her nose with the back of her hand. She runs her hand under the faucet and dries it on the towel slung over her shoulder. She goes back to the vegetables and hip bumps him. He smiles. Then he kisses her cheek. This loud, wet, raspberry of a kiss.

"For a moment I think they've forgotten I'm there. I'm just sitting on the scooter watching. It was nothing, but it was everything at the same time." She stopped for a moment, stared at the painting on the wall. Pastel palm trees on an empty beach.

"That must sound totally weird," she said.

"No, not at all. Sounds pretty cool. What about one that isn't real? One you think you made up in your head?"

Maya picked up her fork and stabbed a piece of macaroni. She popped it in her mouth and put her fork on the table as she chewed. Ran a hand through her hair and pulled her knees up to her chin. Wrapped her arms around her legs and clasped her hands, ankles crossed.

Jeremy watched the movements of her limbs, the tangling and untangling as she sifted through her memories.

"I have this one I know can't be real. I'm little, so my mom could still be alive. The three of us are climbing these grey stone steps. Lots of steps that seem to go up to the sky. I'm between them, and they're each holding one of my hands. Once in a while we do the 'One, two, three, *wheeeeeee!*' yell and they swing me up a step. I'm giggling and squealing. Eventually we get to the top, and my parents are so happy they were able to take me there. My dad picks me up and puts me on his shoulders so I can see the view. It goes on forever." She rested her chin on her knees.

"Where are you?"

"Oh, sorry, of course you wouldn't know! I didn't either at first. Then I started playing around on the internet and figured it out. It's Chichen Itza, the pyramid there. My dad must have shown me pictures when I was growing up and it became this fantasy of mine." Maya looked at Jeremy. He wasn't following.

"Mayan ruins." She explained the Saturday night story ritual she shared with her father. "He used to mention them from time to time as part of the Raymond Adventures. I think he planned we would go there someday as a family. He hasn't given up on the two of us going so I can see where my name came from.

"Anyway, I think I created this memory from the actual pictures he showed me and some of his stories. It never happened. But it makes me feel good, so I hold onto it."

She took their bowls to the sink, rinsed them, and placed them in the dishwasher.

"You should," he said. He stood and placed a hand on the small of her back. "You definitely should."

~

One afternoon in the fall they were sitting on the patio doing homework. A water fountain bubbled in the corner, muffling the noise from the occasional passing car. Jeremy pushed his book away and grabbed his iced tea. The condensation left a ring on the glass table.

"Was there ever anything special you wanted to do when you were a kid? Like a dream job?" he asked Maya. He popped a piece of ice in his mouth.

She put down her pen, propped her feet up on the edge of his chair.

"You mean like be a rock star? Like you?" She nudged his leg with her bare foot and nodded toward the guitar laying across the next chair.

He put down his cup and pushed away from the table. Picked up his guitar and strummed a few chords.

"Maya, oh Maya, won't you run away with me." He tilted his head back and sang to the sky, pounding the strings three more times for emphasis before returning the instrument to the chair and winking at his girlfriend.

"Yeah, something like that," he said. "I used to sit at my desk in high school and dream up names of punk rock bands. Just by stringing a few words together. Recumbent Pancake. Skinny Beach Balls. Mangoes of Sarcasm."

"How about, Maya's Ruined?" she said. A breeze blew across the yard. She put her pen in her book and closed the cover.

He sat back and watched her chin drop. Self-doubt stole the glow from her skin. "Why would you say that?"

"I don't know. I guess I'm just feeling antsy, like I should be doing something different." She put her feet down and leaned forward, her elbows on her knees, her face in her hands. "Like I'm not making progress." She looked up at him. "There must be more to life than living in Key West and fixing boat engines."

He set his cup on the table and sat up in his chair, sensing an opening. He was finishing his associate's degree and would be studying mechanical engineering at the University of Florida. By next semester he needed to be on campus, an eight-hour drive from Key West on a good day. He hoped Maya would join him, but each time he brought up a move she changed the subject.

"Well, if you're tired of Key West, you could come up to Gainesville and finish your AA at the community college up there. Your dad would be thrilled." He knew this was both true and his only hope of convincing her. He drummed his pencil on his notebook.

She scanned his face. She recognized the expression her father wore as she packed her bags to leave Seaport. Sad but resigned. She wanted to go to Jeremy, to wrap her arms around his neck and kiss the scruff beneath his collar. To pick up his guitar and sing his love songs back to him. The verses he wrote in bed after they'd made love, her head on his chest, his humming lulling her to sleep.

Something gnawed at her, held her back. She reached over and rubbed his arm. She hoped it would be enough to comfort him.

"I don't know," she said. "I'd like to finish what I started here. Then figure out what's next." She paused. "Plus I don't know if UF is the answer for me. But we can try the long distance thing."

"Come on, Maya," he said, pulling away. "You actually think we can make it work? You barely tolerate the phone. Other than your dad, have you spoken to anyone from home in the last six months?"

He leaned back in his chair and adjusted his ball cap. He looked through the gate as a couple walked along the fence toward Duval Street. The man's hands moved with his words as if he was drawing a picture or playing charades. Jeremy couldn't hear him over the gurgle of the water fountain. He sighed and moved his chair toward Maya's.

"Listen, forget it. I'll come down and maybe you can come up once in a while. We'll just see how it goes." He took her hand, wondered how much time would pass before she'd let go. Let him go.

"Of course," she said, smiling. She reached over and touched his cheek.

They tried and failed. Jeremy buried himself in his engineering classes. Maya forgot to return calls. The chorus of his last love song began to fade. After a few months they had a talk. They agreed to be friends, to stay in touch. They didn't.

Fourteen

MAYA CYCLED THROUGH HER FIRST set of roommates and found her second. Before long their late nights proved too much for her early mornings. She told them she'd be moving at the end of the lease. She found a room to rent from an older conch woman named Gladys who had a small house on Catherine Street.

"You're from here?" Maya asked. It was their first evening together. They sat in the family room off the kitchen. Gladys shifted in her recliner, cranked the lever until her feet popped up in front of her. Maya sprawled across the couch. They'd just finished watching *Jeopardy*.

"Yes, I'm a conch," Gladys said, muting the television. "I've lived here all my life. My husband was from Cuba. We met here. Raised our boys here. Anthony, my older boy, teaches history at a small college in Minnesota. He's married, two kids. My younger son, Thomas, lives in Brooklyn and works on Wall Street. I don't understand what he does," she said, waving her hand. "Anyway, the boys couldn't wait to get out. But I like it here. I wish my sons were closer, and my grandchildren of course. But they visit. It's enough."

Short, if not small, Gladys loved to cook and bake. She took rice and beans to church suppers and traded key lime cookies for the electric bill when the letter carrier delivered the mail. Her hip slowed her to a shuffle as she lugged flour and sugar from the cupboard to the table, but she rolled out doughs and mixed batters. She stirred milk and eggs into a creamy custard that she transformed into a golden caramel flan.

While she worked, the radio sprinkled bits of news into her sauces and stews. Gladys shouted her contempt when she disagreed, mumbled acknowledgment when she didn't. Even a grown son could steal a cookie from a cooling rack in exchange for a peck on the cheek. But he knew better than to discuss politics or religion with his feisty mother.

Gladys had spent many years serving food at the Key West High School cafeteria. Her husband died a few years after they both retired, and rather than keep all the bedrooms in her house empty she rented one to a student from time to time. When she found Maya, she saw the shyness, the sweetness, and knew she had a winner. Gladys, like Maya, was early to bed and early to rise. That they both liked *Jeopardy* was a bonus.

Maya moved into Anthony's room. Gladys had replaced the mattress and bedding when she had her first renter. She left the desk, chair, and dresser empty for whoever slept in the bed. For less rent than she paid in the apartment, Maya had a quiet space with room to think.

Maya's new job came as a result of both hard work and luck. Joe had given her as many hours as he could, but he was limited by the marina's needs and budget. One morning a local charter boat captain stormed into the dockmaster's office and slammed the door.

"I'm going to kill that guy!" George yelled.

"What is it this time? No-show or hung over?" Joe asked.

"Complete no-show. Hung over I can handle. But a no-show is a killer. I drove by his apartment and banged on the door. No answer. I've got to find someone new."

"Why don't you offer Maya the job? You know she's a good worker. She'll show up every day, on time, and she'll do anything you ask."

"I know, but I don't think she can handle the heavy lifting. She can't be strong enough."

"Try her out for a couple of days. You don't have to fire the other guy yet. Just give her a chance."

It was early May, the beginning of the best time of year for redfish fishing and a busy period for George. The fish were already running for the season. He had few options. Other boats were set with their mates, and the few floaters he knew around town were no more reliable than his guy. With charters booked through the summer, he needed help now.

A mate's days start early and end late. As George's mate,

Maya would have to be at the dock by six thirty to prepare for the day's trip. Set up the rods. Collect the bait. Fill the coolers with ice. He would have a list of chores for her.

George had his boat, the *Great Catch*, custom-built for charter fishing. The inside was air-conditioned, had a head, and offered some respite for clients looking for a break from the South Florida sun. Simple but comfortable.

The captain ran the boat from the flying bridge above the cabin. The perch allowed George to see in all directions, whether he was looking for fish, birds, or other boats. With room for two, occasionally a client would climb up for the ride if George slowed to trolling speed.

George earned his living and reputation in the stern of the *Great Catch*, a forty-foot sport fisherman. A fighting chair sat in the center of the open space, and a string of rod holders lined the back lip of the flying bridge, overhead but within reach. Outriggers extended the boat's lines out into the ocean. When a fish hit off a trolling rig, the mate's job was to shout up to the captain to stop the boat. The mate would grab the rod out of the holder and hand it to a client. If the fish was of any decent size, the client would sit in the fighting chair, place the rod in the holder at the base of the seat, and reel in the fish. Sometimes they had a quick fight. Other times the angler had to let the fish run, tire itself out. Ten minutes. Twenty. An hour or more. Depending on the species and size, an angler could face a battle to earn the coveted photo of catch in hand.

The morning of George's frustration, he was expecting four guys from Orlando who hoped to leave Key West with mahi mahi. If successful the guys would return to work on Monday and brag to their buddies in the office. Tourists from outside Florida were great, but Orlando was close enough to provide a regular stream of anglers. George wanted this trip to go well as it could help fill up some of the open days on his summer calendar.

"Where is she?" George asked Joe.

"Doing the regular early morning stuff. Opening up."

"Can I steal her from you today?"

"Sure. But when you hire her, and I said when, not if, because you'll love her, you have to find me a replacement."

"Deal. You can have my guy."

Joe found Maya hosing down the dock. On the way to the office, he explained George's predicament. Maya knew George, but only as one of the charter boat captains who came and went each day. She asked Joe if he thought she could handle the work, and she watched for a wince, a moment's hesitation. She wasn't sure herself, but she trusted him.

"You can do this," he said. "George is as good to learn from as any of the guys here at the marina. I've seen him with his kids. They're a little younger than you. He's patient and a good teacher. As soon as he sees you can handle the mate's duties, he'll teach you everything he knows. More than you could ever learn in school."

Maya walked into the office and shook George's hand. He explained what he needed, that this would be a tryout to see if they could work together. That it would be a long day.

"I understand," she told him. "I'm ready."

He led her on board the *Great Catch* and gave her a rundown of the boat. "Since this is new for you, I'm going to handle some of the chores today that typically a mate would do.

You'll catch on. And we'll see if we can work together. If I'm up on the bridge, you may have to shout for me to hear you, so don't be shy. I'll try not to yell at you if you mess up, but don't get upset if I do. Sometimes it happens in the heat of the moment."

George had already performed the prep duties that normally would be Maya's responsibility. He'd filled the fuel and water tanks, gathered the rods and reels and set them in their holders, and lugged the coolers and ice on board. He'd checked the engines and rigged lines with bait so they were ready for trolling.

He stood in the stern, looked around, lifted his hat to scratch the top of his head. "I think we'll be okay," he said. "If you jump in and help when I need you, we can avoid any disasters."

Maya's first lesson was how to prepare the lures for trolling.

"Here, sit next to me and I'll show you how to rig a ballyhoo." He took a fish out of the bait cooler and a hook and bright pink lure from the tackle box. The ballyhoo was long and skinny, more than a foot from its tail fin to the end of its bill.

George sat on the edge of the gunwale and motioned for Maya to sit beside him. He held the fish in one hand and squeezed the body. "You want to get some of the innards out and pop the spine. That'll loosen it up so it looks more natural in the water, like it's swimming." He dumped the guts of the fish over the side of the boat and ran his thumb and finger down the spine of the fish until he felt it give. He held the fish up and wiggled the body. "See?"

"Yeah, I got it."

He snapped off part of the fish's bill, leaving a stump. Next he popped out the eyes and threw them overboard.

Ew, Maya thought, I forgot how nasty this is. She took a deep breath and leaned forward to gather her focus. Followed the movement of George's hands.

"To rig it, I'm going to thread the hook through the body from the head. Before I do that I place the hook against the side of the fish to measure where the end of the hook will come out." He held the hook up to the body. "Once I find the right spot, I puncture a hole in the fish to mark the exit point." He made a small hole with the end of the hook. "Then I thread the hook in below the gills and out through my exit point." He inserted the hook near the head of the fish, moving it through the interior and out the hole. "When I'm done I tie the whole thing up." He pushed a pin rigged on the lure through the lower and upper jaws of the fish, looping a rubber band over it and around the fish's mouth to hold the lure at the top of the hook.

"You see?" He held out the fish and lure to show her the finished product. "The bright colors of the lure attract the mahi mahi to the ballyhoo." He waved the fish as if it was swimming through the water. "And the way it moves makes it more likely to convince the dolphin to bite." He placed the rig into the bucket of water by his feet.

"You get how I did that? We can go through it again later."

"I think I've got the general idea, but I'll need to practice."

"Okay, good. Here's the game plan." He slapped his hands together. "I'm not going to troll right away. I want to get a little farther offshore. But keep an eye out for birds or weed lines or floating stuff along the way. You know the drill, right?"

"I think so." She'd been out fishing for mahi mahi a couple of times with friends, though she still had to remind herself it wasn't Flipper they were after. Mahi mahi, also known as dorado, dolphinfish, or dolphin to the locals, were predictable.

They liked to feed on the smaller fish that hid below the cover of anything floating on the surface of the water.

"First we're looking for weed lines. We can usually find good lines after a storm like we had a couple of days ago. Also keep an eye out for something floating. A cooler, broken buoy. Any kind of trash. If you see anything like that, holler. The smaller fish tend to gather underneath that stuff. And the dolphin feed on the smaller fish. We're also looking for frigates. You know what they look like?"

"Are those the skinny, black birds?"

"Yeah. If you see a few flying around in circles up high, there could be fish in the water. Or if you see one flying low above the water or diving below the surface, that may be something. Mahi and frigates eat the same fish. If a frigate is finding fish, dolphin may be close by."

"With weed lines and buoys and frigates, do you always find fish?"

"Most of the time we hit on something. No guarantees though. A few years ago I worked on a boat out of Marathon. From there we could get out pretty quickly to the West Hump. You heard of that? It's great for fishing. Always did well there."

Maya shook her head.

"It's like a hill that comes out of nowhere on the ocean floor. You have this dramatic change in water depth from about a thousand feet to less than five hundred at the top." He motioned the rise of a hill with his hand. "The Gulf Stream flies over the Hump so the current pushes the water up the hill toward the surface, and with that all sorts of baitfish. Dolphin, wahoo, they love the area. From here I won't run that far. But it was fun back in the day.

"Anyway, for today keep an eye out for weed lines, birds,

coolers. If we find something we'll throw some lures and baitfish on the outriggers and troll. If we get a hit on a ballyhoo, we might luck into a school and get all our guys going one right after the other."

Maya nodded in the direction of four men in their early forties heading down the dock. "Looks like the clients are here."

After introductions, the men boarded the boat. Maya untied the lines, coiled them on the dock, and jumped on.

"You guys can put whatever food or drinks you brought in the cooler in the cabin," she said. "Make yourselves comfortable, and let me know if you need anything." She enjoyed being their host. Like they were in her care as they headed out to sea.

George had the engines humming before the sun snuck too far above the horizon. He reeled off a quick safety briefing and instructed the men on life preservers. "You all can relax if you like," he said. "It'll be a little while before we're offshore."

"That's okay," one said. "We had a bit of a late night at Sloppy Joe's." He reached for the cabin door and turned back to his buddies. "Power nap," he said, waving his coffee cup toward the salon. They mumbled agreement and followed him inside.

"Rough night," Maya whispered to George.

"Often is," he said, smiling. The last of the men closed the door.

"Okay, here we go." George climbed the ladder and stood at the wheel in front of the captain's chair. He entered the coordinates for the first stop into the GPS and nudged the boat out of the slip at idle speed. As he crossed into open water, he pushed up on the throttle. The engines revved as the boat carved a wake behind the stern. Maya held onto the ladder and looked out at the white caps disappearing behind the boat. She wiped the salt spray from her cheek and turned to face the morning sky.

In the search for fish, George had the best view from the flying bridge. He'd scan the ocean and sky over the bow as he headed into deeper blue. Maya took the stern, sipped a bottle of water as she considered the day ahead. Sun on her skin. The first hours of a new life.

"Maya, port side, weed line!" George yelled a few minutes later. He yanked the throttle into neutral and scrambled down the ladder. "Let's get the outriggers set up!"

Maya startled to attention and grabbed the ballyhoo rigs out of the bucket.

"Here, I'll show you." He placed the rods in the holders and fed the lines out along the outriggers to prepare for trolling. She shoved her hands in her pockets and watched, wanting to help but not quite knowing how.

The Orlando Four, as Maya thought of them, emerged from the cabin. She had forgotten their names but had numbered them One through Four in her head.

"See something?" Three asked.

"A nice looking weed line," George said. "Let's see what we can shake up."

In minutes they were trolling, George back upstairs and The Four standing around and scanning the waters with Maya. A dolphin was one of the most beautiful fish in the ocean. The head and top half of the body generally ran a deep green color, the bottom a bright yellow. Blue dots speckled the skin, and the fish had a noticeable dorsal fin that tended to run blue as well. A dolphin jumping out of the water to fight a hook flashed color through the air.

"Fish on!" yelled Two.

George throttled back to neutral and jumped down the ladder. "Okay," he said to Two. "You spotted the first one, so it's yours. Take a seat. Maya, hand him the rod."

Maya grabbed the rod just as the dolphin started to run. She stumbled toward the chair but righted herself as George lunged to help her. Together they placed the rod in the chair's rod holder. Two hung on while George gave him some direction.

"Let him run a bit if he wants to. Give him some line."

Two gave the fish a bit of line before reeling him back in. The fish was almost to the boat when he tugged the line again. Two let him run some more, watched him jump a couple of times. When it seemed the fish had exhausted itself, Two reeled him closer to the boat.

"Let him hang out next to the boat a minute or so. Maybe he has a few buddies who are slow swimmers," George said. Two left the fish in the water. After a few minutes, George told him to bring the dolphin on board. Maya opened the fish box, and George gaffed the fish and deposited the first catch.

"Nice size fish you got there. Probably about twenty pounds. Great start guys. Let's see if he has any cousins who've been lagging behind," George said. He leaned over the port side. "I think I see something coming. Maya, toss out some chum."

Maya scooped the fish guts from a bucket at her feet and dumped them in the water. Gross, she thought, but another part of the job I'll have to get used to. She turned back to the bucket as George touched her arm.

"That's enough for now," he said.

"Oh, okay," she said, her cheeks reddening. She rinsed her

hands with the saltwater hose and shook them out before wiping them on her shorts. Guess these are fishing shorts now, she thought.

In a moment, two more dolphin found the food. One and Three spent the next twenty minutes reuniting them with their friend.

After the first three fish made the cooler, George had Maya help him reset the outriggers. They trolled the area, found another weed line, and within an hour Four had caught a large bull and Two and Three were working on their second fish. At the end of the day, after a hit under a lost buoy and another chasing a frigate, George closed the fish box and headed the *Great Catch* back to the marina. Two sat in the fighting chair. The rest leaned against the sides of the boat, sunburnt and happy.

"That was an awesome day," Three said to his buddies. "Maya, you and George make a great team."

"You think so? It was our first day together."

"Wow, really?" Four said. "You'd never know it."

"Seriously, you guys were great," One said.

Two sat back in the chair and took the cap off his water bottle. "Can't wait to see what kind of day we have when we come back next year." He smiled at Maya and took a long drink.

Maya adjusted her sunglasses as she processed the day. She looked off to the western sky. If this works out, I probably won't be making too many sunset celebrations on Mallory Square, she thought. That's okay. I don't feel so homesick anymore.

"Great work today," George said after they finished cleaning the boat.

"Thanks. Though I felt like I stumbled around the boat all day."

"Nah. That's just because you don't know what your job is yet. You were great on the water. You didn't get seasick, took good care of the clients, and stayed out of the way. When I asked you to do something, you did it. And just now, when we cleaned the boat and the rods and put everything away, you did exactly what I needed you to do. A few more trips and I won't have to tell you anything. You'll just know. What do you say? Want to give it a week and see if you like it?"

"If I like it? I love it! I just want to make sure I can do a good job."

"I think you can, but no pressure. Let's see how you feel after a full week. Meet me here around six tomorrow morning. I don't usually get here as early as you'll have to, but I will for the first few days until you're ready to fly solo. Sound good?"

"Yeah, sounds great! Thanks, George. I'll see you tomorrow."

She picked up her bag and walked the few blocks to Gladys's house. Her mind churned. She felt like she had something. Like she could reach out and cup the air and when she opened her hands she'd see her life dancing in her palms. Maybe not see it but feel it. Within her grasp.

She walked in the back door off the carport, humming "Here Comes the Sun" to herself. Dad's old Beatles tunes tended to meander through her mind when she was happy. She should call him tonight, she thought. Tell him the good news.

"Wow, it smells great in here," Maya said as she entered the kitchen. She leaned over the stove to inhale the garlic, onions, and peppers sizzling in the pot. Gladys had just added the chicken and was stirring in cans of tomatoes and turning down the heat.

"You think so? Good, you're joining me for dinner," Gladys replied. She pointed a wooden spoon at Maya.

"No, no, I didn't mean that. I have plenty of food. I don't want to take yours."

"Food? That crap macaroni and cheese you eat out of the blue box? That's not food. And you're too skinny. You eat with me. I have plenty. Besides, I like having someone to cook for." Gladys turned back to the stove.

"I'm not just going to take your food without paying you," Maya said to Gladys's back. Gladys reached over to turn up the radio. She turned back to Maya and mouthed "I can't hear you" before returning to the stove. Maya shook her head and threw her hands up before heading off to shower.

I'm going to have to do something about that, she thought. But for now, if it makes her happy, I'll let her win. "Well, we'll both win," she muttered as she walked into her room.

In the bathroom, Maya peeled off her clothes and piled them in the corner. As the water heated, she looked at her face in the mirror. "Too much sun today. Need to be more careful."

She stepped into the shower and pulled the curtain, turned toward the showerhead to let the warm water run down her face. She licked her lips to catch the last bits of salt before the day washed away.

I hope George is right and I catch on before he runs out of patience, she thought. She squeezed shampoo into her palm and massaged her head until all she heard was the fall of water and the fading reprise of the Beatles.

After she showered, Maya joined Gladys in the kitchen and

set the table. When they sat down, Gladys said, "How was your day?"

"Today was great." She explained how George's mate had skipped work and she'd had a chance to replace him. She described the dolphin and her struggles with the bait. How happy the clients seemed to be when they left, and George's comments to her about her work and invitation to stay on for a week. "I like it a lot. I just hope I can learn fast enough. I'm a little nervous."

Gladys shook her head as she chewed a piece of bread. "Don't worry about that. George is a good man. I've known him all his life. And I think that work suits you. Something tells me you couldn't work at a desk. Maybe not even under a roof." She pointed a piece of crust at Maya as she spoke.

Maya sopped up the last of the tomato sauce on her plate with the end of the loaf. She was surprised someone she'd just met could see her so clearly. I don't get it, she thought. I'm quiet. I don't tap my foot or fidget. How can she know?

"I can tell," Gladys said, as if reading her mind. "You need to be outdoors. You like watching *Jeopardy* with an old lady, which is good, because I like the company. But you seem content when you're outside. Like you could live there."

As Maya settled into bed that night, she thought about her day. The work was exciting. Joe was right. She could learn a lot from George. Maybe she had a future here. It felt like the beginning of something. On the edge of her fingertips.

Gladys seemed to sense the change in her as well. Content, she'd said. A word Maya had always loved. No matter the pronunciation, it was a word with weight. She was content in the outdoors. Where she found peace. She also felt a life worth living had to have content. Had to mean something. Maybe this was the start of her path. Maybe this would lead her somewhere.

Crap, she thought. Forgot to call Dad.

She sat up and grabbed the phone off the nightstand. It was only nine o'clock. He would still be awake. She punched in his number. It rang several times before he picked up.

"Hello?" he said. At least, she thought it was him.

"Dad, are you okay?" she asked. "Were you sleeping?"

"No, good, I'm fine, sweetheart. I'm awake. Just watching TV." His words were slow, damp. Like he was under water.

"You don't sound fine." She got out of bed, turned on the light. "I know it's Friday night, but it takes more than a few beers to make Charlie Raymond drunk, right?"

"Oh, don't worry about that. I'm drinking scotch."

Maya sat down on the edge of the bed. She sighed and ran a hand through her hair. Apparently the irony of his response was still swimming around the bottom of his glass.

He wasn't expecting me to call tonight, she thought. I never call on Fridays. Maybe I need to change my pattern, call him when he's not on his best behavior waiting to hear from me.

She started to tell him about her day, but he didn't seem to be listening. She ended the call and told him she'd call him the next night for a story. She wondered if he'd remember their conversation when they spoke the following evening. She stared at the receiver. I'm so far away, she thought. I should be there. Caring for him. Worry crept into her belly, seeped out her skin.

She placed the phone in the cradle and turned off the light. Climbed into bed, rolled over on her side, pulled the covers up to her chin. A sound stirred in her ear. Like a train coming from far away. Odd, she thought, half in sleep. There are no trains in

Key West anymore. She heard the locomotive enter her head. The engine chugged along, the sound slow, methodical, as it grew to a roaring din. It swept through her mind as she fell asleep.

The next week was a blur. On Saturday George had two half-day charters. The morning was a single guy, and the afternoon was a couple. Other days were three-quarter or full days. One day he had no one. Staying at the dock, they did some extra cleaning of the boat and equipment in the morning and took the afternoon off. At the end of the week, he offered her the job.

"I know you like working for Joe, but if you want the job it's yours. You learn quick. You work hard. There's not much you haven't been able to do. And you'll get stronger."

~

When she started, Maya feared her small size would be a liability. After a few weeks, she forgot she'd ever had a doubt. Occasionally she encountered a heavy chest she couldn't lift, but she knew many men wouldn't be able to either. She used the dock cart for moving gear to the boat, made a few extra trips, but she managed. George helped with whatever needed an extra hand.

Her confidence grew as her t-shirts tightened over her back and arms. As she learned to move around the boat without thinking.

Fifteen

2006

MAYA AND GEORGE BECAME A TEAM. Tourists came and went. George taught Maya the ups and downs of the charter fishing business.

"Hard work. Unpredictable. Weather-dependent," he told her. "But if you love it, there's not much you can do but get up every morning and thank God your office is the Atlantic Ocean and the Gulf of Mexico."

"Come to dinner tomorrow night," George said one morning as they prepared the boat. "Linda's been after me to have you over. We've got a half-day in the morning. Nothing in the afternoon. Should have plenty of time to clean fish and the boat and still make it an early evening without everyone falling asleep in their plates. What do you say?"

"Sure, I'd love to."

After work the following night, Maya went home and showered. She walked the few blocks to George's house.

"It's so hot out. I don't know why I bothered showering," Maya said as Linda welcomed her at the door. "Well, I guess I do. Otherwise I'd smell like fish." She handed Linda a small bouquet of yellow roses and daisies from the convenience store on the corner. "I didn't know what to bring. I'm not old enough to buy wine yet. And I don't have a fake ID."

"You have your associate's degree, right?" Linda asked. "So you must be turning twenty-one soon?" She took the flowers and closed the door behind Maya. "By the way, you didn't have to bring anything, but these are beautiful. I love fresh flowers." She buried her nose in the center of the bouquet and inhaled. "Lovely."

"I turn twenty-one in September. Can't believe how fast the time has gone. Sometimes I feel like I just got here."

Linda walked into the kitchen and pulled a vase down from an upper cabinet. "What day? The twins are September, too. They'll be sixteen on the fifth."

Maya followed Linda into the kitchen. "Paul and Manny? Wow, I didn't know that. Mine's the ninth. Right around the peak of hurricane season. I hope it's not a bad omen for my life in Florida."

Linda poured Maya a glass of sweet tea and offered her a seat at the bar.

"Do you think you'll stay?" she asked, pouring herself a glass and placing a dish of smoked fish dip and crackers on the counter. "Help yourself. The males are still primping." She took a pile of napkins from the pantry and set it next to the plate.

"I don't know." Maya spread fish dip on a cracker and bit

into the smoky creaminess. "This stuff is so good. It may be my favorite food." She wiped her mouth with a napkin. "Um, as far as staying, I'm not sure. I love Key West. The work and the weather. I just don't know where my roots are meant to be planted."

"You don't need to know. You're young. Enjoy your freedom. Someday you'll have other people to take care of."

Linda moved toward the stove and stirred the pot of black beans, turned down the flame on the back burner. She peered under the lid of the rice before stirring the chicken simmering in the pan in front.

"Anything I can do to help?"

"No, thank you, please just sit and enjoy. I have to chop an onion for the beans and then I'm done." Linda reached in the drawer below the oven and removed a chopping board. She took a knife from the block on the counter and an onion from the fridge and ran cold water in the sink to peel the onion. "Just a few tears, then I'll be fine." She smiled at Maya and turned to the chopping board.

"Are you from here?" Maya asked.

"No, I'm from Miami," Linda said as she diced the onion into bits. "*Whew*, these always get me." She dabbed her eyes with a dish towel and scraped the onions into a bowl. "I came down after college to teach, thinking it would be a fun place to live for a few years. And then when I got older, I'd move back up. I didn't count on meeting George. He convinced me to stay." She sniffled and grinned at Maya. Washed and dried her hands and hung the towel on the oven door handle. "Okay, now I can relax a little bit." She dipped a cracker into the fish dip and took a bite. "I love this stuff, too. George's uncle made this batch. He's got the best smoker."

"Do you still teach?"

"Yes. Spanish at Key West High." Linda wiped her mouth on a napkin.

"Oh, do you know Gladys? From the cafeteria? She's my roommate, or my landlady I guess. I don't know what to call her."

"Of course! Everyone knows Gladys. She's wonderful! Don't give up that spot. You won't find a better roommate or landlady in Key West."

"No, I know. And she's a great cook, too."

Linda gave Maya a Key West primer. Who the local families were. How the city had changed over the years with the influx of tourists.

"It's an interesting place to live. Still feels like a small town. That's good for raising children. Bad for keeping secrets, but we don't have any to keep. It's comfortable, but if it's not for you, you'll know. Sometimes falling in love forces you to make a decision you're not otherwise ready to make. That's what happened to me. If it doesn't for you, just make sure you eventually make some decision.

"The danger of living in a place like this is you get complacent. You don't want to wake up one day and wonder where the time went. If you love it, great. Just be conscious." She sipped her tea, chewed a piece of ice. "People come down here and say they'll leave next summer. Next summer never comes. They end up weathered and don't look happy. They look, I don't know," she searched for the word. "Hardened. Maybe regretful? Wondering if there was more somewhere else.

"I'm sorry," she said, patting Maya's hand. She stood and grabbed the pitcher from the fridge. "I don't mean to lecture you. George mentioned your mom died when you were young, so I wanted to offer you a woman's perspective. It's none of my business. You keep doing what you're doing." She refilled their glasses.

"No, no, it's fine. Actually, I really appreciate it. I'm struggling with this a bit." Maya turned to face Linda. "I feel like I should know more about what I want, and I can't seem to get there. I see lots of people around town just a few years older than me. They look like they're on the cusp. Either they leave soon, somewhere between twenty-five and thirty, or they'll never go. And I think it's fine if they don't, as long as, like you said, it's a conscious decision.

"I think there are a lot of people down here who confuse carefree with careless. I mean, it's so easy, right? You wait tables or tend bar. You're up half the night, first working, then partying. You spend half the day on the beach or the boat. Everyone's doing it, so it must be okay. Like the first one to jump off the cliff is crazy, but the second guy, not so much. Before long everyone's jumping and not realizing it's a stupid idea to follow the guy in front of you off the cliff." She paused, took a drink.

"I went to college with some of these kids, and I can see they're already at the edge of the cliff. I want to shake them and tell them to stop. Like 'Hey, look over the edge! Make sure you want to jump!' But I think if I grab one, he's going to look at me like I'm the crazy one. And then I have to look in the mirror and ask myself. Am I? Maybe I should jump, too."

Maya sipped her iced tea. "Sorry, I don't know why I said all that."

"Because you're smart and thoughtful. I'm not worried about you. You'll decide when it's your time. And it will be the right decision." Linda reached over and touched her arm. "I can tell you're going to be just fine." She turned to the doorway. "Well, look who finally decided to join us."

"Smells good in here," George said. He kissed Linda's cheek and squeezed Maya's shoulder as he surveyed the kitchen. "I'll grab another chair for the table."

"Yeah, Mom, smells great," Paul said, putting an arm around his mother's shoulder. "Hey, Maya."

"Hi, Paul, Manny."

"Sup." Manny lifted his chin toward Maya and shuffled to the stove, hands buried in the front pockets of his shorts. He raised the lid from the pot of beans and inhaled the garlic and oregano, cumin and pepper. "I'm starving." He turned to his mother. "Everything ready?"

"All done. If you boys set the table we can eat."

Manny took the plates and glasses from the cabinet while Paul gathered silverware and napkins. The boys jostled for the last of the fish dip before a stern look from George sent them to their seats at the table.

"What happened at work today?" George asked as he spooned beans over his rice. "Paulie, did you talk to your boss about your hours once football practice starts?"

"He was too busy talking to the new girl on register two," Manny said, smirking at his brother.

Paul's cheeks reddened as he elbowed his brother's ribs. "Not cool, dude," he whispered. "I forgot, Dad. I'll talk to him tomorrow."

Manny buried his face behind his fist and choked his food down amidst his laughter.

"Manny, that's enough," Linda said. Her stare melted Manny's giggles into quiet convulsions and finally a polite clearing of the throat.

"Yes, ma'am."

"And you? You didn't talk to any cute girls today?" George asked Manny.

"They're all taller than him. He's too chicken."

"Shut up, Paulie." Manny scowled at his brother. "You're barely an inch taller than me, dude. And anyway I'm better looking." He sat up straighter in his chair and looked over at his brother, moving his hand from above Paul's head back and forth above his own. "See, practically the same."

Paul elbowed Manny again and they both laughed before returning to their plates.

George and Linda glanced across the table at each other, shaking their heads and failing to hide their smiles. Maya watched the four, chewing quietly and taking in the movements, the tenderness. The family shared a warmth that wrapped the five of them in the cocoon of a late June evening. Maya felt like their blanket covered her. Like she belonged.

After tres leches cake and café con leche for Linda and George, the boys cleared the table and excused themselves.

"Night, Maya," Paul said, heading down the hall.

"See ya," Manny said, saluting Maya and following his brother.

Maya laughed. "Night, guys." She turned back to George and Linda. "Are they always like that? They were hilarious."

"They tease each other, but they definitely dialed it up a notch for you," Linda said.

"Huh," George chuckled. "You can say that again. You were treated to a special performance."

Maya yawned behind her hand. "I'm sorry. I am so rude."

Linda laughed. "No, you're not. He's just working you too hard." She smiled at her husband.

"It's true. I'm a tyrant." George winked at his wife. "I'll drive her home. Come on, Maya."

"No, thank you, though. I'd rather walk. Thanks so much for dinner and for having me in your home. It means a lot. More than just a meal. And it was a great meal." She hugged Linda and headed for the front door. "Good night."

Maya faced the street, but instead of heading home she walked toward the marina. The air settled around her. In a few minutes the chill of the air-conditioned house left her skin.

She strolled down the dock past the *Great Catch* to the end of the walkway. A few fishermen were still cleaning their catch, having a beer to wind down the day. A light went on in a sailboat at the next dock. A dog barked.

She thought about what Linda said. About making decisions when the time was right. How did you know when you were at the edge of the cliff? What if you'd already jumped and didn't realize it? She looked up at the sky. The moon was almost full. Months had passed without her noticing.

She remembered the Saturday night after her first day on George's boat. Her dad had updated her on a new house he was building in Newburyport for a local doctor. He'd had a Raymond Adventure story ready. She and her mom and dad traveling to Breckenridge to ski powder. Nights sitting by the fire in the lodge, the hearth eight feet wide and five feet tall, the stones on the fireplace rising three stories to the top of the great room. Drinking hot chocolate and bragging about moguls and triple black diamonds. Maya had shivered against the cold. She'd smelled the cocoa. Felt her mother near.

She hadn't brought up the phone conversation from the night before, after her first day of work with George, when Charlie had been drinking. When her words seemed to fall away into the phone. She didn't know what to say, and her dad seemed fine as he set the scene in Colorado.

Probably just an end of the week thing, she thought now. Long week, knock a few back. She looked up at the moon. The memory nagged at her. She needed to go home and see him.

One evening as Maya hosed off the rods and reels, George sat down on the side of the boat and pulled out his laptop. "We'll probably have a slow period in the middle of September. Some businesses close completely, and I have no bookings for almost a week. Isn't your birthday around then? Maybe you could go home for a few days."

"How did you know that?" Maya asked as she put the hose away.

"I can't take credit for it. Linda wrote it down when you came for dinner. I don't remember any of that stuff. We were looking at my calendar last night and she mentioned your birthday was coming up and I should give you some time off. It's okay with me, and I'm not saying you have to go home. But if you want to, you should go."

"THERE SHE IS!" CHARLIE SHOUTED as Maya dragged her suitcase past security. She smiled and stood her bag on end as her father wrapped her in a hug. He held her an extra moment before letting go. "Let me take that. You must be hungry. What do you think? North End for pizza? Want to walk Quincy Market and eat whatever you see first? Name it. Lady's choice."

"Gert's."

"Really?" He turned to look at her. "The clam shack in Seaport? You don't want to hang out here in town?"

"No, I want to get home. I want to eat fried clams at a picnic table at Gert's. They're still open, right?"

"Yeah. They don't close until after Columbus Day. Fried clams it is."

They walked to the parking garage, Maya stealing glances at her father. Same old work boots, dirty from construction sites. Same old jeans with the right back pocket worn down from his wallet. He had on a new shirt though, probably just for her arrival. Navy blue polo.

"You dressed up for my homecoming," she said. "Even took the pencil out from behind your ear. I thought that only happened on Christmas." She nudged his arm.

"Aw, come on. I take it out at least once a week when I wash my hair." He swung her bag into the bed of the truck and unlocked the doors, grinned at his daughter.

As they pulled out of the parking garage, she touched her father's arm. "Can we take the back roads home? I mean, if you're not too hungry. And if you don't mind the drive. I'd like to see more than Route 1."

"Of course." He turned and looked at his daughter, happy for her nostalgia. Maybe it would bring her home more often. "It's early. We've got plenty of time."

Charlie drove the truck up Route 1A, through Lynn and Swampscott and Salem. Occasionally he turned off for a short detour, a jaunt through Gloucester to see the fisherman's statue. He parked the truck on Western Avenue, and they walked over to look at the memorial to fishermen lost at sea.

"You know, I worry about you. I know you're just on day charters and you're not far offshore. And George is a great guy and from what you've told me treats you like you're his daughter. But every once in a while I think about this statue. Just be careful, okay? You're all I have." He put his arm around Maya and drew her to his side.

"Dad, I'm very careful. So is George. Plus we don't do anything like what these guys did or what the commercial guys up here do now. It's not dangerous. No more than what you do anyway." She looked away from the statue, pictured a day on the ocean. George's boat jetting into open water. Bright sun. Salt spray. The buzz of the line when a fish ran. It seemed familiar now. Safe.

She considered her father's days and realized she'd been away so long, she couldn't recall them anymore. Was he in the office most of the time now that the company was growing? Was he running from job to job checking on his crews? As they walked back to the truck, she let her thoughts of his days drift to his evenings. Was he home alone every night? She remembered the phone call after her first day on George's boat. She had to find a way to talk to him about his drinking. A serious talk. Something they never did.

Late in the afternoon, Charlie pulled the truck into the dirt lot by the clam shack.

"*Mmmm*, smell that grease! I've been waiting for that," Maya said as she jumped out.

"What, there's no grease in Key West? Your chefs down there too fancy for a little old-fashioned peanut oil?"

"Oh, we have our share. But I miss New England grease. It dates back to the pilgrims."

Charlie laughed as he slammed the door. He put his arm around his daughter, kissed the side of her head, and walked her to the window. "That would have to be corn oil. In any case, order anything you want. I trust you will ensure we're well fed."

She ordered a plate of whole belly clams, a plate of fries, and two lobster rolls.

"I'll share a plate of clams with you, since the serving is so big they're falling over the sides." She set their food on the picnic table and sat on the bench, faced the sun. The wind picked up as she tucked her hair behind her ears. "But there is no way I'm sharing a lobster roll with you. This baby's all mine." She held up the end of the buttered frankfurter roll and bit through a piece of sweet claw meat. "Oh my God this is totally amazing." She wiped mayonnaise from her mouth with a paper towel from the roll on the table. "I've stayed away too long!"

"I'm glad to hear you missed the food so much," Charlie said. He dipped a clam in tartar sauce and popped it in his mouth. "I was beginning to think you weren't ever going to come home." He took a sip of his iced tea. "Beautiful day today. We've had a lot of rain lately. You must have brought some of that Florida sunshine with you."

Maya watched him look at the ocean. Away from her. Frustration welled in her chest, curled her hands into fists that landed hard on the table.

"Don't do that, Dad! Don't make this about food or talk about the weather!" He turned toward her, confused, and her face softened. She paused, leaned back, settled her hands in her lap. "I'm here. Can we have a real conversation now? About what's really going on?"

"Aw, come on, I'm just teasing you. What's to talk about?" He leaned forward, elbows on the table, ready to change the subject. "Tell me about work. Are you learning a lot from George?"

"Yeah, it's fine, but that's not what I want to talk about." She wiped her mouth. Picked up her tea, swirled the ice with her straw. She took a deep breath, released it as she met his gaze. "Remember the night I called to tell you about my first day of work?"

"Of course. You were all excited. And then I told you a Raymond Adventure story. A ski one maybe?"

"That was the *second* phone call. I called you the night before, on Friday. *That* was my first day of work. But you'd had a few drinks and weren't paying attention, so I told you about it again on Saturday. Do you remember that?"

"Sure, I remember." He dipped some fries into ketchup and chewed, thought back to the Friday night phone call. The salt lingered on his tongue. He brushed off his hands and looked at his daughter. "I was probably tired on Friday. From work. Saturdays I'm always much better." He smiled at her. "Why, you worried? Think your old man has a drinking problem?"

He picked an ice cube out of his cup, put it in his mouth, chewed. He shook his head. "I'm fine. I don't drink that much. You caught me on an off night. Mikey was home, and we'd been out to dinner. You know he and I can get a little carried away."

"Uncle Mike was home? Why didn't you tell me? How is he?"

Maya adored Mike, or Uncle Mike to her. When she was growing up, whenever he'd come home from school or wherever he was working, he made sure to visit with her as well, not just Charlie. He brought her shells and sharks' teeth, and he was one of the reasons she'd been interested in marine science. He'd earned a doctorate degree, worked out of Woods Hole, and traveled frequently for research or to lecture.

"He's doing well. Spent some time in Antarctica. Said he may be down your way one of these days. Might be doing some work in Islamorada."

"Seriously?" Maya's face brightened.

"Yes, and he'll let me know if it happens. You know Mikey. There's no way he'd get that close and not see you."

A seagull landed on the other end of the table. "Shoo, get out of here," Maya said. "You're not taking my clams." She waved the bird away. It squawked in protest as it fluttered to the next table. Maya watched the quick flap of the wings, the ease of the escape. She sensed a moment hanging between her and her father. He'd provided the diversion of Uncle Mike. A trail through the woods, away from her questions. She could follow him along that path or lead him back to hers.

"That answers the question of what he's up to. Doesn't explain why you didn't tell me about it that night."

"Are we still on this?" Charlie asked, raising his voice. "Can you let it go?"

Maya sighed, looked at her father. He seemed older, she thought. But it was more than that. He was about the same age as The Four from her first charter. Those guys, though, they had an energy about them he didn't have. Sure, they were on vacation, but Charlie was excited to have her home. For him, her visit was better than any vacation. What was it?

"We can let it go." She figured she could talk to her grandparents and her Aunt Karen. They saw Charlie every week. If anything was off, they'd know. Maybe they'd tell her.

As Maya cleared the table, Charlie thought back to the Friday night of the phone call. Mike had lectured in Boston that day. He'd come home to have dinner with Charlie and spend the night with his parents before leaving the following afternoon on a research trip.

They'd met at the pub. Charlie had ordered a burger and fries. Mike a veggie burger and salad.

"What's up with you? Mikey turning into a rabbit?" Charlie grinned at his old friend.

"Little bit. We're not getting any younger, and I'm trying to keep my weight in check. Traveling this much I can pack it on. What about you? Still eating crap and drinking too much?"

"Not as much. I've cut back. A beer or two here or there. A scotch when I need to keep the ghosts away."

Mike looked up from his plate. "What do you mean, ghosts?"

"Nothing, I mean, nothing really." He sipped his beer. "It's just that since Maya left, the house is so quiet. Archie's getting older, and he never had much of a bark to him. It's weird. Even though Sierra never lived in the house, I feel her there. Sometimes I'm in the kitchen making dinner, and I see something out of the corner of my eye. I turn my head real quick and it's gone. I know it's just wishful thinking, that I'd love to have her around. Even if she's just standing next to me while I cook. Like she used to.

"Then sometimes I feel like she's been there and she's gone. Bums me out. You know?"

Mike nodded.

"Times like that, I have a scotch or two, no big deal. To be honest, I've had the same fifth in the house for the last six months. I don't drink it very often. Just when I need to dull the cold she leaves behind."

Mike sat back in the booth and crossed his arms, sighed.

"You know, man, you can't live this way forever. I didn't say much when Maya was growing up, because you were so focused on raising her right. And you did a hell of a job. Then when she left, I thought, give him some time, let him adjust. Eventually he'll venture out and try to meet someone. At least go on a date. But it's been three years now, Mit. You can't shut that part of your life down. You're too young. You can't just live with a ghost."

Charlie looked up from his plate, a half smile on his face. "I know. There's a new woman working over at the concrete plant.

I saw her when I was in there the other day. Thought I might ask her out. What do you think? Charlie Raymond still have a chance?"

Mike smiled, relieved. "Definitely. It's a great idea. Let me know how it goes."

They finished dinner and caught up on each other's lives. Work, family. Mike was dating a marine biologist who lived in Los Angeles.

"I love her, and I think it's time for me to do something about it." He smiled at Charlie. "Maybe that's why I'm busting your chops. I understand now how great it feels to be happy."

They paid the check and walked out the door, gave each other a brief hug.

"Call me, Mit, all right? I want to hear about you sweeping this concrete plant woman off her feet. Okay?"

"Yeah, man, you got it. Stay in touch. Let me know when you'll be back up here or if you'll be in Florida. Maya would love to see you. And give me a heads up when you pop the question." He punched Mike's arm and headed for his truck.

Charlie drove home and pulled in the driveway. He turned off the ignition and sat until the engine quieted. He wanted to get inside, and he didn't. She'd be there.

"I'm home," he said when he walked in the door. He threw his keys on the table. Archie jumped off the couch, stretched his legs, came over for a pat. Charlie scratched his head.

"How you doing old boy? You alone tonight or you have company?" Charlie sat down on the couch and turned on the TV. He flipped through some channels and threw down the remote.

"Fuck it." He stood and walked into the kitchen, took the bottle from the top shelf in the cabinet. He poured a shot, threw it back, poured another, and took it to the couch. He sipped as he watched the game. The Red Sox were in Seattle. Long day, he thought. Long week. Long life. The Mariner's first baseman hit a line drive over the wall in center field. The crowd cheered. Archie jumped up on the couch and laid his head in Charlie's lap. Charlie petted Archie's back without feeling whether the dog was really there.

"It's you and me, bud. Just you and me." He sipped his drink. "Have to remember to make up a new woman next time Mike asks."

Charlie fell asleep. He was walking along the edge of a lake under a full moon, droplets of light reflecting off the water. She was there. At least, he thought so. He heard a splash. Sierra? He waded into the water. What would she look like? He reached for her, but she was falling away. He looked around and saw a rope on the beach. He trudged back through the water, grabbed it, and threw it toward her.

"Take this! I'll pull you out!" The rope went taut in his hands. He tugged against the weight. The rough fibers burned his skin.

He kept pulling, hand over hand until his fingers bled. He felt a slackening and yanked once more, harder, stumbling backward before catching himself. The end of the rope dripped in his hands.

"No! Sierra! Where are you?"

He dove under the water and swam around. The lake was murky, the bottom thick and spongy. He grasped at the muck but found only mud and sticks and rocks. No hand reached for him. No breath bubbled beneath the surface.

"Sierra!"

Charlie searched until his lungs squeezed the last of the air from his chest. He dragged himself to the shore and picked up the frayed rope. He knelt in the sand and sobbed.

The phone rang and jolted him awake. He grabbed the portable.

"Hello?" he said, wiping sweat from his forehead.

"Dad, are you okay?"

Charlie remembered that night well.

After his brief talk with Maya, he'd turned off the TV and let Archie out. He'd rinsed his glass and picked up the bottle of scotch. He'd opened the cabinet to put it away, and then stopped and stared at the label before unscrewing the cap and pouring the rest of the liquor into the sink.

"Enough. If there are ghosts, I need to face them."

Seventeen

MAYA HAD A QUIET WEEK AT HOME. She saw family, some high school friends, and the guys at the marina. Sat in the backyard sketching pictures of Archie, ran along the beach. One afternoon after a long, slow run, she came in the house and found her father in the kitchen making dinner.

"Salmon? Wow, nice Dad. I had no idea you were so healthy."

"Your old man has expanded his horizons. Besides, everyone's coming over so we can all celebrate together. I wanted to do something special. Open the back door for me so I can get the grill ready. We'll eat in the backyard."

Maya showered and wiped the fog off the mirror with her damp towel. "Twenty-one," she said to her reflection. "How did that happen?" She dressed and threaded the towel through the bar opposite the sink. As she opened the door to the cooler air of the hallway, she paused once more to look in the mirror. "It's been three years since you left. What have you accomplished?" She sighed and turned to greet the voices down the hall.

"Hi, Grammy." She hugged Carolyn before taking the covered dish from her hands. "Is this?"

"Yup, macaroni and cheese. Your favorite." Carolyn pecked Maya's cheek.

"Sweeeeet!" Maya kissed her grandfather and carried the dish to the kitchen. Sierra's parents, Pat and Jim, arrived a few minutes later bearing hugs and green beans. As the grandparents settled in the backyard, Karen hustled her husband and sons through the front door with a bowl of black bean salad dotted with red onions and yellow peppers.

With each arrival, Maya fawned over the food and tried to ignore the birthday presents, embarrassed for the attention. She knew her dad and grandparents would give her cash. Her aunt and uncle surprised her with a gift card to a sunglass store.

"Pick out something you like," Karen told her. "Something good for the Florida sun."

After her birthday favorite, a mint chocolate chip ice cream cake, Maya and Karen collected the dishes and took them in the house. Karen stacked the dishes in the sink and rinsed, handed plates and glasses to Maya to arrange in the dishwasher.

"How is he?" Maya asked her aunt.

"Your dad?" Karen asked. She looked out the window screen as her little brother cracked a joke, his smile wide. The cackle of the family members echoed through the backyard. "He's good. Now. I mean, he misses you like crazy, but he's doing well. Dialed down the drinking. Eating better and getting some exercise. Lost a few pounds over the summer. I think he's finally accepted that you're not coming home. At least, not anytime soon. So he has to stop with this limbo he's been living in. Why? Did you notice something?"

"Not this time." She told her aunt about the Friday night phone conversation from a few months back. "He seems better now. But I still worry."

"You shouldn't. Your uncle and I have him over at least once a week, as does Grammy. He goes to Pat and Jim's, too. I wish he'd meet someone, but he doesn't seem interested. I ask him from time to time. He always has some story about a woman he saw and might ask out. But I know he's full of it. He's never gotten over losing your mother. I don't know if he ever will."

"So he's lonely, and that's not good." Maya pushed the bottom rack back in the dishwasher and closed the door. She dried her hands, leaned up against the counter. "Don't they say lonely people die younger? He's probably depressed. He never used to be a loner, right?"

"No, not Charlie. He was the life of the party." Karen turned off the faucet and wiped her hands on the apron. She untied it, pulled it over her head, and hung it back on the hook on the wall, the Boston Celtics leprechaun smiling back at her. "When he was a kid, he was everyone's favorite. Teachers loved him, the principal. It always got him out of trouble when he pulled a prank, the fact that everyone loved him so much.

"He's always had a good heart. I bet the day he walked up to your mother, he wasn't doing it to hit on her. She was the new girl, and he wanted to show everyone he thought she was okay. So people would be nice to her, maybe accept her.

"Charlie's like that. My mom tells this story that one day when he was little, maybe five or six, he came in the house all upset. He'd been playing in the backyard and found a bird with a broken wing, probably the victim of the neighbor's cat. The poor little bird was flopping around out there. Charlie came running in to my mother, yelling at her to fix the bird. He was crying and dragging her by the hand out the back door. She didn't know what to do. He was inconsolable. So she put the bird in a shoebox and took it and my brother to the vet. He sat in the waiting room, and my mom and the vet went in back. In a little while, my mom came out and told Charlie they'd fixed its wing and it flew away. He was disappointed he didn't get to say goodbye to the bird, but he was very happy it survived and would be safe from the cat. Mom was so relieved."

"That the bird made it?"

"Maya, please. The only place that bird made it to was birdie heaven. But that's not the point. My brother has been a fixer since he was little. He looks at an old building and doesn't see why you need to tear it down when you can preserve its beauty and build it back up. He looks at people the same way. Everyone's worth helping. Saving.

"I think that's why he devoted himself to you. He couldn't imagine giving an ounce of himself to someone else and risk not having that ounce left for you if you needed it. That's why we all worried about him so much after your mom died. I stayed on him. Got him to a few therapy sessions, but before too long he decided it wasn't for him. Either he'd said all he had to say, or he wasn't ready to say whatever else was bothering him. I'm not sure which. He's kind of worked his way through it over the years, though he's not quite there. He's still got a little bit of a broken wing, flopping around in the yard.

"Don't you worry, okay? I'm looking out for my little brother. I won't let anything happen to him. You go back to

Florida and keep working hard. And if you decide to go back to school, that's great." She touched Maya's cheek.

"You figure out what makes Maya happy. I'll take care of Charlie." She moved her hand to Maya's arm. "I may force him to go on a blind date with one of my co-workers. She knows his story and said she'd be happy to do it. Knows it won't lead anywhere, but she's charitable like that. Says it will be a good deed to get him out. I think I can convince him. Okay? So don't fret. Auntie Karen's got it under control."

"Can I ask you something else, Auntie?"

"Sure, honey, anything. You know that."

"Did you know my mom very well? I don't remember much. I get stories from Dad, but you know how that goes. I'm not sure how much of it is real and how much is him wanting to make me feel better. I don't know what she was like."

"Well, I don't know what your father told you, but your mom was his perfect match. When they met, I was a senior, so I saw the whole thing play out. He liked her from the start. He'd had a few girlfriends. Some lasted a few days. Others a few weeks. Nothing longer than that. When he met Sierra, he was finished." Karen laughed. "It was fun to watch.

"By my last semester in high school, they were spending a lot of time together. Sierra was over our house all the time. You know we had these big family dinners on Sunday nights. My grandparents would come. Sometimes the aunts and uncles and cousins. Whenever Charlie could convince her, Sierra would come, too. It wasn't that she didn't want to, just that she didn't want to impose. After a few months with Charlie, I think she figured out she wasn't an imposition. We had plenty of food and were happy to have her. That's when we got to know her. She wasn't a wallflower by any means. Your grandfather was always teasing her.

"I remember one night he asked what she was studying in school. She said they were reading *Romeo and Juliet* in her English class. He told her it was a complete waste of time, that she should be taking practical classes so she could get a job. 'If you want to go to college, take math and become an engineer.' That was his attitude. 'And while you're at it, take home ec so you can learn how to cook.' That one really got her going. But she gave it right back to him. Told him she needed literature since there were too many Neanderthals in the world. She looked him right in the eye when she said it. Then she said she could still take home ec if she wanted to, and shop class, since the Neanderthals weren't smart enough to cook or build a birdhouse."

Karen laughed at the memory. She wiped her eyes.

"The whole table erupted." She sighed, dried the counter with the dish towel. "Your mother could keep up with anyone. She was smart and funny and very quick. But that wasn't the best part about her. The best part was she had a heart every bit as big as your dad's. She didn't make a joke at anyone's expense. She cared about people. Always wanted to help. If she was at our house, she wasn't just there to see Charlie. She'd ask me about college. Hang out with my mom. She'd wander into the garage and find my dad tinkering with something and ask if he needed someone to hand him a wrench. Sierra became part of the family before any of us realized it was happening. Grampa was teasing her about home ec at the dinner table, and she probably helped my mom make the meal without him even knowing it."

Karen shook her head, searching for the memory of that day so many years before. Maya crossed her arms, shifted her feet. She waited as she watched Karen's face change. As the story unraveled for her aunt like a ball of yarn rolling across the floor at their feet.

Sierra had come over to their house that Sunday afternoon as the snow started falling. She and Charlie finished their homework, and when the flakes dwindled Charlie went out to shovel the driveway and front walk. Sierra put her books away and looked out the living room window at the white blanket draped across the lawn. The tired fingers of the last rays of sun picked through the empty tree branches, tickling the fresh snow until a few final sparkles gave way to the pink and purple sky.

She waved at Charlie and walked into the kitchen. Carolyn was chopping garlic and onions. Water boiled on the stove. A large bowl sat on the counter.

Sierra opened the fridge and began taking out vegetables for the salad. She looked at Carolyn, who surveyed the pile on the counter and nodded. Sierra washed and peeled and chopped. She arranged everything in the bowl and looked at Charlie's mom again. Carolyn pointed to the lettuce, and Sierra washed a few more leaves. Sausage sizzled in the pot. Carolyn smiled and squeezed Sierra's shoulder. She hummed a Sinatra tune as she stirred the sauce.

Karen shook her head as she roused herself from the memory. "Your mother fit wherever she went. She had a way of making everyone fall in love with her."

She hugged her niece and pulled away. Pushed a strand of hair out of Maya's eyes. "Some days I see Charlie. Other days all I see is Sierra." She looked away, sniffled. "Let's get back outside, okay? Everyone will need to get going soon. You doing anything special to mark your twenty-first? Going out drinking with your old chums? Or is everyone away at school?"

"Most are away. Some live here and commute, but I'm not interested in going out tonight. I live in Key West. If I want to party, it can wait a few days."

"A very mature response. Exactly what I would expect from you." She pushed open the screen door. They rejoined the family in the yard as the door closed quietly behind them.

Eighteen

MAYA RETURNED TO FLORIDA AND EARLY MORNINGS on the water. The seasons changed as did the catch. Over the winter and into the spring, certain clients came to the Keys to chase sailfish. Maya loved this beautiful creature. It had a Pinocchio-like bill, which she liked to think of as its snout, and a navy blue sail that ran along the center of its back. It was fast in the water and a challenge to catch. When it jumped to escape a hook, Maya marveled at the shimmering blue breaking the surface, fighting for survival.

George did everything he could to bring a sailfish to the boat for a client, but he went just as far to make sure the client released the creature safely to the sea after snapping a few photos. He felt if someone wanted a wall mount, they could take the photo to a taxidermist and order a replica. No need to kill for decoration. Few people enjoyed eating this particular catch.

Anglers have different options when fishing for sailfish. George liked to use kites and live bait, a popular technique in the Keys.

"Let me show you how to rig one of these kites," he told her one morning. He pulled a kite out of the cabin. Square, the bright pink nylon supported by plastic rods that crossed in the center. Though not far removed from the diamond-shaped versions of beach days with her dad, it lacked the colorful tails that would whip in the wind and streak across the sky. She cleared the old image from her mind and stepped closer to watch.

George clipped the kite to a line attached to a fishing rod. "It connects like that." He held the rig up to show her. "I stick this rod in a holder, and as long as we have some wind while we're drifting the kite will stay up.

"Then I take some live baitfish and hook it to a line on a different rod. I attach the baitfish line to the kite's line by another short line. That connecting line is held onto the bait line by a clip." He held up the connecting line, showed her how the two clip together. "If we get a bite, the clip will release and the bait line and kite line will separate so we don't have to deal with the connecting line or the kite. You follow?"

She nodded.

"Sometimes I'll bait two or three lines, all clipped to one kite. As the kite lifts with the wind, it brings all those little baitfish near the surface. The lift from the kite makes it look like they're swimming." He motioned with his hand, mimicking the baitfish moving with the current. "Looks more natural."

Maya nodded again, absorbing the intricate instruction, chuckling to herself when she realized her head was swimming as well.

"We good?" George opened the door of the cabin to stow the kite.

"Yeah, good." Maya paused. "Hey, George?"

He looked back at her, raised his eyebrows.

"Thanks. I mean, for everything. You're a good teacher." She blushed. "I just wanted you to know how much I appreciate all you've done for me."

He smiled. "My pleasure." He winked at her and closed the cabin door behind him.

As the air cooled, George began bringing them coffee in the morning. He purchased an extra insulated cup for Maya and filled it each day. One morning he added a third cup.

"What's that one for?" Maya asked. "Stay up too late watching Letterman?"

"Ha, ha, are you kidding? I don't make it past ten. No, I forgot to tell you. My nephew's coming this morning. I take him once a year to try to get him a sailfish. He's a firefighter."

Maya was pulling out some lures when she heard someone jump on board.

"Hi. You must be Maya. My uncle told me about you. I'm Chris." She shook his extended hand. His palm was warm, his smile bright, unrestrained, like the air during the first hour after sunrise. Before the heat of the day smothers the nascent golden rays of innocent morning.

A breeze kissed the back of her neck. "Nice to meet you." She turned away as her smile widened, her cheeks flushed.

When George climbed the ladder to the flying bridge, Chris followed. He spent the first few minutes of the trip catching his uncle up on family news before excusing himself to use the head. Rather than return to George's perch, he stopped to chat with Maya.

They talked about his life as a firefighter and growing up in the Keys, her life in New England and migration south. He came from Cudjoe Key, about twenty miles north of Key West. He was a few years older than Maya and had always known he wanted to be a firefighter.

"For real?" she asked. "I mean, I get having a fantasy of being a firefighter or police officer when you're little. Like a lot of kids I wanted to be a veterinarian for about a minute. But it's not often the fantasy sticks. That it turns out to be the thing you were born to do."

"I know. I went through that same thought process. Like, is this it? Will it be enough? But I love it. It's honest work. I get to help people. I'm lucky. I have this career that makes me feel grateful every day. You?"

"Still trying to figure that out. I love being outside. Being on the water. I like physical work. But I don't know if this is it for me. I almost feel like I'll just wake up one day and have some sort of epiphany.

"I feel like I'm running in place, or treading water. If that makes sense. You seem like you're moving forward, full speed crawl stroke. Like you're getting somewhere."

The sky was lightening. She reached for the sunscreen. Added an extra layer to her nose and ears and offered him the bottle.

"Thanks." He squirted lotion on his arms and applied more to his face and the back of his neck. "You shouldn't worry. You may be treading water now, but you won't be for long." He winked at her as he closed the top of the bottle. He carried the confidence of a man old enough to utter such reassurances.

Young enough to lack the wisdom to leave them unsaid.

Maya nodded, took the sunscreen, and entered the cabin. She stowed the bottle and paused in the stillness before returning to the movement of water and conversation. He seems so sure of himself, she thought. About his career, my future. Maya trusted the counsel of the adults around her. Linda, Gladys, Joe. Chris is only a few years older than me, she thought. How can he know? She leaned against the side of the cabin. He can't, she thought. Not about life. Not about me. Not yet. She smiled as she gathered the kite and her baseball cap. Maybe someday. If I let him.

Before the air warmed they were offshore. Soon they had their first bite.

"Fish on!" Maya yelled, grabbing the rod and handing it to Chris. He stuck the rod in a holder attached to a belt around his waist and reeled in the slack. He jerked the line to release the clip, separating his rod's line from the line connected to the kite's rod. He reeled in the slack and took a breath.

"*Whew!* That's usually the trickiest part for me. If I can keep the fish on the line and get my line tight after the clip releases, I have a chance."

Chris gave out more line. He let the fish run and then reeled in a bit more. The rod bent. He lifted up to fight the fish.

"*Whoa!*" he yelled as the sailfish leapt from the water. Its head snapped around and body shuddered before it disappeared below the surface. The fish jumped twice more as he reeled against it.

"Nice fight you got going," George yelled down. "Keep at it."

Chris worked the fish until it lost its will. Twenty minutes later, Maya grabbed the line as he brought the fish toward the side of the boat. George hopped down the ladder to help. Chris smiled for his uncle, who took a few pictures of his proud nephew leaning over the side. With Maya's help, Chris removed the hook and released the fish. It disappeared below the boat.

"Oh, man, that was great! Thanks, George!" Chris said, returning the rod to the holder on the side of the boat. "I don't think I've hooked up with one the last couple of trips. That was pretty special."

"Glad we got one," George said, slapping his nephew on the back. "Let's see if we can find another."

They spent the rest of the day chasing sailfish. One hit broke off before they managed to land another, about fifty pounds. Chris fought it for over a half hour before the fish surrendered.

At the end of the day, George climbed the ladder and pointed the boat back to the marina. At the dock, rather than disappear like a typical client, Chris stayed and helped them hose off the boat, put the rods and lures away. He kissed the kite before tucking it inside the cabin.

"Love that thing!" he exclaimed, and then grabbed George. "And you, too, Uncle!" He planted a kiss on George's cheek. "Great day! Thank you so much!"

"You are quite welcome. Just keep working hard and looking out for your mother. You know she needs you."

"I will. No worries there. Anyone want to celebrate my success? A beer on me?" He looked from one to the other.

George looked at Chris, then at Maya. "Not me. But you two go. You deserve it. And Maya, we don't have anyone tomorrow, so just come by around eight. I'll show you some small repairs I'm going to make to the boat. It'll be good for you to learn." He watched Chris jump off the boat and reach down to take Maya's hand. He knows she can get off the boat herself,

George thought. But I like that it doesn't matter.

Chris and Maya wandered down the dock and out of the marina.

"What do you like? Sloppy Joe's?" he asked.

"Not really. Too many tourists. Something a bit divier."

"My kind of woman. Come on. I know just the place."

Hidden between the marina and a hotel was a sliver of a place with a few tables and a dozen or so seats at the bar.

"Wow, I didn't even know this was here," she said.

"Most people don't. That's why I like it."

They sat at the bar and clinked long necks.

"To a good day on the ocean," he said.

"Cheers to that."

"Tell me about yourself. You said you came down from Massachusetts for school and to work on the water. Your parents were cool with that?"

Maya twisted the bottle in her hands. She scratched at the label with a fingernail.

"Sort of. It's just me and my dad. My mom died when I was little."

"Oh, geez, I'm sorry. George didn't mention that." He started to reach for her, then pulled away. "You must miss her a lot."

Maya ran a finger down the smooth, brown glass of the bottle. This exchange with a first date or new friend was delicate, fraught. At the mention of the death of her mother, the person often recoiled, offered apologies. In her teens she hated hearing, "I'm so sorry." She wanted to scream, "Why are you apologizing? You didn't kill her!" By her twenties, she began to notice the ache in the voice, the wrinkled brow. She sat back and watched the unwinding into tenderness. She wanted to reach out, to offer comfort, to tell the person, "It's okay. I'm okay. It's just what happened."

But it wasn't that simple. People needed an explanation of how a person went on. How a young girl grew into a woman. They needed to connect, to give some kind of affection. Some sign of strength.

So Maya pictured herself standing before each new person, her palms cupped and extended. In her hands she envisioned a collection of animals made of glass. A jumble of figurines, each thin as a wafer. She looked at the pile, then down at the table next to them, before turning back to gaze into the eyes of the person before her. This potential friend or lover. Her look said, "If you want to know me, I need your help. I can't do this without you. You must decide whether to reach into this pile and extract each tiny animal. Whether it's worth the effort. The risk of what could shatter."

Maya found that each person held her stare, nodded. And as they talked, as she explained how a girl could grow without a mother, could become whatever Maya would become, the person took each figurine, one by one, and placed them gently on the table. Until all were safe. Until Maya's outstretched hands were all that remained.

Maya looked at Chris. She had a feeling he would gladly take her glass animals, one by one, and lay them softly wherever she wanted. If she asked, he'd carry them all the way to the edge of the sea.

"I never really knew her, so I don't think it's her that I miss. It's the idea of her. Of having a mother." She paused, sipped her beer. "I'm kind of split. Part of me thinks it's literally the old saying, 'You don't know what you're missing.' She died when I was so young, I'm not sure I know what to miss. But another part of me has this fantasy that she's hanging around. And every once in a while I get this feeling that she's just over my shoulder or waiting around the corner. That part feels pretty good.

"Anyway, she got sick right after I turned three and died a few months later. My dad never remarried. So to answer your question, he wasn't thrilled about me leaving. But he would never force me to stay."

"Is he really protective?"

"Not as much as you'd think. He lets me try whatever I want. Though I always feel like he's right behind me in case I fall. Or fail. Which is sort of nice."

Chris looked at Maya. Her eyes were clear, thoughtful. She smiled at him, glanced down at the bar. The years of names etched into the wood had worn away the polish. She traced a carving of "Spring Break 1997" with her index finger and sipped her beer.

"Can I ask what it was like? Growing up without a mom?"

"Yeah, of course." She paused. "Mostly it was normal. My dad did everything, but in dad style, you know? Halloween costumes came from the party store, which was awesome. My friends had homemade costumes and were jealous as hell." She leaned back and laughed, shook her head at the memory. "He helped me with science projects, which tended to be construction-related since that's his business. Lots of cranes and concrete." She reached into the bowl on the bar and took a pretzel, broke off a piece, popped it in her mouth. She thought back to her last science project in eighth grade. How to make concrete. She chewed on the pretzel piece and smiled at the memory. He was disappointed she only got a B.

"The best thing was my proms. He actually took me dress shopping. My aunt offered to go instead, but he insisted."

"He was probably just afraid your aunt would buy you something too revealing." Chris smiled and nudged her arm.

Maya laughed as beer sputtered from her mouth. "*Ha!* That's exactly what my aunt said!" She reached over the bar and lifted a cocktail napkin from the stack next to the plastic containers of lime wedges and maraschino cherries. She wiped her mouth and took another sip of beer. "Sorry about that." She blushed and shook her head.

He smiled and rubbed her shoulder. "Nothing to apologize for."

She nodded, leaned in toward him. "Anyway, he's a good dad." She looked down at her lap. Her palms were open and empty.

They talked for a couple of hours. More stories of family and childhood. Hobbies. They both liked sports, though neither cared much for golf. Chris considered himself a decent cook, and on two occasions during the evening promised to prove that to Maya. After three bowls of pretzels and another beer, he looked down at his watch.

"I'm sorry to say I have to get going. I have to do some work around my mom's house tomorrow, and I have an early shift the following morning. If I don't get my sleep tonight I won't be much use if I have to save someone's life." He smiled. "But maybe we can have a proper meal together next time I'm off? Next week? How about Blue Heaven? It's my favorite. Have you been?"

"Once, for a friend's birthday. Her parents' treat. It was great!"

"Then it's a date," he said. He looked up and blushed. "I mean, we don't have to call it a date. You know what I mean."

"It's a date," she said, smiling.

2007

To George's credit, he asked very few questions of Maya and Chris as their dating life began. Linda played by different rules.

"She wants you two to come for dinner," George said one morning. "And you know my wife. She won't take 'no' for an answer."

After a few more dinners at George and Linda's house, Maya felt like she'd melted into the family. She would come early and help Linda cook. Chris would pop into the kitchen, kiss the women, and put on an apron.

"How did it go with your mom?" Linda whispered to him one evening. They were standing at the sink rinsing dishes.

"It was great," he replied quietly.

"Did you expect anything different?"

"No, of course not. I knew they'd love each other."

Chris's dad had died a few years before, but his mother still lived on Cudjoe Key. After he assured Maya that his mom would love her, she finally agreed to dinner at his mother's house. His sister was away at college, so it would be just the three of them.

Elise greeted them at the door with up-stretched arms. As petite as Maya was, Chris's mom was inches shorter.

"So nice to meet you." She hugged the young woman, then stood back to look in her face. She saw the shyness, the small self-doubt, and pulled her in again. "I'm very happy to have you in my home." She patted Maya's back, led her to the family room, and offered her sweet tea. Chris settled next to Maya on the couch, rested his arm behind her. He watched the women warm to each other as they moved from careful to inquisitive to comfortable. His hand brushed the back of Maya's neck as he rose.

"I'm going to get dinner on the table. You two keep chatting."

Over dinner Maya learned more about Chris. Elise kept leaving the table to pull pictures off shelves and from the walls of the hallway.

"Look, this is Cub Scouts, second grade. And here's one with his sister. They adore each other. She was his little shadow when she was growing up." She placed the photo on the pile growing beside her plate.

"Oh, and this one is soccer." Elise tapped a framed photo of a smiling Chris, his left foot resting on a soccer ball. "I think this was middle school."

"Mom, please, enough." Chris reached for the picture as his mother snatched it away.

"No! My house, my bragging. You don't like it, clear the table and get dessert out of the fridge."

Maya smiled as Chris shook his head and reached for her plate. "What else can you tell me about him?" She looked up at the blushing man as he carried the dishes into the kitchen.

"Here, let me show you some pictures of him in uniform. Very handsome." She smiled at Maya. After a few more, Elise laid the last photo on the table. She leaned back, looked closely at the young woman.

"I can brag all night about his sports and his work, but the most important thing I can tell you about my son is he has a heart of gold. About five years before he died, my husband had a bad fall off a ladder. Shattered his hip. He didn't get around so well after that, so Chris would come over to trim trees, put up hurricane shutters. Never said anything to his father. He knew his dad had too much pride to ask for help.

"Then my husband was diagnosed with lung cancer." She paused, sipped her tea. "Chris was a good son. He was here all the time." Elise searched through the pile and selected one of the photos of Chris and his dad together. She stood it on the table and peered at the two men grinning at her misty eyes.

Maya shifted in her chair. She picked up the photo and held it out to Elise. "Did you take this picture?"

Elise wrinkled her forehead, remembering. "Yes, I think I did. Why do you ask?"

"Looks like two guys who love the person behind the camera very much."

Elise reached over and patted Maya's arm. The setting sun

crept in through the front window and painted the tablecloth with the last oranges and pinks of the day. The clock in the hall chimed half past the hour.

Chris stood at the edge of the dining room, dessert plates in one hand, flan in the other. He'd stepped back into the kitchen at the mention of the accident, the death.

He remembered the long line of mourners shuffling into the funeral home. The women, each with a tight embrace, lingering a moment before release, unsure how to pass along their sympathy and sorrow. The men, the handshakes coarse. Grips of masculinity, endurance.

Yet for all the sobbing and emotion of the women, it was the men who broke him. Because with the handshake came the free hand placed gently on the side of the arm or the shoulder or, worse, looped around the back to pull him in. It was the men. The uncles and cousins and friends, with their love for his father. The love that had no place to rest. The love that stumbled around the halls of the funeral home and rustled in the swaying palm trees of Key West and drained from that free hand. The love that trickled into Chris until he was awash, until he was overflowing. Until he had no place left to put his own.

As he leaned against the wall of the kitchen, he remembered the weight of the casket, the soft leather seats of the limousine, the quiet tears of his sister as the procession weaved through town toward the cemetery. He remembered the grave, the dirt, the ends of his shirt cuffs as he pulled on the sleeves of his suit jacket. He remembered when months later, as the family marked the grave with his father's stone, how he looked at the date and thought it was the beginning of a new chapter. He was the man of the family now. He would care for them.

He cleared his throat, entered the dining room, forced a smile. "Who's ready for flan?"

~

"Your mom's really sweet." They were driving back to Key West. Chris had been quiet during dessert. He seemed rushed to get home. Maya placed a hand on his arm. "You okay?"

"What? Yeah, fine." He looked at her, smiled. "I'm fine." He took her hand and kissed the back. "I heard my mom telling you about my dad. Sometimes when I'm at the house and think about his death, I get a little sad. I'm okay." They drove for a few minutes in silence.

"I worry about my mom. With my sister away at school, I need to come by more often. Her health is good, but I know she's lonely." He looked at Maya. "I need to be here for her."

Maya squeezed his hand. She loved that Chris was generous with his heart, with affection. He wanted to help, to rescue, to comfort. He embraced the needs of others, found small ways to offer a bit more care, an extra blanket of protection. His kindness reminded her of her father. The people in his life came first. Making sure they were safe, they were loved.

~

On Easter Sunday, George's extended family gathered at his house for dinner. He spurned charters that day, went to church with his family, ate all afternoon.

"This is why I work so hard," he told Maya. They were sitting in the backyard, drinking beer. Manny was playing catch with one of his younger cousins. Linda sat with her mother and sister at the picnic table, laughing over the latest gossip from their old neighborhood. "So that when I'm not working, I can enjoy this." George waved his bottle at the scene before him. He looked at her. "It doesn't get any better. Family. It's not about the car you drive or the diploma on your wall. When it's all over, this will be what mattered."

Maya sipped her beer. With one hand she rotated the rope bracelet she wore on her other wrist. It was grey and soft and fit close to her skin. She remembered when she bought it. Her first semester in Key West, three and a half years earlier. She was browsing the gift shops with a friend from class. The girl wore one from childhood. She was from a sailing family, and each of her siblings donned the bracelet as a badge of honor. They're cool, Maya thought. I'll buy one. It'll help mark the passage of time on the water.

She moved the bracelet up her wrist and looked at her tan line. With summer coming, her skin would darken again. Months and years were passing. Full moons and new ones. She was learning how to earn a living on the water. George was teaching her how to catch different types of fish, how to make repairs to the boat and tackle she hadn't learned in school. How to deal with clients. He explained the books and encouraged her to think about the business, not just the physical work. Someday, he told her, you're going to want a boat of your own. You won't be a mate forever.

Twenty

SUMMER PASSED. CHARLIE CAME FOR A VISIT over Maya's birthday when the charter business slowed. She and George took him out for a day of fishing, and they filled a cooler with mahi mahi. At dinner that night, father and daughter enjoyed some of the day's catch.

"This is the way to live," Charlie said as he finished his meal and leaned back in his chair. "Catch food, eat food. I could get used to this."

"Except it's a lot cheaper to buy it at the fish market. It's fun, but not a way to live. At least not for normal people."

"Oh, I know. It's the vacation glow talking." He finished his beer. "This isn't real life. Well, not for me. Does it feel like real life to you?"

"Sometimes." She pushed the last of her rice around her

plate. "Some days it feels like the only work I could ever do. And then other times, when I'm standing in the back of the boat and staring at the horizon, I feel uneasy. Like I should be going somewhere. I keep thinking there's something else out there I should be looking for. Something more important I should be doing. Ever since that guy from high school was killed, it's been on my mind."

One of Maya's classmates had stepped on an IED in Afghanistan.

"These guys are out there dying, and for what? And what am I doing? Helping people catch fish." She looked down at her plate and shook her head. "Doesn't seem right. I'm young and healthy. Why not me?" She pushed her plate away.

"Is that what you want to do? Or is it that you feel guilty or just want to make a difference? What is it?"

She sighed. "I don't want to go to war. I guess I feel a little guilty. I just want to do something to help someone. Something that matters. Maybe somewhere else." She looked at her father for an answer.

He stared at his daughter. Watched her shift in her seat, cross and uncross her arms. His face softened. "What you don't realize is you're already doing that here." He leaned toward her, rested his elbows on the table, folded his hands. "Who are your clients?"

"Mostly tourists from different parts of the country. Sometimes from Canada or Europe or somewhere else."

"That's right. And you know what those people are doing? Getting away from their troubles. That guy from Wednesday's charter who hooked a dolphin? His wife left him for another guy. His cousin who's with him on the trip? He lost his mom last year to breast cancer. The guy on the next trip? Hates his job, barely gets through each day. He has to, has a family to support. So he slogs his way through the commute and the hours and the difficult boss.

"People come here to escape. To find some comfort and release for a few days. They drink, they get on the boat with you, and they let the salt air clear out their lungs. Because in a few days they have to go back to whatever led them to you." He laid his arms on the table.

She looked around the room. Her eyes moistened.

"Look at me," Charlie said. She turned to her father.

"Are you hunting down terrorists or saving someone's life? No. But that doesn't mean what you're doing isn't important. The world is crazy. Look what happened on 9/11. What's happening now. People are scared. You and George, you give them a reprieve from whatever they're running from. They're running to you. They may not know it, you may not know it, but that's what they're doing.

"People have wounds. You put a little salt water on them and help them heal."

Maya heard her father. Wanted to believe him. Yet despite his efforts, doubt nagged at her. For periods of time her mind quieted, and when she was at peace she focused on work. The sun and tropical breezes soothed her. Gladys was her rock. George and Linda and the boys became her extended family. Chris provided the companionship and love she craved. She enjoyed the time they spent with his mother, who'd already started treating her like a daughter. To keep herself in motion, she took more classes and earned her captain's license.

Her relationship with Chris was different from those she'd had before. Chris wasn't a boy trying to figure out how to become a man. He had a career he loved, but he explained early on that something was missing: a partner and children. He didn't seem desperate or rushed. But finding the right person was important to him, as was having kids while he was still young enough to coach them at soccer and carry them on his shoulders. He'd had trouble meeting women in Key West who shared a desire for permanence. Most of the women he knew and liked from childhood had left. Many of the ones who'd moved to Key West wanted to party. He wanted someone fun but serious. Someone like Maya.

"You are something else," he told her one night after they'd made love. "Smart, funny, beautiful. I don't know how those New England boys let you get away."

"Yeah, yeah, whatever. Talk to me when you're washing dishes or tired from work and want to be left alone. Right now, you have no credibility." She nudged him and smiled.

"That's not completely true. If we hadn't done it in a couple of weeks and I was desperate to get in your pants, then I'd have no credibility. For me, sex is the ultimate truth serum. Besides, I talk the same way when I am washing dishes or tired from work. You know that." He rolled over on his side and brushed the hair out of her face. "You're the one for me."

Maya reached up and touched Chris's face. He was a special guy. He would make someone a great husband. She kissed him.

"I love you." She meant it. But she didn't know what it meant.

She decided not to dwell on her future. Work became her

focus, the lifeline she clung to when she stared too long at the horizon. When thoughts of leaving Key West crept into her mind.

One night after a long day on the water, she came home, showered, and crashed on the couch.

"I've got some bean soup going, you want?" Gladys asked.

Maya had long ago surrendered the idea that she and Gladys were merely roommates. Gladys cooked. Maya ate. The arrangement gave both of them pleasure. After much arguing, Gladys had agreed to allow Maya to contribute to the grocery bill.

"But only because you'll drive me nuts if I don't accept," Gladys had said. "It's not necessary. I used to cook for hundreds. I've cooked for four and for three and for two and then for one. I prefer two over one. Letting me cook for you, it's a gift to me."

They were in the kitchen one night, Maya washing the dishes. She insisted on doing the washing whenever Gladys cooked.

"I understand. But your gift back to me will be allowing me to contribute something. Let me at least do that. And your dishes." She smiled and put the last plate away.

"Bean soup sounds perfect," Maya said, mindful of her surrender to their arrangement. She stood up and fell backward onto the couch. "*Whew*, I'm tired."

"Sit, sit. I'll get the trays. Alex is coming on in a few minutes anyway."

Gladys set up the TV trays and placed a steaming bowl of ham and bean soup in front of Maya. She tore off a piece of Cuban bread, buttered it, and set it on a plate on Maya's tray.

"This is great." Maya spooned through the lentils, white

beans, and tomato broth. She bit into a chunk of salty ham and sat back with a sigh. "One of my favorites."

"There's plenty, have as much as you want. You seem more tired than usual. Too much sun today?"

Maya drained her bowl and stood up to refill it. She grabbed Gladys's and took them both to the kitchen.

"I don't think so," she said over her shoulder. "We caught a bunch of tuna today with some clients, a family from Ohio. They had a couple of middle-school-aged kids with them, so I was dancing around them a little bit. But I don't think that's it either. I'm just worn out." She handed Gladys her bowl and placed her own on her tray. "I know I have a dream job, but maybe I need a vacation."

She hadn't taken time off in over a year. Charlie came down for visits every few months, so Maya never felt compelled to go home. She had no thoughts of going anywhere else.

"You're young. Yes, you should get your rest, but I don't think that's it. What's the matter? You miss home?"

"A little. I miss my dad, my family, New England. It's made me think more about my mom, too." Maya settled back in her seat. She dipped her spoon into the bowl and savored the rich liquid. She wondered what it would have been like to have a mother present when she was young. What kind of soup her mom would have made. She sipped a spoonful. Maybe it was the earthy broth that warmed her, she thought. Maybe it was her mother, lingering in the evening air.

"Do you ever wonder if your husband is around?" she asked. "Looking out for you or keeping you company?"

Gladys believed in ghosts. After her husband died, her family stayed with her until they felt she was ready to be alone. When she closed the door behind the last relative, she turned to face her small home. The purple orchid on the windowsill. The frayed, crocheted pillow on the sofa. Her husband's recliner next to hers, facing the TV.

She sat in her chair and looked at his. She pictured him snoring, a crossword puzzle resting against his chest and pen dangling from his hand. Late afternoon sunlight streamed between the blinds. Dust settled. She picked up the remote from the side table. As she turned toward the TV, something shifted beside her. An impression on the seat cushion. A flutter in the still air. She reached over and patted the arm of his chair. She sat back, placed the remote in her lap. Listened to the quiet.

Gladys returned to normal life. She cleaned the bathroom and mopped the floors. She shopped for groceries. Cooked beans and rice. At the end of a day, tired and achy, she turned back the worn sheet and blanket, climbed into bed, settled in. As she drifted off to sleep, the mattress creaked.

"Yes," Gladys said to Maya. "I think he visits me. He's not here all the time, but he lets me know he's around." Gladys muted the TV. She listened to the whirr of the ceiling fan, the chain clinking against the motor. She looked at Maya. So young, she thought. Too young to have lost a mother.

"I think they're with us," she said. "Not all the time. But when we need them."

Jeopardy started. Gladys turned up the volume. They returned to their bowls, each shouting out answers. Gladys knew three in the historical fiction category. Maya knew two of the lakes and four of the national parks.

"You're awfully worldly for someone who hasn't traveled much," Gladys said after *Jeopardy* ended. "Must be all that storytelling. Or did your dad take you when you were growing up?"

"Not too much. Actually, I think it's the storytelling." Over the years, and particularly since the Disney trip, both she and Charlie brought a little more effort to Saturday nights. Their stories were no longer random fantasies of famous places. The Eiffel Tower and Big Ben appeared, but so did remote regions of the Yukon and small islands in the South Pacific. They both read and prepared like honor students.

Maya sat back in her chair. She licked the last few drops of soup from her spoon as she remembered last Saturday night.

"You upped the ante this week," Charlie had said to her. She pictured him stretching his legs the length of the couch. Adjusting the volume on the handheld phone to better hear his sleepy daughter. "That trip to Java was pretty detailed. Where'd you get that stuff?"

Maya remembered rolling over, fighting to keep her eyes open. Pulling up the sheet and comforter. Gladys blasted the air conditioning. Her nose was always cold.

"*National Geographic*. There was an article and some cool photos. I picked it up at the library. You should check it out."

"That's okay. I like your story better. No reason to bring reality into it."

Maya stood to clear their soup bowls as her father's words faded away. "The storytelling keeps me motivated. It's kind of an unspoken competition at this point, forces me to read things that matter. I can travel the world without leaving Key West. Much more cost effective."

"But is it enough?" Gladys rose, stored the trays behind the couch. "You can't live your life through a story once a week. You're young. There are things to see."

"Trying to get rid of me already?" Maya smiled, touched the older woman's arm.

"Never! My dear, you can stay as long as you like. For me,

this is all I need." She reached up to stifle a yawn. "I'm tired, too. I think I'll go to bed. Good night."

"Night. See you in the morning."

Maya finished the dishes, shut off the TV. She brushed her teeth and turned out the lights. It was early. She'd read for a while. In bed she pulled a novel off her nightstand. College kids lost in the mountains on spring break. They were hiking into the backcountry with their skis. A rumble in the distance. Avalanche. The snow rushed over them, buried one of the young men, tossed another down the side of the mountain. The fiction felt real. Maya nodded off as two more tumbled beneath a wave of powder. Her eyes fluttered as the men rolled under the surface, unsure of where to dig, how to find air. She woke with a start, heard a thud.

"What was that?" She jumped out of bed, opened her door, and wandered into the hallway. It was quiet, but she heard a shallow breath. Then silence. She felt the wall for the switch. Under the soft light, she saw Gladys slumped on the floor.

"Gladys!"

Maya called 911 and started CPR, but Gladys didn't respond. In minutes the paramedics arrived with a defibrillator.

"Clear!" one of the paramedics shouted. She jolted Gladys's body and looked at the screen. The jagged line changed. Her heart was coming back. "Let's get her on the gurney." The paramedic turned to Maya. They knew each other through Chris. "You know I can't let you in the ambulance since you're not family, right? I'm really sorry."

"It's okay. I'll call her family and meet you there."

Maya phoned Gladys's sons and George. The brothers said they'd fly down in the morning. George arrived in minutes and drove her to the hospital. They spent the next few hours pacing through the waiting room, taking turns wandering down the hall for coffee. Sometime around midnight the doctor came out to greet them.

"You're not family, correct?" she asked.

"No," Maya said. "I rent a room from her, but I've been speaking with both her sons who live out of state. They're coming down tomorrow. I know you'll be calling them, but can you tell me anything?"

"I will call them. But I can tell you we put in a stent. She's stable now, but let's see how she looks in the morning."

Maya thanked the doctor, and she and George headed for the entrance. "Thanks, George, for coming and staying. I think I should come back in a few hours, if that's okay."

"Of course. You take whatever time you need. Listen, I can handle a few days on my own, or find someone around town to help. And don't worry about money. I'll help you if you need it." He put his arm around her shoulder and walked her out.

Maya rose early and was at the hospital before eight. The cardiologist met her at the desk, gave her an update. "She's awake. You can go in."

She stopped before approaching the bed, the flashing lights of the monitors startling in the grey morning light. Her eyes tracked the changing numbers, the radiant green zigzag. Would it have been like this for my mom, she wondered. She was so young then. She couldn't recall.

She shook the distraction from her mind. Be here, she thought. Be here for someone you love. Even if it's difficult.

"Hey there. Looks like you had a bit of a heart attack. Just can't accept when I beat you at *Jeopardy*, huh?" She bent over and kissed Gladys's cheek under the oxygen tube. "Guess I'll have to start throwing the game."

"What are you talking about?" Gladys whispered. "You'll never beat me in fine arts. You were lucky with the categories last night." She coughed.

"Okay, okay, you're right, I got lucky. Enough talking." She sat down on the edge of the bed. "You gave me quite a scare. They won't say much since I'm not family, but the doctor was kind enough to tell me they put in a stent and you're going to be fine in a couple of days. The boys are coming. They'll be here soon." She rested her hand on Gladys's arm. "You should sleep some more. I'll be outside if you need me."

Gladys patted Maya's hand and closed her eyes. Maya sat a moment longer before she left the room.

Gladys's sons arrived just after noon. The three spent the rest of the day at the hospital before retreating to the house for a quick dinner break. One moved into his old room, the other dropped his bags by the couch. They refused to take Maya's room.

"Are you kidding?" Anthony said when Maya raised the issue. "First of all, you saved our mother's life. And second, you pay to live here. That room is yours, not mine. I don't want to hear another word about it."

Thomas agreed. They spent the next three days shuttling back and forth to the hospital and worrying how to care for Gladys. After they took her home, Anthony flew back to Minnesota and Thomas stayed. He arranged to work from Key West for a few weeks to help his mother through her recovery. By the end of the first week, Maya was back at work and Thomas was cooking dinners for the three of them. He and Maya were in the kitchen one night cleaning up after Gladys went to bed.

"Cup of tea?" he asked.

"That would be nice." They sat at the table in front of mugs of steaming pomegranate. "Tell me about Brooklyn."

"Oh, Brooklyn's great. It's lively. There are phenomenal restaurants and bars and shops. People everywhere. Sometimes I miss being able to take a walk without sirens blaring, but it's a small price to pay. There's something about being in a city, where no one knows you and you can just fade into the background whenever you want to. For all the noise, you can get lost in the aloneness of a big place. In Key West I knew everyone, and everyone knew me. I had to get away from that. Be invisible for a while. Know what I mean?"

Maya nodded, sipped her tea. "Yeah. I know the feeling of having to get away from wherever 'here' is. At first I thought it was just Seaport. That I had to leave the small town I grew up in. But I've been here a few years, and I'm starting to wonder if it's less about that and more about being in motion. Do you feel that way in Brooklyn?"

"Not really. It's different for me. I needed to leave this place in particular. My dad and mom knew I was gay. And I knew they loved me, but it was difficult for them, with the religious thing and all. I think my parents always blamed Key West for who I am, and by extension blamed themselves. I thought if I moved to a place like New York, they would see it wasn't geography that made me this way. I think they figured that out eventually and made their peace with it. And in the process I fell in love with Brooklyn. It's my home. I don't think I'll ever leave." He tilted his head to look at her. Such an important time in her life, he thought.

"There are lots of people who wander. And lots of reasons they feel like they have to go somewhere else. My only advice is if you leave a place, especially a place as great as this, make sure it's because you're running *to* something, not running away from anything. Otherwise it's hard to find permanence.

"When I left, I was running away. I had to stand still long enough to make sure the place was no longer the problem. Well, that and sit through a few years of therapy. Brooklyn's good for that, too. But eventually I found my peacefulness about it. I found a place." Thomas sipped from his cup. He looked at Maya. "How is it for you?"

Maya finished her last few drops of tea and set the mug on the table.

"I think I'm where you were. Still running away." She sighed, sat back in her chair. "Lately I've been feeling like it's time to go again. I've been here almost four years. But I don't think this is my place."

"Is it Chris? Are you running from him?"

"No, I don't think so. Might be why I've stayed this long. Chris and Gladys and George and his family. It's comfortable. But it's not my Brooklyn."

"Then you need to find your Brooklyn."

Maya nodded. She took their mugs to the sink, rinsed them, and put them in the dishwasher. She opened the cabinet and reached up to the top shelf for the roll of heavy nylon tucked next to the popcorn maker. She paused a moment. Wondered about the pain he'd suffered. Her chest tightened. I hate that he hurts, she thought. That the world hurts so many. She unfurled the rainbow flag and handed it to Thomas.

"By the way, you're right about your parents. They more than made their peace with who you are. Your mom carries this every year in the Pride Parade."

Thomas held the flag and rubbed the stitching, turning it over in his hands. He wiped his eyes and spread the crinkly fabric out on the table. "I love my son Thomas," he read. Underneath it, PRIDE was sewn in all capital letters. He looked up at Maya. "She did this?"

"Yeah. She wanted all of Key West to know she wasn't just a supporter of the movement, she supports you. That she loves you and is proud of you. She bought the flag at a shop on Duval Street and stitched in the lettering herself. Then she and your father would walk the parade. They did it together for years. She still does it. She never told you?"

"No. My dad, too?"

"Yup. They did it together. You know your mom. She doesn't talk about her feelings. She shows you she loves you by cooking, nagging at you to eat and get your rest. Maybe next year you can walk with her."

"I think that's very likely to happen." He paused, cleared his throat. "Thank you." He put his head in his hands and wept. Maya brought him the box of tissues from the bathroom and kissed the top of his head.

"Company or alone?"

"I think alone is good," he said, looking up at her and wiping his eyes with a tissue. "Thanks."

Twenty-one

GLADYS STRENGTHENED. THOMAS PREPARED to leave. As he piled his bags into the cab, he kissed and hugged his mother and turned to Maya.

"Remember what we talked about. Figure it out, okay? And don't worry about this place. I think I've shown my boss I can work from here when I need to. My mom is even talking about coming up to Brooklyn for a few weeks at a time. We can make it work."

Maya nodded. She hugged Thomas an extra moment and rubbed his back. She felt like she'd gained a friend. She didn't want to lose him.

One night a few months later, she and Chris sat down to dinner. He'd grilled steaks, filled their plates with baked potatoes and sour cream and steamed broccoli. They were in his kitchen, sharing a rare evening when they were both off work the next day.

Maya pushed the last few pieces of potato around her plate. "I'm stuffed. That was delicious." She smiled at him, her mind eager to move past the niceties of food and the news of their respective days. When he finished his meal and the details of his last rescue call, she asked him what he knew about Islamorada.

"Nothing much. Good fishing. Decent tourist area, shops and restaurants. A couple of fire stations. Not much else to know. Why, you want to go on a trip?"

"Not exactly a trip." She shifted in her chair, rubbed her damp palms on her shorts. She thought spending the night together would give her time to explain why she needed to go. Give him time to see she was only leaving Key West. Not him.

"I'm thinking of moving there."

Chris sat motionless, his napkin still in hand.

"Moving? Why? You're not happy here?"

"Yes and no. I love you and everyone here, and I love working for George. But I feel like I have to keep exploring. I don't feel like this is my last stop."

"Uh, okay, well, it's not that far away. Won't be as easy for us to see each other with our schedules. And we certainly can't commute that far, but we can make it work. I mean, if that's what you want." He looked at his plate. Then he stood and cleared the table. His mind reeled.

"Chris, come on, let's talk about this. It's not about us. It's about me. It's this feeling that I need to do something different, progress somehow. Don't you get it?"

He hovered over the sink, gazed out the window. The yard was dark. His reflection stared back at him, grim and smoldering. He turned and glared at Maya, crossed his arms.

"No, frankly, I don't get it. I don't get telling me you love me in one breath and saying you want to leave in the next. I know it's not that far away, but it is away. And that's the point with you, isn't it? It's always away. The next Raymond Adventure. You and your dad, you concoct these stories like there's a better place out there. Guess what? There isn't. This is as good a place as any. Better than most."

He stood for a moment. His thoughts simmered.

"Don't you see? It's not about whether you have sand between your toes or you're scraping ice off your windshield. It's about who you sit next to on the beach, or who is on the other side of the car, scraping away in the cold with you. Anything else is pure fantasy. It's bullshit. And you and your dad believe your own bullshit. Here's the reality. This is all there is."

Maya looked up from her chair. Her eyes flashed across the room. The black chip on the edge of the range's white enamel. The tattered kitchen towel with the faded cows. All so familiar. So soon to be gone.

She picked up her napkin from her lap and wiped her mouth. Her hand shook as she set the napkin on the table.

"I guess I don't get it then. Because I don't think this is all there is. At least not for me, not now. I'm sorry. I have to do this. I thought maybe you could look into whether you could find a spot in Islamorada. Like you said, they have fire stations. Maybe there's more opportunity. You might even get a promotion."

She'd had so many ideas of how this would go. None like this. She'd pictured them lying in bed, holding hands, the TV muted across the room. He'd be excited for her, she'd thought, for the new chapter their lives would enter. She couldn't look at him now. Couldn't bear the pain seeping into his skin.

"Is that what this is about? I'm not ambitious enough for you?"

"No, it's not about anything like that. Geez, Chris, can't you see this has nothing to do with who *you* are or what choices *you've* made? This is about *my* life, *my* future. I'm trying to figure out what that looks like."

He stared at her, turned away. He shifted his feet and looked back at her.

"So what does it look like?" he asked quietly. "When you see into the future, am I in it?"

She hesitated. "I don't know. I hope so. But I don't know."

He reached into his pocket and pulled out a black velvet box. He walked over toward her and sat down, placed the box on the table. He laughed once, his voice catching on the burrs lodged in his throat.

"This wasn't the way I saw this night going. I thought we'd go for a walk, sit on the beach." He ran his hand through his hair, opened the box. The diamond sparkled under the overhead light of the kitchen.

He leaned back in his chair, threw his hands up, dropped them in his lap. Shook his head.

Disbelief fluttered across the warm kitchen. Anger chased it into the family room and out into the night. Grief stayed behind, leaned against the refrigerator, folded its arms and waited. Waited for this man and woman to find it.

"I love you, Maya. I've loved you since that first day on the boat. I don't think I knew it that day, but I knew it pretty soon after. I'm a simple guy. I told you that from the beginning. I want to work and come home and be with you and whatever other little creatures we have or don't have." His voice splintered. "Is that too much to ask?"

Maya looked at the ring and then at Chris. She sat back in her chair, mouth agape. What to say to this man I love, she thought. How do I speak without breaking him, breaking me? Breaking us.

She shook her head, reached deep inside to find her voice. "No, it's not too much to ask. But it's too much to answer." She took his hand. "I can't say yes right now. Maybe one day I'll be able to, but for now it wouldn't be right. I would love for you to come with me, but I know your family is here and they need you and if you don't want to do that I won't push you. We can make it work. We just won't see each other quite as much."

He sighed, rubbed her fingers.

"You really believe that, don't you? That this can work if we don't see each other as often? It's hard enough now with our schedules. You think it'll be easier if you're an hour and a half away?"

"I don't think it'll be easier, which is why I hoped you'd consider coming. I think if you stay here it'll be more of a challenge, but we can still do it."

Chris shook his head. He pulled his hand away, closed the box, rose from the table.

"I think you knew I wouldn't come and that's what you hoped for. I think you want to leave both Key West and me. It's just easier to break up with Key West because you don't have to talk about it. Islamorada's your first stop. It won't be your last."

He walked into the bedroom and shut the door. Maya sat for a moment, listened to the hush of early evening. A scooter sped up the street. She stood and walked to the bedroom, leaned her head against the door.

"Chris. It's not what you think. I don't want to leave you." She traced her index finger along the groove of the door panel.

"I want to leave me," she whispered.

She lifted her head, waited a moment. When he didn't

respond, she picked up her bag and left the house. Tears didn't pass her cheek until she was halfway home. Running for her life.

Telling everyone else was no easier. Gladys was happy for her but sad to lose her companion.

"You must go. Don't worry about this old lady. I'll be fine."

Thomas had been coming down every few weeks, and Gladys had already taken long trips to visit both sons. She was wearing an alert button now, but the doctor said she was healthy. "It's just to keep the boys happy," she said the first time she put it on. "I'm not going anywhere but Brooklyn and Minnesota."

George and Linda were disappointed but supportive. Maya told George she would stay as long as he needed her. George had a friend in Islamorada with a larger charter boat. He had an opening for a first mate, and Maya was the perfect choice. The job would give her a place to stay as she could live on the boat.

The next few weeks were a blur. She wasn't going far, but losing regular meals with George and Linda and the boys and nightly chats with Gladys was burrowing a dark hole in her heart. Then there was Chris. Maybe this is the wrong decision, she thought. Maybe I'll regret it.

She remembered the night with Thomas in the kitchen. She thought about how he'd found his place, how she needed to find hers. Key West is not my Brooklyn, she thought. Time for me to leave.

As Maya skirted delicately around the edges of her sadness, Chris charged into the vast sphere of his anguish until it rolled into waves of anger. He stomped through the firehouse, hacked at trees in his mother's yard. He drank more, and then not at all. After a few weeks, his rage dwindled, his fire lost the crackle of its flames. But the embers lay hot underneath.

He kept his distance. George reminded him she would be leaving soon, but he couldn't bring himself to return any of her calls. Couldn't bear to utter her name into the evening breeze.

"Ready to go?" George asked Maya on her last morning with him.

"I guess so. I'm excited, a little sad. But I know I can come back and see you guys whenever I want." She paused. "I'll miss you all, though."

"We'll miss you, too." George placed his hands on her shoulders, looked in her eyes. "But you're doing the right thing. This will be good for you." He dropped his hands and turned away, cleared his throat. "Have you heard from Chris?"

"No. Six weeks and he still won't take my calls." She sighed. "I know this is the right decision for my career, but I'm not sure it's the right decision. You know?" She wiped her eyes.

He nodded.

Six weeks, she thought. What was the old saying? Days pass slowly, years fly by? The past six weeks had fled from her, a flurry of packing and last stops around town. Strolls with friends through the sunset carnival of Mallory Square. A grilled grouper sandwich at B.O.'s Fish Wagon, the key lime mayo dripping down her arm. Some evenings she'd walk over to Higgs

Beach and sit under a palm tree, stare up into the fronds that waved with the last whispers of the day. The rustle a chorus of goodbye, goodbye, goodbye.

Weeks flew, but moments stood still. Next to her. Across the room. On the other side of the rocking boat. Wherever, whenever she paused. The moments without Chris halted time.

"I miss him."

"I know you do, sweetheart." George stepped forward, put his arms around her. "Give him some time. I know it's difficult. But just know he's suffering, too."

"You think so?"

"I do."

She buried her face in his chest, the gravity of her leaving heavy on her back. She pictured the frothy wake of her departure, the loved ones bobbing in the waves. Her tears dampened his shirt.

George hugged her closer. "It's okay." He let her cry until the heaving slowed, her breath returned. Then the wind shifted. And she gently pulled away.

Twenty-two

THE STREETS OF KEY WEST keep their stories close, hidden behind iron gates and trellises drenched in pink and purple bougainvillea. Some homes, dark and quiet, sag with their aging, creased by decades of chipping away. Others stand tall, bright white, their shutters vivid with the colors of new life. Violet, royal blue. The hot coral of a sunset draped across the western sky.

Visitors spend days wandering the neighborhoods, studying the architecture, inhaling the dense perfume of frangipani. Listening for ghosts. By late afternoon the pictures are all taken, the t-shirts bought. The ramblers settle onto bar stools and salute the sunshine, the bartender, the forgetting. Some fish or follow Hemingway. Others come to the end of the island chain to marry. But for many, the drink is the thing.

Islamorada's bar stools are smaller in number, a gathering, more a troop than army. Key West neighborhoods bump up against one another, tumble into each other. Tourists meander from Mallory Square to Duval Street to the quiet, shaded sidewalks of the Truman Annex.

Islamorada is a relay down U.S. 1, the baton passing from one island to the next by car. Visitors don't stroll from Whale Harbor to Venetian Shores. People arrive, unpack rods and reels, back boats off trailers. Fish. They wake before the sun rises and tuck in soon after it sets. Kayakers paddle up and down canals or out to Indian Key to walk among the settlement ruins. Still, history here sleeps quietly, less a part of a visitor's agenda than in Key West. Some find bar stools and celebrate life's short reprieve. But for most, the fishing is the thing.

Giant yachts. Forty, fifty, sixty feet long. Roaring diesel engines hidden below, churning clear water to reach the dark blue ocean faster than last year or the year before that or the year before that. Charging across the vast sea.

Small flats boats. Sixteen, seventeen, eighteen feet long. A quiet outboard puttering behind the stern, nimble enough to flit among the mangrove islands, float in water inches deep. Boats capable of running. Or hiding.

Key West offers little such shelter, few places to lie in shadow away from the world. In Islamorada, tiny keys dot the seascape. Near the shores of Lower Matecumbe alone, one can find the cover of red mangrove that with time and persistence has grown into a small island. A great blue heron or white ibis might perch in the branches, waiting for the ripple of water following a young snapper or snook. Or for the tide to recede, leaving the bottom open to the scurry of a small crab.

In Key West, crowds mill about Mallory Square, waiting for the final blaze of the day to disappear behind the edge of the Gulf. Fierce reds, purples, magentas fading to black, leaving the evening to draw the mayhem back to Duval. Back to the whirr of blenders, the strum of a Buffett tune, the stumbling embraces of drunken release. The colors, for the moment so alive, so quickly, dramatically, disappear into darkest night.

Color in Islamorada is a slow, seeping creature. It crawls in on its belly when the first rays tiptoe across the Atlantic, bringing baby blue sky to lighten the navy ocean. Against the mangroves and sandy beaches, the early morning water lightens to a rich turquoise, and by midmorning a mint green that reflects the startling glint of the powder blue sky. By noon, the waves of grass below dance under seafoam green. As the sun saunters into the afternoon, the water ripples to sage, the sky a cornflower blue, dotted with white clouds leaving long shadows across the heated earth. Finally, as the sun wanders away, the skies to the east melt into the sea. All teal above and below, no distinction between blue and green. The horizon gone to sleep.

So many reasons to stay in Key West. So many reasons to leave.

Twenty-three

2008

George's friend in Islamorada had a sixty-foot custom boat with a large cabin. His first mate had left a few months before. He'd found other help, but the guys he'd hired were not willing to commit long-term to the schedule and pay he offered —tips only—given the recent downturn in the economy. With a lighter schedule, Bill thought he could survive with someone less experienced, if that person could survive on the scant tips currently available. And since George trusted this woman, he'd let her stay on the boat. Unusual for Bill, but a fair compromise under the circumstances.

"I don't know," Bill said when George first called him about Maya. "She sounds a little small for this kind of work."

"Look, I'm not going to lie. You may need to give her a hand with a few boxes or coolers, but she can do just about anything. Besides, aren't you trying to save money right now?"

"Yeah, this housing bubble killed my business. I'm down

sixty percent from last year, and my reservations over the next few months are worse. Shit, man, I'm really worried this time. Hope it blows over soon."

"I know, me too." George leaned against the cabin door, squinted into the early morning sun. He'd decided not to replace Maya with a full-time helper. His boys would pick up some of the slack, and Chris had a couple of buddies looking for extra work. He would make do for now.

Bill rubbed his whiskered chin, looked out over the marina. Too many boats still in their slips for this time of day. He needed help. But not as much as he used to.

"Okay, let's do it. I trust you wouldn't steer me wrong. When can she start?"

~

Maya arrived at the *Wake Up* ready to work, to put the last few weeks behind her.

She soon learned boats and captains differed in many ways. Bill was a good boss but less of a teacher than George. More like a mentor. He was patient, but he expected her to keep her business and her life in check and the boat in shape. Occasionally when they had more than four anglers aboard, he would bring on additional help. For four or less he expected Maya to handle everything from morning setup to evening cleaning. Hard work, and she did most of it alone, but she enjoyed the solitude.

Since business was slow, Maya had more days off than she liked. It affected her pay, but she survived on what she made. Bill kept her because he had other businesses and needed someone to care for the boat.

In spite of his gruff manner, Bill warmed up to Maya, wanted to help her. If they were offshore and having a slow day trolling for dolphin, he'd tell her to pull in the outriggers. Then he'd set the GPS for the 409 Hump or Islamorada Hump to catch amberjack. First she had to learn how. He offered her a lesson one weekday afternoon when they had no charters scheduled.

"Clients might prefer to catch dolphin, but they'd rather catch amberjack than nothing. And amberjack are usually easy to catch." Bill entered the coordinates for the 409 into the GPS. "Blackfin tuna is another nice consolation prize. I'll show you how to jig for amberjack and blackfin."

He drove out to the 409 Hump and checked the fish finder. Plenty of activity below.

"So when you jig, first you figure out where the fish are congregating, and then how the boat is going to drift with the current over the top of the school. These fish will bite on a plain old metal lure, as long as the lure looks like it's swimming. Once you have the current sorted out, you position the boat and drop in a line. Just let the line run to the bottom for some period of time. I start with a count of about thirty or forty seconds, but it varies with the depth of the school. Then you start jigging. You reel in, allow the line to drop, and you keep repeating the process up and down, real quick.

"If you don't get a hit, let it out again. Maybe go up to fifty or sixty seconds and reel. If you're fast you can get a few in before you have to reposition the boat so you're over the school again. But usually you get a hit on at least one line for each drift. Sometimes on the way down, sometimes on the way back up when you're reeling in. You'll be amazed at how many hits you get. It's the closest thing I've ever seen to shooting fish in a barrel."

"Why's it so easy?"

"Because you're not fishing for hungry fish. You're just trying to piss them off. Jigging is about finding where the fish live and pushing their buttons. They see this shiny metal thing invading their space and it irritates them. So they grab at it to make it go away. You poke the fish until it can't stand you anymore. Except when it pokes you back, it gets more than it bargained for. Doesn't work for all fish. But with amberjack, grouper, any territorial fish that makes a home somewhere, it tends to go fairly well.

"The other good thing about amberjack is they're fun to catch. They like to run. Don't always eat so good, so we usually release them unless the clients are familiar with the taste and want to take some home. Maybe smoke some. Generally we let the clients take a few pictures and throw 'em back. Most of these guys don't care if they go home empty-handed as long as they have pictures to send their friends or post online."

Maya thought about someone poking her, trespassing in her home, her life. I'd fight back, she thought. I'd protect myself and the ones I love.

Summer lumbered across the island chain. The sun's early morning pilot lit the air, baking the sky all day into the red glow of sunset. On an August afternoon, the earth itself was hot to the touch.

Chris came in the back door of his mother's house, walked to the sink, and turned on the faucet with his elbow. He pumped soap into his hands and washed the grime and specs of palm fronds away under the cool water, splashed his face.

"What are you doing in my kitchen? You want to bathe? Go down the hall and take a shower," Elise teased him.

"Mom, please." He took a towel from the drawer. He leaned against the counter and dried his forehead, pushed back his hair.

His mother watched his movements. Sharp, jagged. So much anger lingering just under the skin, she thought. He's still carving everything in his path into tiny pieces. I ache for him. For both of them.

She chewed her lip. "You have clothes in the truck?"

He wrinkled his brow. "Yeah, why?"

"Go shower, change. I made chicken cutlets. You'll stay and eat."

"Thanks, but I need to get back."

"You don't have anywhere you have to be. You need to sit with your mother and eat a good meal. Go."

He opened his mouth to argue but caught her eye. She held his gaze. He wouldn't win this fight. He nodded, threw the towel over his shoulder, and left to get his bag.

"Smells good," he said when he entered the kitchen, clean from his shower.

"Good. You smell much better, too." She kissed his cheek and handed him the silverware to set the table. She noticed the wrinkles around his eyes as he turned away. This talk will not be easy, she thought. Please, God, help me find the words.

As she placed bowls of yellow rice and steamed asparagus on the table, she remembered the time she'd spanked him. He was four and had run into the road to chase a squirrel. In seconds she'd crossed the yard, grabbed his hand, lost in the madness of worry, of how to respond. How to imbue a respect for danger without a fear of the world. She'd led him inside, spread him across her lap on a kitchen chair. Swatted him three times.

She recalled how he'd wailed. Not from the pain, but from the betrayal. How she'd held him afterward, whispered tenderness and regret in his ear until the agony had subsided. Until the sadness had drained from mother and child.

This conversation will feel like that, she thought as she pulled in her chair. We close the wound with a bandage of love. But the salve we apply underneath is another layer of pain.

They ate quietly, talked of the weather. After they finished, when each fork and knife laid in repose across their plates, Elise pushed back her chair, folded her hands in her lap, and lowered her head for a moment of prayer. Then she told her son what he didn't want to hear.

That he was wrong. That if he loved Maya, he needed to let her go and yet keep after her. That the only thing worse than his heart breaking now would be if she broke it later. After a few years of marriage, maybe a couple of kids. When the shoreline of the small island closed in around her. When she felt trapped. Desperate enough to pen a note for the family she would leave behind.

She spoke with warmth and ferocity. She waded slowly into the moat surrounding his broken heart.

"Christopher, I'm going to tell you the truth. Love is not easy. Marriage is even harder. But if you love her, you have to let her do what's right for her. She's still figuring out what she wants out of life. You have to give her time. That doesn't mean you stay away, or you clomp around here like you're trying to kick a hole in my floor. It means you go see her and you apologize."

His eyes opened wide, his cheeks flushed. "Apologize? For what? For wanting to marry her?"

"No. For not understanding she might not be ready to marry you. For demanding she be someone she hasn't yet become. Buying her a ring might make you a husband. It doesn't make you a partner. You want a happy marriage? Learn how to be a good partner. Then you can be a good husband."

Chris listened to his mother. He watched the line of her jaw, heard the pull in her voice. She's never spoken to me like this, he thought. She has this strength, this insight I've never noticed. How have I lived this long and not seen her for who she is? He wondered what else he'd missed about his mother, his sister, Maya. About what it meant to care for the people you loved and allow yourself to be cared for in return. He wasn't good at that. He would learn to be better.

He sighed, leaned forward in his chair, put his head in his hands.

"Okay." He looked up at her, nodded. "Okay."

~

Three days later Maya was putting some lures in a tackle box when she heard footsteps on the dock.

"Hey."

She turned toward the familiar voice, lips parted. "Uh, hi. What are you doing here? Is everything okay? Your mom?"

"Yeah, yeah, everything's fine. I just wanted to talk to you. Is that okay? Can we talk?"

"Sure. Come on board."

They went into the salon and closed the door.

"You want something to drink?"

"No, thanks, I'm fine." He slid into the banquette, leaving room at the end of the seat. She won't sit here yet, he thought. Not that I blame her.

Maya moved toward the table. She wanted to be close to

him, their legs touching, her hand in his. Then she backed away. Maybe he's not ready to be so close to me, she thought. She leaned against the counter, crossed her arms, uncrossed them. They dangled at her sides as her hands clenched and unclenched. "Look, I'm sorry," she began.

"No, let me go first. Please. I'm sorry for the things I said. I shouldn't have come at you like that. You had every right to leave. Doesn't mean you were trying to leave me. Right?"

"No, right, you're right. It doesn't mean that." She paused. "But maybe I was."

The last few weeks flashed through her mind. The long days on the boat, when she'd had time to think about their relationship. Whether she was running from him. Whether Key West was an excuse. Whether Islamorada was just one stop that would allow her to break up with him without guilt. Had they stayed together, he would tire of her, of the distance. He'd give up like Jeremy. She'd be free to go wherever she pleased. Is that what I want? She'd asked herself the question time and again. Chris looked at her like he was reading her mind.

"No, I don't think so. I don't think you know what you want, so the easiest thing to do was leave. That's fine. I get that you needed to go. At least it's not Seaport or San Diego or the South Pacific. We can still see each other, we just have to work harder at it. Like you said." He stood up, stepped toward her, took her hand. "I'm willing to do that. I'm not giving up just because you need a change of scenery. You'll have to fight me off." He kissed the back of her hand and put it up to his cheek.

"Besides, I blame George." He moved next to her, put his arm around her. "He made your life too boring, and now you want to work on a bigger boat. So, I'll chase you up here. Maybe I'll join you someday. We'll see."

Maya laid her head on his shoulder. "Okay. We'll see." She hesitated. "Does your mom hate me?"

"*Ha!* Are you kidding? She's the reason I came to my senses. She reminded me about the women I've dated before. Most of them didn't have any idea what to do with their lives, so even if they weren't sure about marrying me they might have taken the ring if I'd asked. You have hopes and dreams. That's one of the things I love about you. My mother understands that, too. Actually, I think it makes her a little wistful, thinking about what she might have done if she'd had the courage. She thinks you're really brave. I do, too."

Maya turned toward him, placed her head on his chest and wrapped her arms around him. She inhaled the deep scent of his cologne, rubbed the familiar muscles across his back. She closed her eyes. Just breathe, she thought. For now, just breathe.

Twenty-four

2009

One evening the following spring, Bill and Maya were reviewing the schedule for the upcoming week. "We've got some clients in from Anchorage on Wednesday," he said. "Two brothers. Patrick and Garrett. They've fished with me before. They're also spending a couple of days on a backcountry charter. Like to get the whole experience when they come down."

Tall and lean, light-haired and in their thirties, the guys grew up on the water in Palm Beach County and were expert anglers. Job opportunities in technology sales led them to Alaska, but every year or two they came to the Keys to warm up.

On their first day in town, the wind was blowing about fifteen to twenty knots. The waves outside the marina wore white caps. Still, the brothers wanted to see if the fish were biting, so Bill fired up the boat and idled out of the slip. He stayed within a few miles of shore, figuring if the guys had a change of heart he could circle back quickly. They were experienced, but rough seas could turn the stomach of the best angler. Before long, Patrick and Garrett each had two photos to send home. As Patrick leaned over the side of the boat to release his second catch, his partially digested granola bar followed.

"I told you not to eat this morning, man," Garrett laughed. "Wind's always a problem for you." He slapped his brother on the back. "Amateur."

"I think it's as much about the rum runners last night as the wind," Patrick said, rinsing his mouth with salt water and wiping it with the back of his arm. "But it's worth it." He smiled at Maya. "You seem to be doing okay."

"I've had my share of rough days, and that's without rum runners. I'm good today."

They motored around the rest of the morning without another bite. Given the uncertainties of the weather this time of year, they'd gambled on two half days with Bill rather than a full. He drove them back to shore and told them he'd see them tomorrow.

"Thanks for the business, guys. It's been a little slow lately. You know, with the economy. Appreciate you coming back."

"We appreciate you putting us on fish every time we come down," Garrett said. "Why don't you guys join us for dinner tonight? Our treat."

"Thanks, I've got a family thing. But take Maya. She could use a decent meal."

"What do you say? We don't bite," Patrick said. "We'll pick you up at seven and get you back early. And we'll put you on a five rum runner limit so you don't look like me today."

She laughed. "I'm up for dinner, but I probably won't limit out on the rum runners."

Garrett and Patrick spent the evening entertaining Maya with tales from the Alaskan backcountry. Float plane landings on remote rivers and lakes. Hikes in Denali National Park in search of grizzlies and black bears, moose and wolves.

"There's a beauty in Alaska you don't find in South Florida, or in many other places in the Lower 48," Garrett said. "You can drive for hundreds of miles, and all you see is unspoiled land. You should get up there one day. No one goes to Alaska without it changing their life. We're tiny, which occurs to you once in a while when you live here. Maybe when you're offshore or looking up at the stars at night. But in Alaska, it's in your face every day."

"Enough preaching to the young lady," Patrick said. "Geez, man, how many beers have you had?"

"This is not alcohol talking." Garrett lifted his bottle and saluted his brother before taking a sip. "This is the gospel that is Alaska. Anyway, who are you kidding? You feel the same way."

"I do, but I save it for family. People who already know I'm a freak and won't slowly back away when I get on my soapbox and lecture them on the wonder of open space."

Maya watched the two go back and forth, each volleying with either a virtue of teaching the uneducated about Alaska or a reason to keep the revelation to themselves. We don't want to overrun the place with developers looking to pave it over, one said. But we do need the tourism, the other offered. Beats more drilling.

Maya's mind drifted as they continued their match. She loved watching siblings spar. Paul and Manny, George's twin boys, had a playfulness that could lead to an alpha battle. But they always hugged it out in the end. She imagined Patrick and Garrett, just a couple of years apart, grew up the same way. She wondered what it would have been like to have a brother or sister to argue with, scheme with. She couldn't imagine sharing her dad with anyone else. But maybe with another heart in the household there would have been more love to go around.

"You still with us?" Garrett asked, waving his hand in front of her face.

"Oh, yeah, sorry." She smiled, blushed. "I'm sorry, what did you ask me?"

"If we've convinced you to visit the Great Land. Not any time soon, but someday. What do you think? Are we an effective marketing team? Should we hit up the tourist board for a grant?" He smiled. "You know I'm just kidding, right? We love the place, so we brag about it. No pressure."

"Actually, you've given me something to think about. I don't have a plan for what's next. My dad used to take me hiking in New Hampshire and Maine when I was a kid. And I loved it. There's something about the mountains, the burn you feel when you grind up a trail. And then you get to the peak and see valleys and lakes and small towns for miles. The wind is blowing, the air is cold. The whole world is out there right in front of you. And it's all yours." Maya looked at the brothers and down at her plate. "Wow. I don't know where that came from. I must sound like a weirdo."

"You sound like us. Like the little sister we never had," Patrick said. "Which doesn't preclude you from being a weirdo. Just ask our family. They think we're nuts living up in the cold. Doesn't mean there's anything wrong with you. Just means you're different from other folks. Have to figure out where you belong."

"I keep hearing that. And that I have plenty of time to figure it out. I wish I knew if the second part was true."

The next day, after their last trip on the *Wake Up*, Patrick and Garrett said their goodbyes. Garrett handed Maya a slip of paper. "Here's our information. If you ever want to check out Alaska, you let us know and we'll show you why we love it. You may leave the Lower 48 forever." He winked at her, and they left the boat.

Maya stashed the paper in a drawer in her cabin and tackled her chores. She thought about the mountains as she scrubbed the deck of the boat. How she felt an inner peace at elevation she wasn't sure she'd found at sea level. She didn't know if it was the thinner air or the views or the accomplishment of the climb. Or if she might be a mountain girl at heart.

She looked out at the water. The same view that had drawn her gaze in Seaport, when she first felt the urge to wander. She wondered if it was the unknown lurking past the edge of the horizon that drew her, rather than the fact that the horizon separated sea from sky. Maybe it wasn't about water or warm weather. Maybe the view from a mountaintop would be enough, wouldn't leave her yearning. She hosed off the boat and went inside to shower.

Twenty-five

2010

THE *WAKE UP* CONSUMED MOST of Maya's days, but occasionally a clean boat and empty calendar left Bill and Maya some free time. On those days, Bill had Maya meet him at his house where he kept a small flats boat, the *Flat and Happy*. Bill preferred flats fishing to the open water, found it more peaceful to float atop the shallow waters close to shore. He enjoyed pulling the boat up behind a small island, dropping a pole in the sand, seeing what hungry fish would come out to bite. With the economy still in shambles, he wasn't ready to operate a second boat. But he wanted to prepare Maya for when tourism picked up and he could run both an offshore business on the *Wake Up* and a backcountry business on the *Flat and Happy*. He planned to train her to run the small boat on her own. He trusted her, and the smaller boat was a good fit for her size and skill set. He'd find a new mate to accompany him offshore.

Maya took to flats fishing as easily as open water work. She maneuvered around the little boat with ease, climbing the platform to pole through short water. Bill taught her where to look for tarpon and when to anchor under the bridges to catch them. She learned new tricks, like bonefish will bite some days on live shrimp, other days on rubbery, artificial shrimp scented to mimic live bait. And that ladyfish, skinny, long and silvery, were okay to catch but not worth keeping. Flats fishing was a smaller universe to Maya. She appreciated the clear, green bay water and sandy bottom that greeted her each morning. Like Bill, she longed for the quiet moments on the *Flat and Happy*.

She'd been in Islamorada more than two years now. People here knew her, and on some days she felt settled. The flutter of the breeze didn't always nudge her to leave like it had in Key West. If she decided to stay, learning the backcountry would allow her to run her own boat one day. Not quite a plan, she thought, but an idea.

Chris shared her temporary contentment, or at least offered the impression. He and Maya managed to see each other almost weekly, and he'd long since recovered from her rejection of his proposal. They were together. For now, it was enough.

~

One evening after a full day on the *Wake Up*, Bill came out of the cabin as Maya was finishing the last of the cleaning. He held his laptop in one hand and two beers in another.

"Come sit." He handed her a beer, sat down in the fighting chair, and flipped open the laptop. She pulled a folding chair out of the cabin and sat beside him.

"What's up?"

"Have you noticed we haven't been out on the *Flat and Happy* much lately?"

"Yeah, but I'm not complaining. Business has been picking up."

"Right. And look at this." He handed her the laptop open to the calendar for the next six months. "We're up thirty percent in comparison to this time last year. I've been talking to some of the flats fishing guides and their business is up, too. I'm thinking it might be time to find your replacement. Get you started on your own. You ready?"

Maya's mind raced. "Am I ready? Hell yeah!" She paused. "But do you trust me? That's the bigger question."

He took the laptop from her, closed it, and set it behind him. He picked up his beer, nodded. "I do. I wasn't sure when we started this arrangement whether I'd ever be able to say that, but I trust you'll take good care of my boat and my clients. Of course you'll have to find a place to live. Have you thought about that?"

"I've asked around. I know people looking for roommates. A couple of places. I can find something."

"Okay. I'll start looking for your replacement." He lifted his beer and they clinked bottles. "To new horizons."

"To new horizons." She slowly raised the bottle to her lips as she looked at the sky darkening over the ocean. Same horizon, she thought. Her skin tingled. The hair on the back of her neck stirred. What was that? Not excitement, she thought, not like when she left Seaport. Not exactly fear, though something akin. She shuddered.

Bill finished his beer and headed home. Maya leaned back in her chair, watched stars begin to peek out of the sky. When the breeze picked up she went inside and threw a frozen dinner in the microwave. She sat in the salon, stared at her food, nudged curls of pasta around the black plastic dish.

What was she afraid of? Change? That like those before, the next chapter wouldn't be the answer? Wouldn't be the paradise waiting at the edge of the dream, the bed warm and soft, until the alarm clock shrilled and the cold morning intruded?

Or did she fear the opposite? That this new adventure would finally answer whatever question blew in with the afternoon breeze. The wind rustling her hair, whispering to stay, settle, unpack whatever bags she still carried. Maybe her hair stood on end not from fear she'd want to leave. But that she'd want to remain. Running was her craft, her gift, her departure the graceful stride of a gazelle on an African plain. Staying was achy, gangly. The unraveling of limbs fallen asleep, tucked under, pins and needles. The forgetting of how to move, how to be. To stay meant she had to rise, regain her footing, feel the blood flow back to the ends. It meant she was part of something. That something was part of her.

She shook her head, stabbed a noodle, ate. This is a good change, she told herself. You'll see. She wriggled a piece of whole wheat bread out of its plastic bag and sopped up the last few drops of marinara.

~

Within weeks Bill found a new mate, and Maya found a new home. She moved into a three-bedroom house shared by two other fishing guides. Andy was a third generation fisherman. He'd grown up in Marathon and learned the trade from his father and grandfather. He'd come to Islamorada because he preferred the backcountry here and some distance from family.

Mark was from Miami and grew up fishing on his father's

boat. He'd tried college, but he'd spent more time staring out the library window than studying. After two interminable semesters, Mark pitched the idea of a guide business to his father. When the tuition bill for fall semester arrived, patriarchal wisdom led to one conclusion: the better return on investment was floating on the water. Prescience. Mark paid him back within five years. The house was his second investment. He rented it to Mark, and Mark sublet rooms to people he trusted. The arrangement held the son responsible to his landlord. And there was just enough tension in that line to keep the roommates in check and his father in Miami.

Mark and Andy weren't in the habit of cooking, but the night Maya moved in they grilled steaks for their new roommate. They assured her this was a special occasion, and that if not for the threat of random visits by Mark's father, the place might be littered with pizza boxes. Andy confirmed Mark ran a tight ship. He acknowledged as well that it was good training for his future. Someday, he told her, he'd want to share space with someone other than a roommate.

The three sat together on the patio.

"Ready to fly solo?" Mark asked.

"I think so. I mean, I'm sure I can run the boat. I know where to take clients. How to find fish. I'm a little concerned about the other guides. There aren't many women on the water. You think the guys will have a problem with me? I heard things from time to time as a mate, but I think since I wasn't the captain I wasn't a threat. Bill hasn't said anything, but I worry."

"I wouldn't," Andy said. "There are some women out there already. Maybe talk to them. I know some guys bitch about women captains, but not many. I don't think they'll mess with you. They may be pissed because they think you'll take business away, but they'd be pissed at a new guy coming to town, too. Besides, you're working for Bill. If it wasn't you, he'd hire someone else. You have a license. You deserve to run your own boat."

Bill gave Maya a day to settle in before springing the first clients on her. She spent the time visiting some of the spots they'd fished together as well as others he'd plotted for her on the GPS. She looked at the weather report for the next day and collected pinfish for bait from the trap he set in the bay.

At the end of the day, she realized she needed more baitfish. She returned to the marina, grabbed some chum and her cast net, and headed out into Florida Bay as the sun started to set. After finding a spot and dropping the chum in the water, she pitched the pile of mesh into the grassy flats. Gathering the net. Setting her feet. Tossing the nylon mass into the shallow water. Hauling it into the boat. Picking out the fish. Again and again. The repetition cleared her mind. Her breathing slowed. She stopped when her arms tired and the sun receded.

She arrived at the marina the next morning an hour before her clients. The previous night she'd deposited her pinfish catch into a holding pen tied to the dock. In the morning she transferred some of the pinfish into her live well. She filled the gas tank and loaded the boat with rods, lures, coolers, and life preservers. She loved that on the boat everything had a spot. A place where it belonged.

Her clients were a couple of retirees from northern Wisconsin. They'd traveled to Florida by RV and were stopping in locales around the state to fish. They'd spent a couple of days in Boca Grande on the west coast fishing offshore for big game. In Islamorada they wanted to slow the pace.

Maya started the engine and launched the boat away from the dock. When she reached the edge of the marina, she turned north and followed the channel markers across the green glass of early morning. No wind, she thought. Should be a good day.

She pushed up on the throttle and pointed the boat toward the wheel ditch, a narrow passage amidst the mangroves that flats boats, wave runners, and a few larger boats darted through to save time. To her it was like a tunnel closed to the behemoths of the ocean. She cherished the short excursion, the closeness of the trees. The nod to the fish and birds living in this little neighborhood she commuted through.

Morning stirred early here. As the dark seawater paled with the first rays of sunrise, schools of glass minnows weaved among the mangrove roots, slipping past snapper and down to the sandy floor through flowing blades of seagrass. Soon the clear water would turn cloudy with upturned mud, the surface white with the intrusion of propellers and hulls. But for the moment, before Maya and others entered the sanctuary, silence. Dapples of light. Bright with hope.

On the west side of the wheel ditch, Maya headed out into Florida Bay. She watched for depth changes on her Garmin, though this boat could run almost anywhere. She maneuvered around some small islands and found a hidden spot. Since her clients had been fishing longer than she'd been alive, once she baited their hooks she turned them loose to cast on their own. In the quiet sanctuary of the mangroves, they reeled in sea trout and redfish. The buzzing of their lines was the only noise of the day, other than an occasional "Got one!" shouted over a rocking shoulder. Once an angler reeled in a catch, Maya netted the fish, dropped it in the cooler, and baited another hook, all with a smile and a few words of congratulations. Otherwise, the day passed in relative silence.

Back at the marina, she filleted the fish, accepted her clients' gratitude in praise and cash, and wished them a good trip. She cleaned the boat, went home to shower. As evening settled along the treetops, she collapsed on the couch, remote and cell lined up beside her. She and Gladys still watched *Jeopardy* together at least once a week.

Her first day churned into days, weeks, months. The work became routine as with her previous stops, and the routine provided comfort for periods of time. At other moments she paused, wondered, questioned. But she pushed thoughts of flight away. She was building her reputation. The other guides were learning she was capable. For the most part, she felt she belonged.

Twenty-six

FROM TIME TO TIME, MAYA FELT the maleness of her peers. Wade, a guide about her age, was a local who believed outsiders should go back to their own waters to fish for a living. He didn't say much to the men who came to town. But a female interloper was an easy target.

Guides often asked each other over the radio where the fish were biting on a particular day. Most were willing to share at least some information, believing they were compatriots as much as competitors. After all, a good day today could precede a bad outing tomorrow. One online review could kill business.

The first few times Maya checked in on the radio, guys were helpful. One morning Wade responded. He sent her to a bridge where no fish were biting, having just abandoned the area to try somewhere else. She saw him back at the dock later that day.

"Catch anything, sweetheart?" Wade asked, laughing.

"You did that on purpose?"

"Aw, don't sweat it. You're new. You'll learn."

She shook her head as she walked away. She asked Andy and Mark about Wade that night.

"That guy? He's a complete dick," Andy said. "Ignore him. He's probably just messing with you since you just started on your own. And if anyone else heard him and didn't say anything, don't worry. They'll give him one jab at you. After that, they'll sort him out."

"You don't think the 'sweetheart' thing is any indication?"

"Nah," said Mark. "He's just pushing your buttons."

Andy was right about the other guides. The next time Wade tried to send Maya off on a chase for wild geese rather than fish, two other guides set him straight. But he didn't let up.

One afternoon Maya was packing up to leave the Channel 5 bridge. Another guide asked over the radio whether anyone had seen any bonefish, and Maya said they'd had some luck earlier in the nearby flats. Wade spoke next.

"Why don't you take your little boat back home and make dinner for Chris, okay little girl?" Maya's face reddened as Wade's voice filled her boat. Not because the jab was any worse than any of the other ribbing he'd given her, but because her clients had heard. Two guys from Fort Lauderdale were aboard. They froze as they waited to see how she would respond.

"Sorry, buddy, I'm too busy catching all your fish," she replied as the air left her lungs. Her clients laughed and turned back to their rods. She winked at them and regained her breath.

She returned to the marina and finished up with her clients. When they left, she unloaded her gear and cleaned the boat. As she took her first load of equipment to the truck, she saw a few of the other guides chatting at the end of the dock. Wade stood in the group, eyeing her as she approached.

"Sure you can carry all that? I can get one of the boys to help if it's too much for you."

A few guys chuckled as Maya started to move past the group. She stopped, put her gear down, and turned to face the cause of her rising anger. He was several inches taller and fifty pounds heavier, but she stood toe to toe and looked him in the eye.

"Listen, asshole, I've been putting up with your shit since I started running this boat. I'm done." Maya poked his chest with her index finger. "If you ever embarrass me in front of a client again, or if I ever find out you've been talking shit about me, I will find you and gut you like a fish, motherfucker. You think you're funny making jokes about women? We'll see how funny you are with a gaff stuck through your mouth and coming out your dick hole. Are we clear?"

Wade, jaw hanging, threw his hands up in the air and stepped back. "Yeah, yeah, we're good. Geez, I mean, I was just kidding. You guys knew I was just messing with her 'cause she's new, right? Not 'cause she's a chick or nothing." He looked at the other guides standing around him. They shook their heads and laughed.

"You're such a douche, Wade," one of them said. "Leave her alone. Besides, she may save your sorry ass one of these days. We've all had a turn bailing you out of some mess."

Maya picked up her gear and headed toward the truck, shaking but happy. Sorry, Mom, she thought. She stopped. Sorry, Mom? Where the hell did that come from? She started slowly for the parking lot. She drove home, showered, and ate dinner, but she couldn't shake an odd feeling. She'd never talked to her mother that way before.

As she lay awake that night, Maya tried to picture her

mother's face. She turned on the light, threw the covers off, and went to her closet. She reached for a box of mementos from childhood perched on the top shelf, extracted an old photo of her with her parents. She'd forgotten she had it. She backed up and sat down on the bed, traced the lines of their faces. Sorry, Mom, she thought. I won't forget again.

After that night, she moved through the world a little differently. She'd turn and see a quick flash out of the corner of her eye, and she'd wonder if she'd missed something. If someone was there. She found comfort in believing her mother was close by. The feeling arose on the boat, too. On a calm day, out of nowhere a light wind would brush her cheek. In those moments she felt her mother's presence. Her clients fished. She smiled into the wind. Her body warmed.

She mentioned these experiences to her father one Saturday night. "Does that happen to you? Do you see or sense something and think she's there with you?"

Charlie leaned back against the couch, put his bare feet on the coffee table, and smiled into the phone. "Only all the time. I've tricked myself into thinking all sorts of things are her. If I'm outside and a leaf falls, it's her telling me to be careful, look out for things falling on my head. Or look where I'm walking on a jobsite because I might trip over a tool. If I'm driving and the sun is in my eyes and I don't bother to look for my sunglasses, and then a cloud passes over for a second, I think it's her telling me to pull over and dig them out. Don't be an idiot." He laughed, put his free arm behind his head. "I guess all of it is her telling me not to be an idiot." He shook his head and sighed. "I miss her like she just left. Like she went out for milk."

Maya waited until the last fragments of his sigh passed through the phone. After all these years, he still had these fleeting moments of honesty with her. When the pain grew from a faint echo to the wail escaping a fresh wound, a new sear on the delicate skin. In these moments, she gathered herself, found the courage to speak, to push.

"Dad, you have to do something. Talk to someone. Anyone."

He thought about the dream he'd had the night before. In the dream he was on the couch watching TV. Maya was around somewhere. Maybe in her room studying. He wasn't sure. She was still in high school, that was clear. Sierra had gone to the grocery store. Everything in their life was normal, like she'd always been around, never been sick. The doorbell rang. Nicky Malone from the police department stood on the front step. He looked at Charlie, and before he could say a word Charlie screamed. He saw the accident. The crash, the broken glass. Suddenly he was at the scene, picking apart the car, yelling for her. Where was she? Why couldn't he find her? He saw her jacket in the back seat and grabbed it. The cloth was warm with blood. One long hair rested on the collar. He took the hair and let the jacket fall to the ground. It disappeared in the grass. He stared at the lock. It was all he had left of her.

"I will, honey, don't worry. I've been thinking lately about maybe speaking to someone. I talked to a guy right after your mom died. He was good, and he probably still practices. I'll give him a call."

He remembered his sessions with Keith. He'd left things unsaid. Time had closed the wound but hadn't healed what lay under the scab.

"So you'll go see this guy? Or if he's not around, someone else?"

Charlie agreed and launched into a story about the three Raymonds. They were camping in New Hampshire.

"Haven't we done that one?" She'd heard the story and couldn't remember him repeating one since she was young, when she would forget her mother's face. In those days she often asked her dad to retell a story and show her pictures of Sierra to jog her memory.

"Yes, you've heard this one. But it's real. We haven't done a real one in a while, and this is a good one. Okay?" He was happy to be moving the subject away from therapy.

"Sure. I'd love to hear it again." She settled into bed and pulled up the covers.

It was the summer before Maya turned two. Charlie borrowed his mom's minivan for the weekend and some camping gear from a buddy, and they headed up to Franconia Notch in New Hampshire. They found a campground and began to set up a tent, poles flailing, and he and Sierra laughing while trying to keep Maya from busting out of her stroller.

"You didn't like that your parents were having a blast building this green, nylon play cave while you were strapped into peanut gallery prison." Charlie laughed and mimicked his young daughter. "All we kept hearing was 'Maya out! Maya out!' It was freaking hilarious!"

"Very funny, Dad. I get the point." She smiled as she pictured her young, stubborn self trying to escape stroller jail. I was probably a little pain in the ass, she thought.

Maya's exclamations only made Charlie and Sierra laugh even harder. "We'll get you in a second, honey," Sierra said. "Just sit tight."

"No, out!"

Finally Charlie put his pole down. "You keep at it. Let me get her. She can help me on my end."

Once liberated, the little girl was happy to participate.

"Maya help," she said, smiling at her dad.

He picked up the pole again and fed the first segment through the nylon sleeve. "Here, give me your hand." He put her hand on the fabric and pushed the cloth over the pole. When they hit a seam between two connecting parts of the pole, he slid the nylon back, showed her how to wiggle the fabric over the bump until the pole came out the end. "There we go, it's out!" He looked down at his daughter, clapping with pride. "We did it!"

Sierra watched as her husband high-fived their little girl. He's good at this, she thought. He'd struggled at first with diapers and holding an infant, but once Maya learned his voice and he saw her recognition when he entered a room, he was hooked. When she showed interest in toys, he grabbed them and dropped to the floor to play. When she took her first step, he held her hands and led her across the room. He would do anything to show her the world.

That night they made a fire and cooked hot dogs and beans. Sierra unpacked graham crackers, marshmallows, and Hershey bars.

"Okay, honey, time to learn about s'mores," Charlie told his daughter. He stuck marshmallows on a stick, crouched next to his little girl, and held the stick over the fire. "Hold my arm. You can help toast the marshmallows."

Maya stayed close to her father, away from the fire, a little afraid of the heat and flames. She took his arm and moved a step closer.

"That's close enough," he said.

Her wide eyes darted between the fire and the marshmallows as they browned. One caught fire. "Daddy, look!"

Charlie pulled the stick backward and blew out the flame.

"It's done! Now the fun part." He took the marshmallows to the picnic table, where Sierra sat with a plate of graham crackers and squares of chocolate. He took a cracker, placed three squares of chocolate on it, and smeared the marshmallows over the top, covering the sticky mess with another cracker. He took a bite. "Oh, man," he said, throwing his head back. "That is good stuff!" He bent over to Maya and put the sandwich in front of her face. She bit, chewed, and swallowed, her chin washed in gooey marshmallow and melted chocolate.

She squealed with glee. "Daddy, more!"

Sierra laughed. "Don't worry, Daddy will make more. That's why they call them s'mores. And your daddy is addicted to them."

Maya smiled through the bits of graham cracker dotting her lip as she chewed on her second bite.

Like father like daughter, Sierra thought.

"Dad," Maya said into the phone, "did you ever notice in a lot of the stories, the real ones, Mom is just watching you and me? Like the best part for her was seeing us have fun?"

"Yeah. Your mother was never happier than when you and I were laughing. I would come in the door at night and give her a kiss and ask her about her day. Then I would scoop you up and raspberry your belly until your giggles filled the apartment. As much as your mother loved me and the attention I gave her, nothing gave her more pleasure than watching you and me together, engulfed in joy. She told me that once. That was the pinnacle for her.

"She was a giver, your mother. I think that's why I feel like she's still with me. She was always such a great observer of what we were doing, how we were doing. I feel like she's still around, soaking it all in." He paused. Maya heard a sniffle. "Anyway, it makes me feel better. Whether it's crazy or not, it makes me happy. Brings me peace."

"Me too."

Twenty-seven

2012

MAYA SETTLED INTO THE QUIET WATERS of Islamorada. Her troubles with Wade long past, she developed a reputation as a reliable guide with a good work ethic. The old feelings that nagged at her to move on didn't surface as often. When they didn't, she wondered why. Was she happy here? Was this where she was supposed to be?

She saw Chris almost every week, but the distance was starting to weigh. One afternoon he drove up for an overnight, each off work the next day. She'd planned a simple dinner and early night. After he finished the dishes, he dried his hands and turned to her. "Go for a walk?"

"Now? Aren't you tired?"

"Not really. Come on. It's a nice night."

She looked in the family room and saw her roommates draped over the couch and recliner. She sensed Chris wanted some time to themselves. She grabbed her keys, and they left the house. They walked to the end of the block and turned onto the next road. Chris slowed their pace, looked up at the sky.

"Lots of stars tonight." He reached for her hand. "So, how are you?"

She looked at him in surprise. "Okay." She paused. "How are you?"

"I'm good, I'm good. It just seems like we haven't talked in a while. Not like 'How's your day, dear?' but more like, 'What are we doing?' You know?"

She felt a breeze on the back of her neck. Maybe Mom's listening, she thought.

"Yeah. I know." She hesitated. "I'm good, to answer your question. I'm happy with the way things are, the way things have been going." She dreaded the next question. "Are you?"

"Sort of. I love you, you know that. And I'm happy your work is going well. Bill seems to be taking good care of you. I just was wondering if you'd be willing to come back to Key West one of these days. Maybe get your own boat and work down there?"

They meandered through the neighborhood. Lights were on in most of the kitchens, family rooms. TVs flashed the day's news. Baseball scores. Car crashes. Approaching storms.

She considered her reply. "I don't think I'm ready. I know the waters here now. I'm building a reputation as a good guide. People have accepted me." She thought for a moment. "Would you be willing to move?"

He sighed. "You know I can't do that. My family needs me." He stopped, turned toward her. "I just, I don't know where we're going. I'm not trying to pressure you, but I want to move forward. Get married. Have kids. And I don't feel like you want to do that. Or maybe you do, but not with me and you're afraid to tell me. Or maybe you don't know what you want."

She took his hands in hers, chose her words. "I know I love you, but I don't know what I want. And I don't know when I will."

"Okay. At least I know nothing's changed for you."

"Has it for you?"

"To be honest, a little bit. If I knew there was an end date, when you would take the ring and we could get married, I would wait as long as you needed for that day to come. But the unknown." He paused, shook his head. "I just don't know how long I can wait for an answer. I don't want to keep putting off the next stage of my life." He put his arm around her, pulled her close. "I'm not mad. Just frustrated."

"I get it."

They stood for a moment under a streetlight. He pulled away, looked in her eyes. "I think I will always love you, Maya Raymond. But I think I need to figure out if that's enough."

She wiped away a tear. "Are we ... is this ... over?"

He looked at the ground and up at the sky. He shook his head. "No. I don't know. I was hoping this conversation would go differently." He smiled, sadly. "When it comes to you, I'm both hopeful and hopeless." He wiped his cheek and put his arm around her again. They walked back to the house. He went inside and picked up his bag while she stood in the yard, looked at the stars. A mariner searching for guidance.

He came back outside and kissed her cheek. "I think I should go. A drive might do me good. Are you okay?"

"Yeah," she lied. "But why don't you stay? We can talk more tomorrow."

"I don't think there's much to talk about. Until one of us changes how we feel, we're both going to want different things."

"Will you call me when you get home?"

"Of course." He kissed her again, leaving his breath on her lips. "I love you."

"I love you, too."

After his truck pulled away, she went inside and sat on the arm of the couch.

"Where's Chris?" Andy asked, moving his feet so she could sit down.

She slid onto the cushion. "He left. We're ... not on the same page. He wants me to move back to Key West so we can get married. I'm happy here."

"What about the getting married part?" Mark asked. He muted the TV, turned to her. "You up for that?"

"I don't think I'm there yet. I love him, but I feel like I've got other things to sort out."

"I've seen this movie," Mark said. "It ends with someone getting hurt." He turned the volume up and looked back at the TV. "Take care of yourself, kiddo."

~

Life, briny and sweet, bathed Maya as the days passed. Small, lean, muscular, arms and legs brushed by the sun, skin near her eyes beginning to pleat. The old Red Sox cap, turned backwards as she hauled in a baitfish net, the navy blue fading to white around the red stitching. The freckled nose and cheeks, blond ponytail, pursed lips, faced east each morning, west each afternoon. Imagining places the sun traveled when it left her behind.

Solace drifted in with the morning tide. She focused on her clients, the weather. She and Chris talked, but they decided not to see each other for a while. She thought if she missed him, her choice might become clear. Instead, she fell deeper into the space of life without him. She missed him. But not enough.

One afternoon a couple from Nebraska joined her on the boat. Bryce, mid-thirties, tall and broad, a former college football player whose round face and pale arms tinged to peachy apricot under the bright sun. Leigh, petite, his high school sweetheart. Her dark hair pulled back in the same ponytail she'd worn when she cheered at his games on fall Friday nights.

Maya watched them move around the boat. Bryce helped Leigh with her casting. Leigh rubbed extra sunscreen on his nose. He brushed her cheek, she touched his arm. Maya thought of Chris. She reached for her tackle box but couldn't remember what she was looking for.

In the afternoon, after they'd caught some yellowtail and lost a few lures, they asked Maya to take them on a short boat ride before their time expired.

"Only if you don't mind," Bryce said. "We don't get much of a chance back home."

"Of course," Maya said. She was happy to ride them around the mangrove islands, put a little wake behind them. The afternoon sizzled. Having the wind in her face would feel good.

"Thanks," Leigh said. "This is the first vacation we've taken since the recession hit. We lost our house and had to move in with my parents for a while. Now that we're back on our own, we thought we'd splurge and come down here for a little break. It's nice to be on the water."

Maya thought about what her father had said a few years before. That people needed this time away from their lives. That the salt water healed.

"I'm really sorry to hear that," she said, looking from one to the other. She'd remained insulated from the housing crash, having lived on Bill's boat while the country recovered. She moved toward the front of the boat to pull up the anchor.

"Thanks," Bryce said. "We took our lumps like everyone else. We bought when the market was high and, excuse the pun, were soon under water." He laughed, pulled his hat down over his forehead. "You think you have it all figured out. You go to college, get a degree, get a good job. Get married, buy a house. You do everything right. And then before you know it your mortgage rate skyrockets, your company lets you go, and you can't pay your bills." He shook his head. Looked out at the water.

"I remember when we were kids, we used to play this game called monkey in the middle. Two kids throw a ball back and forth, with a third kid trying to catch it. When the kid in the middle catches the ball, the kid who threw it becomes the new monkey in the middle. Do you remember that?"

Maya nodded. She'd played it with the kids on her street.

"That's what this feels like. You've got banks offering loans, homebuilders offering dream homes, and companies offering great paying jobs. They're all playing catch. There's supposed to be all this money for everyone, but they're just throwing the ball back and forth to each other. We're just trying to catch a happy life, somewhere in the middle of it all. So one throws it to the other, and we chase it over there. Back and forth, but we never quite reach that ball. Turns out we're not the middle class. We're the fools in the middle. The only ones who don't know it's a game. We're just being played."

He looked at Leigh. The bitterness drained from his face as she moved toward him and took his hand.

"It'll be okay," she said. "Things are better now. We've got our bills under control. We have a nice place to live. Eventually, we'll buy again, have kids. Just like we planned, but a little later." She reached up and hugged her husband.

Maya started the engine. The couple sat down behind her. She drove the boat around a few small islands, then headed under the Channel 2 bridge and turned toward Alligator Light.

"Hang on," she told them. She guided the boat through the channel and out into open water, dodging lobster buoys as she sped up. In a few minutes they could see the lighthouse in the distance. She slowed the boat in the gentle waves when they drew near the towering structure.

"I love this place," she said. She turned off the engine and let the boat drift away from the lighthouse with the current. "I have a photo of it on my wall. There's something about the white tower with the powder blue sky behind it meeting the pale green water below. It seems so peaceful. Then I come out here and look at it up close."

Her gaze rose with the height of the lighthouse as a small swell rocked the skiff. She squinted up at the old steel, the painted skin withering from decades of the sun's stare and the salt's hunger. The gales of storms. Some named, others long forgotten. She shielded her eyes with her hand and marveled at the size.

"For some reason, being near this old relic calms me down," she said. "I don't know what it is about lighthouses, why people love them. Maybe we have it ingrained in us that they'll keep us safe. The old beacon in the night. An archetype. Like we've all been lost at sea and we're looking for a safe place to land."

Water lapped the sides of the boat. She surveyed the horizon and turned to the couple.

"I don't think we're monkeys," she said. "I think someone took the bulb out of the lighthouse and didn't tell us. So we crashed into the rocks. We weren't played. We gave the keys to the lighthouse to the wrong keeper. Trusted the wrong person to keep us safe. That doesn't make us fools. It makes us hopeful.

"I wouldn't trade that for every house in Islamorada."

She started the engine and drove them back to the marina. Pulled the boat into the slip and helped the couple unload their gear. She grabbed the fish out of the cooler and carried it to the fish-cleaning station. When she finished, she bagged the fillets and put them on ice.

"You have a few meals here, so you might want to pick up a Styrofoam cooler. I wouldn't save it much longer than a couple of days though."

"Thanks, Maya," Bryce said. He handed her a generous tip. "Thanks for everything." He put his hand on her shoulder, turned, and walked away. Leigh gave Maya a long hug and whispered a thank you. She turned and followed her husband down the dock.

~

That night, Maya was reading in her room when Mark knocked on her open door.

"Got a minute?"

"Sure." She put her book down. "What's up?"

"My dad has a buddy who bought a flats boat, fully outfitted, nice set up. The guy lost his job and wants to sell the boat. My dad knows the market still isn't quite back yet, and he'd like to help the guy out by having him avoid a broker fee, so he thought he'd see if you want to buy it. The guy will give you a great deal because he needs the cash, and my dad will loan you the money. He'll give you a good interest rate, plenty of time to pay it back.

You've been with Bill long enough now I figured you'd at least want to consider it. What do you think? Interested?"

"Yeah, I'm totally interested, but I'm a little scared. I don't know if this is a good idea right now."

"You said the other day you and Bill have been busier than ever. He should be able to find someone to replace you, and business is only going to get better. Maybe it's time to take a chance, get out on your own."

"But why does your dad want to do this for me? He hardly knows me."

"Yeah, but he likes you. And he respects the hell out of you. Ever since I told him the Wade story, he's been your biggest fan. He thinks it's pretty impressive you came down here from Boston on your own and made it. He's a bit of a gambler, and he thinks you're a good investment. Said he'd loan you extra money to get set up with insurance, gear, whatever you need. Like he did with me."

"Let me sleep on it?"

"Sure. No pressure. Just let me know by the end of the week. His buddy wants to make a move soon."

She struggled to find sleep that night. Thoughts darted back and forth, a game of tag among potential worries. What if business slowed again and she couldn't make the loan payments or rent? She had a steady income with Bill's clients. That would disappear. On the other hand, this was a great opportunity. What bank would loan her money to buy a boat after what just happened with the economy? She turned to face the clock. Another hour had passed.

Maya saw Mark the next night. "I'm in. How do we do this?"

"I'll call my dad. The boat's in Key Largo. Andy and I can come check it out with you. We'll grab our buddy who's got the repair shop. He'll look at it for you for cheap."

In a week, Maya was the owner of her own boat. Bill found someone who could take her place temporarily while he found a permanent replacement.

"You've been great," he told her. "I'll owe George forever. If you need anything, you call me. I'm always here for you."

Charlie was thrilled with the news. "I'm so proud of you! But I guess that means no trip home this fall? You'll be too busy?"

"I should probably stay put for a while, save money, focus on the business. Okay?"

"Well, you know I can send you money to come home, but I understand this is an important time for you and you want to concentrate on work. We'll plan a visit this winter."

Chris had a mixed reaction. "I guess this means you're staying in Islamorada." He paused. "Unless you want to start over down here with your own boat?"

"I think I'm staying here. At least for now."

Twenty-eight

MAYA'S FIRST FEW DAYS AS A BOAT OWNER were exhausting. Cleaning and waxing the hull. Securing a slip in a marina and setting up insurance and a web page. Launching her business. Mundane details stole time from the water.

On only her second day at the marina, she had walk-up business. A half-day charter in the afternoon. Two guys eager to fish for permit. As she cleaned the boat that night, she realized she'd made her first dollar on her own. She shut off the hose, the cool water dripped down her arm. Her smile warmed her soul.

She quickly adjusted to her new boat, an eighteen-foot Hewes Redfisher she thought of as Duke. Duke had light yellow sides and a short center console. A padded bench sat behind the console, and the seat back to the bench folded down to add space to the rear deck. A seat in front of the console provided storage underneath, and below the decks in the bow and stern Duke housed compartments for storing dry gear, bait, and catch. An anchor locker filled the center of the bow, and a poling platform stood on the back deck. Maya would climb the platform when she reached the shallows and with a long pole push the boat through inches of water.

Rod holders hugged the sides of the console and platform so the boat appeared to sprout whiskers when she had multiple clients aboard. Along the interior side walls of the boat were bungees for storing more rods. Rods everywhere. An angler's dream.

Duke made the most of his compact space. Maya liked the way the small boat maneuvered both through open water and the backcountry where she did her best work. As petite as she was, she never felt overpowered by the boat or its 130-horsepower engine. She guided Duke, but often she felt like he chose his own route. She enjoyed the hardworking, simple nature of the flats boat. Similar to her two years of fishing on the *Flat and Happy*, but different, too. The fiberglass, the engine, the chrome. All hers. Duke moved through the water with audacity. Her job was to restrain that force, bridle the beast. Make this boat her place.

Duke seemed an appropriate name, but she kept it to herself. She hadn't chosen a name for the side of the boat. She wasn't sure if she would.

Duke had room for four, though Maya had learned over the years that she preferred a smaller group. Her best days were fishing with one client, two at most. Duke seemed to like the less-is-more approach as well. He handled better with Maya at the wheel and one or two passengers on board. Add a third and Maya's stress level rose with the hull lifting off the surface of the bay. True or not, she believed too many anglers could spoil an otherwise promising day.

She risked proving her theory shortly after acquiring the boat. In hopes of scoring a big chunk of her first loan payment in a single day, she took on three guys from New Jersey.

They boarded the boat at eight in the morning with all the proper gear. Maya started from the dock at idle speed, leaving the marina slowly until they passed the no-wake zone. As she approached open water and throttled up the engine, Duke stuck his nose in the air. She worked the trim tab controls until the boat leveled off, but Duke challenged her as she pushed him toward his normal thirty-knot running speed.

Maya moved one of the guys to the front of the boat, legs stretched across the deck, and the rebalancing settled the bronco back to the surface. Evidently having only two men within striking distance of his owner made him feel better, she thought. She drove the boat through the channel without further incident.

She found a spot among a small group of mangrove islands. In shallow water, rather than drop an anchor and disturb the fish, Maya used a motorized pole attached to the back of the boat. The motor dropped the pole into the water without kicking up sand or making noise, both likely to scare fish away in search of quieter waters. She pressed the button, watched the pole descend, and settled the boat behind a small key.

Once her clients were casting, she again questioned her decision to max out capacity on her small boat. The three anglers threw their lines over different sides of the boat, but the current often gathered all three men in the same area. When a fish hit one line, the other two scrambled to move their lines out of the way. The morning was a little more chaotic than she anticipated, and she chastised herself as she stood on the platform, scanning the flats. With two anglers, she thought, the clients would be peacefully catching more fish.

She worried for nothing. The guys were college friends reliving fraternity-brother memories over a long weekend. Each left her boat with permit and snapper. They would enjoy their dinner at a local restaurant, where the chef would prepare the fish they caught and serve it with mashed potatoes dripping in butter and green beans sautéed with garlic and lemon. She pictured them sitting around the table, clinking pints of craft beer, devouring the fresh catch. She provided exactly the experience they sought. But she knew she could do better.

So in spite of her reluctance to turn away business, she promised herself she'd try to limit her trips to no more than two clients. If a group of three requested a charter, she would explain the challenges before accepting. As long as the boat payment wasn't the deciding factor, she reasoned, she'd agree to a larger group.

Life is different, she thought, now that I'm running my own boat. These are my choices. My decisions.

Her life on the water changed little, but on land she had records to keep. She found a lawyer and an accountant, and in a few weeks she felt as if she'd always been her own boss. When she looked at the horizon, she felt content.

One afternoon she finished her work, went home, showered. Toweling her hair, she pulled out her cell phone to see if Chris had called or texted. No messages. No missed calls. They hadn't been in contact in over a week. She was about to put the phone down when it buzzed in her hand.

"Hey!" she said without looking at the number.

"Well, hey yourself. Do you even know who this is?" asked a voice, somewhat familiar.

She blushed. "Uh, no, I guess I don't." She looked at the display. Unknown number.

"*Ha!* Got ya! It's Uncle Mike!"

"Oh my God! How are you? Wait, is everything okay?"

"Yeah, yeah, don't worry, sweetheart, everything's fine. I'm going to be in Islamorada for work so I wanted to get on your calendar."

"Great! When are you coming?"

"In a few weeks. I'm in the midst of a research project on the effect of sea temperature rise on coral reefs. Need to do some diving in your neighborhood. I'll give you a heads up when I know the exact dates. Probably be in Islamorada for a few days, so we should be able to squeeze in dinner one of those nights. Sound good?"

"Sounds great! I'm excited to see you!"

"Me too. It's been too long. I'll text you when I know my schedule. See you soon."

Maya met Mike at a restaurant near his hotel. When she walked in the door, he was standing at the bar drinking a beer and scrolling through his phone. She stopped for a moment, taken with the subtle changes in his profile since their last visit a few years earlier in Seaport. Hair a little thinner, body a bit softer. We're all just clay on a potter's wheel, she thought. Time spins us from one shape to another. Quivering lump to sleek vase to, eventually, a simple bowl that sits in the window and cradles something dear while the days pass.

She thought of her father. Where was he on the wheel? I should be able to picture him, she thought. I should know. She shook her head and walked toward the bar.

"Uncle Mike!" She reached up to give him a hug.

"Maya! You look great!" he said as he hugged her. "Want

something to drink? It'll be a few minutes before our table is ready."

"Just a water. Early day tomorrow."

Over dinner, he quizzed her about life in the Keys. The fishing, the clients, the weather. Most important, her relationship with Chris.

"There's not much to say right now. He wants a commitment I can't give him, so we're not talking very often. I think he's trying to break away slowly, and I don't blame him."

"Is that what you want?"

She shrugged. "I don't know what I want. So maybe that should be telling me something. Anyway, enough about that. Tell me about your work."

He eyed her a moment, let her last words tumble across the table until they rested in the empty space by his water glass. She doesn't want to talk about Chris, he thought. Doesn't want to deal with her feelings. Like father like daughter. His hand brushed the empty space on the table as he reached for his glass and drew a long, cold swig.

He launched into an explanation of the challenges to coral reefs, the bleaching caused by warming waters. He'd already been in town a couple of days, taking samples and filming video. His group would be leaving the next day.

"Sorry I won't see you again," he said as they headed for the door. "But it's good to catch up. By the way, have you seen your dad lately?"

"Not since January. He won't come down when he's busy. Says he doesn't want to give up the work. I think the recession spooked him. I need to get up there for a visit."

"You should. He misses you. I don't see him very often, just when I come to Seaport to see my folks. But I speak to him every few weeks. I know you guys talk, but he could use some face-to-face time with his little girl."

She looked at Mike. Pictured the wheel spinning faster and faster. Dizzying, out of control. She grabbed the side to slow it down, but the friction burned her skin. She pulled away. That's what I do, she thought. Pull away. Maybe I've stayed away too long.

"Is there something I should know?"

"No, nothing specific. And you know he has your grandparents and aunt and uncle and cousins around. I don't want you to worry. But I know he's lonely. I wish he'd get off his ass and meet someone, but I can't get him to do it. I don't know what he's afraid of. Maybe if he met someone else, he'd forget about your mother? I don't know. Do you?"

"That could be it. Or not that he'd forget about her, but maybe no one else could measure up, or he feels guilty. It's crazy. People lose a husband or wife, and they get married again. He won't even go on a date."

"Well, see what you can do about getting home for a visit."

She promised him she would. "What about you? Are you happy?"

"I am." He'd married the marine biologist from Los Angeles he'd dated for years. They lived on Cape Cod with their three kids. "I'm very lucky. I married a great person, my best friend. And our kids are a blast."

Maya's face darkened. She felt the wheel drag beneath her fingers until it slowly rattled to a stop.

He put his arm around her. "It's out there. You'll find it. Sometimes you have to stop looking and it just taps you on the shoulder. That's how life is." He hugged her and let her go. "Be good."

Twenty-nine

2013

MONTHS PASSED AFTER HER DINNER WITH MIKE, but Maya didn't plan a trip home. She was busier than she'd been since she bought the boat, as was Charlie. They spoke and texted often. She thought he was doing well and a visit could wait. Winter turned to spring.

Charlie's company had picked up a commercial job, renovating an old school to transform classrooms into condominium units. A great opportunity, he told her. Couldn't pass it up. The media coverage would spread the Raymond Construction name farther south, closer to Boston.

"I want the company to be a larger player in New England," he told her. "In the next recession, which I know will come at some point, we'll be looking for work well outside of Seaport. This project will help build our reputation. You understand why I can't come down right now, don't you?"

"Of course. Don't worry about it. We'll see each other soon."

One Saturday night he called her for their story ritual. It was early, but within minutes he was yawning. "I'm sorry. We've been working six or seven days a week on this condo. It's killing me. I need a break. Need to plan a visit. I haven't even seen your new boat yet."

"Maybe you should take a day off."

"I am. I told the crew I'm off tomorrow and Monday. It's Patriots' Day, and I want to go into Boston for the race. Haven't done that in years. Head over to Boylston Street, watch the runners come in. Remember when we used to do that when you were a kid?"

"Yeah, I loved that. Forgot the Marathon was Monday. I've got a client scheduled, but call me that night. I want to hear about it. I'd love to be there with you."

~

Maya pulled the boat into the slip, grabbed the lines piled on the dock, and tied them to the bow and stern. She took her dry bag from under the console and climbed out, checked the lines one more time before heading to the café.

"Hey, Gus," she said to the stocky cook as she sat down at the counter. He looked up and grinned, the cleft deepening in his stubbly chin, the wide smile revealing a small space between his front teeth. His brown eyes shined.

"Good morning, sunshine. To what do I owe this great honor? No clients today?"

"Nope, death in the family."

"Oh, I'm so sorry. I didn't know." He turned to her and poured her a cup of coffee.

"No, no, sorry, not my family. I had people coming down

from Miami for the day, but the guy's father died so he had to cancel at the last minute. I don't expect to pick anyone else up today, so I figured I'd have breakfast with my favorite chef." She smiled at him as she added sugar and half-and-half to her cup.

"You are too kind." He winked at her. "What are you in the mood for today? Salty or sweet?"

"Hmm, salty I think." She pulled out her phone to check messages. One from her dad. He was heading into Boston. She'd already forgotten it was race day. Maybe she'd go home early and watch the finish.

In a few minutes, Gus delivered a three-egg omelet loaded with spinach, mushrooms, tomatoes, and feta cheese. She slathered strawberry jam on the buttered wheat toast. "Great stuff, Gus," she said after her first bite. "Just like Dad used to make."

He smiled and topped off her coffee. "How is the old man? Coming down any time soon?"

"I've been trying, but he says he's so busy with work he doesn't want to take the time right now. Maybe in the summer."

"You don't seem convinced." He took a pencil from behind his ear and walked toward a table of four tourists sitting down behind Maya.

"I'm not, but I'll have to see what I can find out Saturday." She'd already planned to confront her dad on story night. "I may have to go up to Boston in the fall if I can't get him to commit to a vacation."

She picked up a mushroom and examined it. Thought about her client whose father was gone and wondered how she would react to such news. She shook her head and shoved her fork in her mouth. No reason to think about that today. No reason to feel that deeply, to glance back at the lengthening shadows, to watch the last rays of sunlight leaving the day. Life was simpler this way. Not dealing with a problem until it exploded into flame, shrieking for water to extinguish the heat and frenzy. With no fire to put out, it was just another day by the ocean.

She pushed the last bit of egg around her plate. Maybe that's my problem, she thought. Maybe I need to look back at the shadows, deal with what's really going on. With my dad. With Chris. With me. Commit to something, somewhere. Someone.

"Okay, Gus, what do I owe you today for this fine breakfast?" She pulled her wallet out of her bag. He handed her the bill. She left the cash on the counter.

As she walked out of the diner, the thought of her client's loss tugged at her sleeve, begged for attention like a small child. She worried about her dad. He was working so hard, probably wasn't taking care of himself. She couldn't bear the idea of losing him. She pushed the thought away. Not now. Another day.

She checked the boat and headed for the truck, pulled out her phone. She texted her dad to see if he was at the race yet. He was probably still walking the streets, mingling in the crowd, she thought. The Marathon was a special time in Boston. People lingered in restaurants, shuffled through camps of spectators. Even though everyone wanted to see the winners, the Boston Marathon was as much about standing in the crowd, anywhere along the route from Hopkinton to Boston, and cheering on all the runners. Being part of the community. Families lined up year after year in the same spots. College kids came out to scream support to strangers. Every person participated. Every runner was celebrated.

Thirty

CHARLIE REVVED THE TRUCK BEFORE the sun peeked above the horizon to get into Boston with time to stroll. To see the city awaken with the excitement of race day. He parked near Quincy Market and grabbed a bagel and coffee at a food stall. Cup in hand, he headed toward Copley Square, walked through Boston Common and the Public Gardens. He went up Newbury Street, watching people come out of cafés or dashing off to meet a friend. The air was sweet with spring. It was a good day to watch the race, he thought. A good day to be part of something.

He meandered until he arrived at Boylston Street. Found a spot on the sidewalk across from the library. A young couple with a toddler stood next to him. He looked at the little girl and she at him. He smiled at her and waved, and she reached up toward him with both arms. Her mother turned to look at him.

"Oh, I'm so sorry, she's really friendly," the young woman

said. "Come on, Sophie, leave the nice man alone. He's here to watch the race."

"Aw, you're a cutie," he said to Sophie. He bent over to touch her small nose with the tip of his finger. She giggled and grabbed at his hand to keep him close. "Do you guys come to the race every year?" he asked the couple.

The mother picked up the little girl, pushed the child's dark hair out of her eyes. The dad answered. "We used to, back when we were at Northeastern. It was a dorm event. That's how we met. Her friends were here and ended up next to mine. We try to come back every year. And now that we have this little one, it's become a family tradition. How about you?"

"I used to from time to time. When my daughter was young, we'd come down together. It was a nice day out. She's grown now and lives in Florida, so I haven't been in a while. Seemed like a good thing to do again."

They chatted for a while as the couple kept their daughter entertained. Before long they heard cheers from the crowd up the street. The young woman picked up her daughter again.

"Look, Sophie, here they come!" All around people yelled as the men's wheelchair division winner broke the tape. Soon others streamed across the finish line, wheelchair racers, runners. The excitement energized the crowd. Sophie covered her ears from time to time, but she seemed to enjoy the revelry. Charlie watched the runners and the child. He marveled at her focus, her joy when another runner finished the race. She clapped and high-fived her dad. Charlie smiled. It was like watching an old home movie. Until it wasn't.

In the months that followed, when Charlie would startle awake from a dream, he'd remember the sound that broke that moment. With time, the pain and smell of burning and images of blood on the sidewalk faded, but the sound came back over and over again. He couldn't remember which came first, the sound of the bomb or the screaming that followed. At times it seemed like the screaming had always been there.

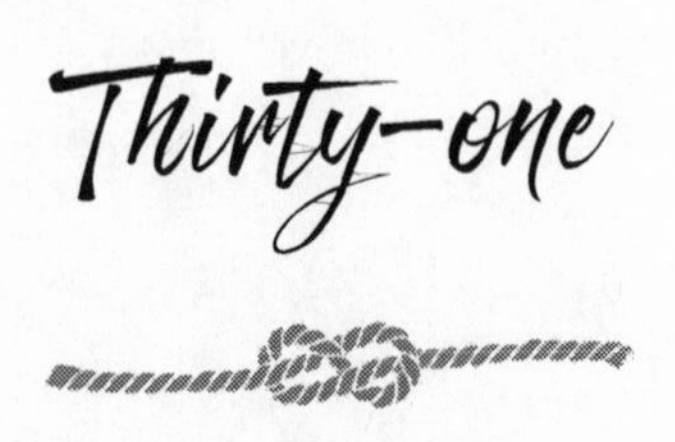

Thirty-one

MAYA MADE IT BACK TO THE HOUSE and turned on her computer. She grabbed her phone to text Charlie but held back. She wanted him to enjoy Boston and the race. She sat down at the kitchen table to do some work, checked the race from time to time.

After a while she got up for water, sat down again, restless. She wasn't used to being still this long, particularly on a beautiful day. Maybe I should go for a run, she thought. Support the marathoners from afar. She smiled and opened up Google to check the news.

Years later, when someone at a dinner party would ask where everyone was on 9/11, she would listen quietly to the responses. At my desk working, one said. Taking my kid to a dentist appointment, another offered. Maya had been young, still in high school. She remembered which class she was in when the announcement came over the PA system. But another memory nagged at her. She was supposed to have a quiz that morning. She'd forgotten to study. Looking back, she thought the relief of avoiding the quiz, not the horror of the day, bound her to 9/11. Guilt hung in the air like the smell of gunpowder.

Others at the dinner party would say, yes, I remember where I was for 9/11, but my parents also talk about where they were when JFK was shot. That it was a moment frozen in time. Maya would nod but not contribute. She was afraid to ask the question that lingered in her mind: Do you remember where you were when you heard about the Boston Marathon bombing?

Maya stood, stumbled backward, knocked over her chair. She clutched the table, read the lines of the story faster than her mind could process them. Grabbed her phone.

"Where are you? Why won't you pick up?" When she couldn't reach Charlie she called Karen.

"Have you heard from him?" she said when Karen answered.

"What do you mean?" Karen worked in a brokerage office, one of the few businesses open in Massachusetts on Patriots' Day. People who didn't have someone at the race gathered in the conference room. Others ran out in search of those they couldn't reach. "Did your dad go to the Marathon?"

"Yes! Yes! He was taking the day off. He said he was going to Boylston Street!"

"Okay, stay calm. I'm leaving work now." She hurried down the hallway to get her purse from her office. Her mind raced. "Look, there's no way he was in that area. I'm sure he's fine." She didn't believe the lie. "The lines are probably jammed so you won't be able to reach him. I'll find him and call you. Okay?"

"Yeah, okay. Please Aunt Karen. Just find him."

Maya stared at her phone. She called her father's number again a few times but couldn't get through. She grabbed the remote and turned up the volume on the TV, searched the screen. Every station told the story, but she couldn't see him. The phone rang. Chris.

"Are you okay?"

"Yeah, I mean, no. How did you know?"

"I saw the news. I figured you'd be freaked out. Do you know anyone running the race?"

She shook her head. "No, but my dad ..." Her words were watery. "He went into Boston to watch. He was supposed to be there. Right there."

"I'm coming. I'll be in the truck in ten minutes. Call me if you hear anything."

She paced. How could this be happening? Who would do this? Where was he?

She sat on the couch, flipped through the channels. People running, tending to the injured. The street littered with empty cups, broken glass, blood.

Thirty-two

"OH MY GOD, SIR, ARE YOU OKAY?" the woman yelled. Charlie looked at her, the little girl's head buried in her shoulder. Sophie and her parents had escaped injury. Charlie sat down on the curb as blood seeped through his jeans.

"What, uh yeah, I think I'm okay." He looked up at the husband.

"Don't move," the man said. "I'll get help." He sprinted off and found a police officer nearby. She ran over, knelt by Charlie, and told him to stay calm.

"I'm going to put some pressure on your leg, okay? We need to stop the bleeding. We'll get you out of here in no time. Is this your dad?" she asked the young man.

"No, we were just standing together watching the race. I don't even know his name."

She turned to Charlie. "Sir, can you tell me your name?"

"Charlie Raymond."

"Okay, Mr. Raymond, you hang on. We're going to get you out of here."

Charlie heard the sirens and the commotion around him. He closed his eyes. When he opened them he was strapped to a gurney being lifted into the back of an ambulance. As the paramedic closed the doors, he saw the young woman looking back at him. He waved goodbye.

Thirty-three

MAYA'S PHONE RANG.

"Karen? Have you found him?"

"Yes, now Maya, he's going to be okay. He's at Mass General. I'm on my way in with your uncle. Your dad's in surgery. But he's very lucky. Shrapnel cut some muscle in his left leg but missed the major artery. He'll be fine. It's just going to take a little time. I'll call you when I get to the hospital and speak to the doctor. From what they've told me, he's going to be okay. You hear me, honey? Are you alone? Is someone with you?"

"Chris is coming. But I want to come home. Can I come home?"

"Let's not make any plans yet. Let me get to him and then we'll talk. We can get you on a flight tomorrow. Just sit tight. He's going to be okay."

Maya placed the phone on the table. She put her head in her hands and wept. Her body shook as fear crawled into the crevices of her mind. She shoved the images away. He's going to be fine, she thought. But he's not right now, and I should be there. She called Chris and gave him the news.

"I'm just a few minutes away."

She sat in front of the TV and watched the news coverage, video replaying over and over. Snippets of the crowd. Was that him? Lying on the ground? She moved closer to the screen but couldn't see the face of the man. I should be there, she thought.

She grabbed her laptop and searched for flights. How soon could she get to Boston? Karen had told her to wait, but she couldn't. She put down her laptop and picked up the remote. People rushed to the injured. A woman sat on a curb. A blanket covered her shoulders, her frizzy hair wild, eyes darting. She held the head of another woman in her lap. They waited. A man stood in the middle of the street, bent over, hands on knees. He straightened, looked at the street and up at the sky.

Chris came in the door. Maya stood. He hugged her, and a new rush of tears dampened his shirt. She told him what she knew about her father. As he rubbed her back, he told her if what Karen said was true, her dad would be okay.

The next morning Chris drove Maya to the Miami airport. They talked sparingly during the two-hour drive. She stared out the window, watched the blue water disappear as they entered the mangroves along the eighteen-mile stretch separating island chain from mainland. Without words to offer as comfort, he occasionally held her hand, kneaded the familiar skin in slow, rhythmic strokes. Each rub of his thumb delivered the same message: I'm here for you now. And I will be.

They pulled into the airport, and he signaled to change lanes for the parking garage.

"You don't have to park," she said. "Just drop me off. I don't want to hold you up." She paused, took his hand again, looked down at her lap. "You've done so much already. I really appreciate it. Don't know if I could have gotten through this without you."

He nodded and drove into the departure area. He pulled up to the curb, and they jumped out. As Maya reached in the back of the truck to take her suitcase, she saw an extra bag.

"What's that?"

"Oh, I brought that in case you wanted me to go to Boston with you." He hugged her and kissed her goodbye. "I told you I was hopeless."

Thirty-four

MAYA SETTLED INTO THE WINDOW SEAT and closed her eyes for takeoff. A man and woman filled the row. Her silence left them to themselves. Once in flight, she pushed up the shade and gazed at the sky.

Flying had intrigued her as a kid. Up in the clouds, she watched shapes turn into wisps. On the ground she marveled at a cloud that resembled a rabbit or butterfly, but they were out of reach. From her seat in the air, she felt like she was in the backyard with them, chasing the bunny until it ducked under the fence. Extending a forearm to give the butterfly a soft place to land.

She had a memory of her mother she wasn't sure was real, could have been a dream or daydream, but it had been with her since she was small. She was in her grandparents' backyard. Early evening in late summer. An ocean breeze rustled the dense maple leaves drooping from heavy limbs stretched overhead. A pair of rabbits munched on grass and dandelions by the fence. They crouched over their food, stone still except for their bobbing noses. The animals saw Maya, but they didn't run. They watched her watch them.

Her mother had been sitting in a lawn chair, trying to finish a book in the last light of day. She looked up and noticed the two babies gazing at her child. She put her book down and carefully made her way the few feet to where her daughter stood.

Maya felt her mother squat beside her, felt the familiar hand on her back. One of the rabbits stopped eating and moved a step closer. The other followed. For a moment the four creatures stared at one another, wide-eyed and silent. The first rabbit blinked, sniffed the air, and scampered for the fence. The second chased after. Maya reached for them, but they were gone.

She turned and looked at Sierra, asked her mother why the bunnies went away. In those few minutes, the rabbits had become her friends.

"Oh, honey," Sierra said to her crying child, head buried in her mother's shoulder. "They were scared. They felt like they had to leave. To protect themselves. They'll be back."

The little girl pulled her head up. "But why are they scared of me? I love them."

"It's not you, sweetie. Sometimes we don't know what to be scared of. Sometimes we run away even from those that love us and that we love. And we don't know why."

The clouds changed shape as the plane flew closer. The rabbit turned into a tree and then was just a cloud. Maya closed her eyes and slept.

Thirty-five

LANDING BUMPED HER AWAKE. She grabbed her phone, found a text from her aunt. Her father was awake and out of bed. The doctors had him plodding the halls with a walker. Thank you, she thought.

On the cab ride to the hospital, she scanned the streets. People hurried into office buildings. That guy looks suspicious, she thought. Was he looking over his shoulder? Watching to see if he's being followed? Is that actually a laptop in his bag? She shook her head and sank back into the seat. He's probably just late for a meeting.

When she arrived at the hospital room, the family surrounded her father. Blue and red balloons bobbed from ribbons tied to the headboard; one shaped like a baseball, flashing a red B at the center. The crowd parted as she stood her suitcase by the door. The women quietly uttered her name, wiped their eyes. The men settled their backs against the cramped walls, sighed, the warm air of their burden fluttering from their lips. She went to the bed and hugged her father, strained to control the tears that threatened to wash the room in the flood of her relief.

"You look good," she said. She leaned back and sniffled. "It's great to see you."

"I'm fine," he said. He pulled himself up against the pillows. "Hit with a few small BBs. They removed the shrapnel, there's some muscle damage, but that'll heal. I've got a few weeks of physical therapy ahead of me. Probably more surgery down the road. But I'll be back at work in a week. Just watch." He winked at her and pulled her close.

Maya had scrambled and made plans to be home for two weeks. Andy and Mark each had days open for some of her clients, and they found two other guides to take the rest of her bookings. Without work to worry her, she focused on her dad. She took him to physical therapy and his follow-up with the surgeon. The majority of the time, they sat together or took short walks. Since leaving the hospital, he walked with a cane.

Some nights they dined with family, but most evenings Maya cooked their meals. She'd marinate chicken, stir sauces, boil water for pasta. Like the old days, she'd tear lettuce and chop tomatoes and cucumbers for a salad. Only now, her father stood by *her* side, sneaking the odd slice of carrot from the cutting board to his daughter's amusement. As garlic simmered in olive oil, the scents of memory wafted through the kitchen and out the old screen door.

Charlie wasn't accustomed to the slow pace set by his injury.

He became frustrated and cursed his clumsiness until he sat in front of the TV again. Then he'd watch the news coverage. The weight of his good fortune quieted him.

When Maya wasn't tending to her dad, she was watching the news. The video of the two suspects. The murder of the young policeman. The violence that ended in Watertown. When the networks showed the fishing boat where the second brother hid, she stared at the screen. The boat, she thought. I'll always remember the boat.

Until he was in custody, she couldn't rest. Her mind returned to the blast, the victims. These were her people, she thought. This was my dad. I should have been here. I should have done something.

Her heart ached for Boston and all of New England. She thought back to the rabbits, running from what they believed they should fear. She thought of the people who stayed, who cared for each other. When she'd turned eighteen, she'd run. She was still running. Like the rabbits, she thought. I have no idea what I'm afraid of. What I'm running from.

One afternoon, Charlie asked Maya if she wanted to walk down to the water.

"Are you sure you're up for it?"

"I think so. The physical therapist wants me to walk a little more anyway. And if I get too tired, you can go back and get the truck."

The day was cool. She went into her father's room to borrow a sweatshirt from his closet. She found a grey crew neck tucked into a back corner of the top shelf. The old Patriots logo screened on the front. The bulky Revolutionary War soldier scowled at her, ready to snap the football to his quarterback. She loved the old mascot with the three-cornered hat. She pulled the shirt over her head and walked out to the family room.

"Where did you find that?" Charlie asked, staring.

"Up on your shelf. Sorry, am I breaking a superstition or something? Should I not wear your shirt?"

"No, it's not that. That sweatshirt was your mother's. I guess I stashed it up there after we moved in and forgot."

"Oh, I'm sorry," she stammered. "I'll put it back."

"No, no, please, wear it. I'm glad you found it. Looks good on you." He paused, cleared his throat, moved toward her. He put his free arm around his daughter and led her to the door. "I always did like that old logo. Come on. Let's go." She followed him outside and closed the door behind them.

"You know, your mom was a huge Patriots fan," he said as they ambled down the street. "And that wasn't so easy back then. We weren't very good. Well, I shouldn't say that. We made it to the Super Bowl in eighty-six. Best part was upsetting the Dolphins in the conference championship. They beat us up all the time in the eighties, so your mother particularly enjoyed that. She hated the Dolphins.

"Everyone in New England, including your mother, was caught up in the mantra: Squish the Fish! We were watching the game at Aunt Karen's house, and after we won your mom jumped up on the couch screaming, 'Squish the Fish! Squish the Fish!' I was laughing so hard when I pulled her down I nearly cracked her head on the coffee table." He shook his head, chuckled at the memory. "And then the Bears beat the snot out of us in the Super Bowl. That was a bummer."

"How'd she take that?" Maya asked, grinning at her father's smile. "Was she sad?"

"Sad? Nah. She was aggravated. Thought we should've

played better. But she was pragmatic. When we won, it was the greatest thing in the world. When we lost, it was just a game. No big deal.

"Your mother felt if her team won, she could celebrate the moment. If they lost, it wasn't her blood and sweat and hours that had been sacrificed, so she didn't deserve to cry. The players could, but she hadn't earned the privilege. I always respected that about her, but I couldn't relate. If the Celtics lost to the Lakers, well, I wouldn't cry, but I was inconsolable. I would mope for at least a day. She'd give me a little space and then tell me to knock it off. Grow up." He laughed again, shook his head.

"Your mother. No matter what, she could always get to me. And I don't mean she had me wrapped around her finger or anything. She did, but that's beside the point. I mean, she knew what to say to calm me down if I was upset, or to make me laugh. She just got me."

They arrived at the seawall. Maya took her father's arm and helped him sit. He watched his daughter as she moved his cane and sat beside him. The ocean breeze ruffled his hair.

"You should keep that sweatshirt. It suits you."

"Are you sure? I don't want to take away your special memories."

"Oh, don't worry about that. I have plenty of great memories of your mother. You having her shirt won't change that." He reached into his jeans pocket. "I've got something else for you, too. I planned to give this to you today anyway, so now you get two gifts." He handed her a ring.

"What's this?"

"Your mom's wedding ring. I've wanted to give it to you for a while but couldn't find the right time."

She looked at the delicate ring lying in her palm. "I can't

take this," she said quietly. "It means too much to you." She held it out to him.

"Yes, you can." He closed her hand around the ring. "I was going to give it to you years ago, but I screwed up." He moved closer to her and resettled himself on the wall. "Do you remember the night we went to the marina and I climbed the fence? When the cops showed up?"

She laughed. "How could I forget?"

"Well, I had a purpose, drunk as I may have been. I'd been keeping the ring in a box on a sailboat at the marina. Remember Todd and I started working on Uncle Rick's old boat? He said we could have the boat if we cleaned it up and made it seaworthy again."

"I remember you used to come down to the marina on Saturdays and work on it once in a while. But I figured you just did that to get out of the house, and because you liked working on the boat. I never figured you'd get it finished. No offense."

"No, none taken. I didn't either. And I still may not. But for some reason, I hid the box with your mom's ring on board. I have no idea why. Maybe I figured if I ever sailed away, a part of her would be with me. We'd still get to travel together, such as it was.

"Anyway, I'd been in your room that day. I wasn't snooping, just putting laundry away, but your laptop was open to the website for Florida Keys Community College. For the first time, I admitted to myself that you were serious, that you were leaving. I didn't know what to do. So I did what I knew really well how to do, and I had a few beers. Then I realized I didn't want you to leave without the ring, so I asked you to take me to the marina. Stupid, I know. Especially since you weren't leaving the next day. I just had this sense of urgency, like I had to get the ring and give it to you. When the police showed up, I was too embarrassed to do anything about it for a while. I just let it go.

"My first visit down to Key West to see you, I had the ring in my pocket. I wanted to give it to you, but the moment never seemed right. I don't know why. Maybe I wasn't ready to let go yet." He paused. "I guess I felt like I'd lost your mother, and in some way I was losing you, too. If I kept the ring, I had a little more of her left. And crazy as it sounds, more reason for you to come back. Not that you even knew about the ring or my plan to give it to you, but I guess that's how crazy works. We rationalize." He took the ring from his daughter and looked at it again. Shook his head. "It belongs with you. Please, honey. I want you to have it."

He took her hand and placed the ring in her palm. She picked up the small gold circle and examined it, turned it over and over. A simple band with "Charlie and Sierra" inscribed on the inside.

"I can't take this." She held it out to her father. He pushed her hand away.

"Yes, you can. I want you to have it. Not Crazy Drunk Dad," he said, making air quotes with his hands, "but this dad who's here with you. You have to understand, it's different for me now. I don't need the things I used to think I needed to remember her. I have pictures and our stories and a few other small mementos. It would mean more to me for you to have it.

"I'm lucky. I had so much time with your mother. You deserve to have more of her things. She would want that, too." He put his arm around his daughter, pulled her close to him. Kissed her forehead. "Besides, I've been thinking over the last few days. I need to make some changes. Work less, see you more. Maybe talk to someone."

"Talk to someone about Mom?"

"Yeah, and about Monday. I used to have dreams about your mother. Sometimes they were good dreams. Like us out on a date or making dinner together. Other times I was trying to save her and couldn't. Nightmares. They faded for a while. The last few nights they've been back. It's probably time to get some help."

The night before he'd had the same dream for the third time. He was at the race. When the first bomb went off, he reached for the young woman. The young man was not there. The mother held her daughter. In his dream, he saw Sierra holding Maya. Sierra looked at him in horror. She backed away, taking Maya with her. He tried to follow, but his feet felt like they were set in concrete. He reached for his wife as she disappeared into the crowd. His daughter turned to face him. Then they were gone.

Maya put her hand on her dad's arm. "I heard you last night. Saying her name, or at least that's what I thought I heard. I figured you were dreaming, maybe from the pain meds. I didn't want to wake you. Are they really bad? The nightmares?"

He bowed his head. Pushed some sand around with the heel of his boot. Picked up a rock and tossed it toward the water. The stone landed just short of the surf.

"I guess, yeah, they can be."

"Why haven't you ever done anything about it? Why suffer all these years?"

He shook his head and smiled. Looked at his daughter.

"You are going to think your old man is a whack job, but I'll tell you what I think. I think I didn't want them to go away. I think part of me figured if the nightmares went away, the good dreams would go with them. And I couldn't live with that. The good dreams, they are just so amazing. It's like she's right there. So I figured I'd rather suffer through the bad to keep the good. I know it's crazy."

"It's not crazy, at least not to us because we don't know any better. But maybe a therapist would help you get rid of the bad and keep the good."

Maya slid the gold band onto the ring finger of her right hand. She stood and offered the hand to her father to help him home.

Thirty-six

"READY TO HEAD BACK TO FLORIDA?" Charlie asked his daughter over pasta with pesto and shrimp her last night in town. He set the serving bowl on the kitchen counter before sprinkling oil and vinegar on his salad.

"Not really." She tore a hunk from the end of a fresh baguette. Dragged the bread across her plate, leaving a jagged stripe through the salty, green sauce. The aroma of parmesan and basil wafted through the kitchen as she lingered over the question. "Aunt Karen promised to keep an eye on you. But I'm still worried."

"Don't be. I'm getting better. And I promise to look into therapy. For real this time." He held her gaze. "In exchange, you have to let me do something for you—pay off your boat loan."

She shook her head. "No way. That's my problem."

"You're being ridiculous. You hardly spent anything on college. If you go back, we can talk about tuition. You're driving my old truck, which cost me nothing. Plus you'll feel better about visiting more often if you have no debt. I'd rather you leave a week open every few months and fly home. Isn't that fair?"

She sat back in her chair. Crunched on a sliver of red pepper as her mind searched for an argument. His company is doing well, she thought. He's saved plenty for retirement. Paying off the loan would be painless to him and would allow me more freedom to travel. He'd give anything to see me more often. She swallowed and sighed.

"Okay. But only because I'll have an easier time getting up here. I still feel guilty."

"You shouldn't. You never ask me for anything. I know you worry about money. Eliminating that stress will give me great pleasure." He smiled, wiped his mouth, and stood. "That and the tiramisu I hid in the back of the fridge."

Maya's return to Florida was a challenge. She thought about her dad when she was on the water, when her mind wandered with the current. What if he fell? He wasn't surefooted with his cane, had no patience to slow down. His physical therapy tired him out, but he pushed himself to go to work after each session. Her grandparents and aunt kept an eye. Still, she worried. She made plans to fly home for his next surgery and every three months after that. Having a plan calmed her.

Chris had surrendered to his inability to stay away, which confused her. He was calling and texting every day. They were spending time together a few times a month. Hopeless seemed to have turned the corner back toward hopeful. She didn't know how she felt about that journey. She had moments, adrift, when she felt she could float back to him. Other times she stood tall, alone on the deck of her boat, wondering if she'd ever find her way to the shore.

One afternoon in October, Bill texted. The two brothers from Alaska were coming to town over the holidays. They'd booked a couple of days with him to fish deep sea. They wanted to spend a day with her in the mangroves. She didn't want to take them away from Bill, but he assured her he was happy to share the business.

Patrick and Garrett arrived a few days after New Years. The morning they set out together, the wind was blowing almost twenty knots. A bit much for her small boat. After a couple of choppy hours tucked behind a small island, the guys suggested she head in.

"But you'll have to join us for dinner," Garrett said. "That's the deal."

She liked these two, so she graciously accepted. At dinner they asked her about life as a guide, having her own boat. Then they started in on her again.

"When are you coming to Alaska?" Patrick asked. "You know you'd love it. Bring your dad." She'd told them about Charlie's injury and recovery. He was almost back to full speed. On occasion, during her quarterly trips home she'd see a hitch in his step or a wince, but rarely.

"Or Chris, or both of them," Garrett said. "We don't care. Just come."

She said she'd think about a trip, and she did. Almost all the time. She'd started sketching again, after years away from her pad. Instinctively she began drawing mountains, the subject most common in her drawings since childhood. She felt pulled to their peaks. Memories of hikes with her father or reimaginations of *National Geographic* photos. She appreciated the flatness of the ocean, the bits of foam scattered on the sand by a retreating wave. But she wondered if she was hard-wired for the majesty of elevation. The muscularity, the icy brawn of a rocky peak.

When she was on the water, gazing at the horizon, she considered what waited beyond the edge of the world. Islands undiscovered. People. Cultures. Spicy curries she hadn't washed down with local lager under a beachside thatched roof. Smiles she hadn't returned hiking a misty, forest path. She'd been at peace for months, at least since she'd bought the boat. But she'd felt settled before. When she moved to Key West for college. The first year working for George and then again with Bill. Moments of respite from doubt, when her mind quieted. The idea of travel to Alaska provoked her again. Intrigued her. The enormity, the remoteness, the solitude. Maybe Dad and I need a real adventure, she thought. Maybe avoiding travel together is holding each of us back.

When she found the courage to mention the brothers' invitation, her father nearly jumped through the phone, surprising his daughter with unrestrained enthusiasm. He suggested they take two weeks in June. Over the solstice, he said. When the days are longest. "We're going," he said. "I'll find some flights and email you."

He remembered the Disney trip, their first vacation away from the family after Sierra's death. He'd avoided travel with his little girl since. Couldn't bear the abyss that filled the third airline seat. The loneliness, the pain. He realized he'd been selfish, that his daughter deserved to experience more than just beach vacations with cousins. How long had it been? Fifteen years? Twenty? He thought he was ready. They were ready.

"I can't believe it's taken all these years for us to go on a trip. This will be the best freaking Raymond Adventure ever! When we hang up, get online and block out your calendar. No back talk."

Maya put down the phone and realized she'd been grinning during her father's diatribe. She grabbed her laptop and marked the dates. Wow, she thought. I'm going on vacation. To Alaska. With my dad! She smiled until her face hurt.

Over the next few weeks, they immersed themselves in planning. Patrick and Garrett sent links to websites of places they should see, but also said to reserve a few days. The boys were planning a trip into the backcountry for river fishing. The four of them would take a float plane to a remote cabin surrounded by snowy peaks and dense pine forests.

Maya looked forward to the fishing trip, but she craved time in the mountains. While Charlie searched flights, she booked rooms in Talkeetna and near the entrance to Denali National Park. She spent hours surfing through photos of the wilderness. Moose and grizzlies. Mountaintops.

Since Christmas, she and Chris had settled into a life together, trading visits every week or two. They spent evenings on the patio grilling mahi mahi under the stars, their beer bottles leaving damp rings on the weathered picnic table. Morning runs along the bike path, racing each other back to the house as sweat and laughter poured out of their tired bodies. Late afternoons sitting by the water, fingers touching, the daylight slipping into the sea. Time swimming away. Tick. Tick. Tick. Tock. Tock. Tock. This existence, this partnership. This love flowed under her delicate skin, flushed her cheeks, and raised the wispy blond hairs at her nape. She wasn't sure what this life meant, but she was content. He seemed to be. Gossamer, airy, a love that billowed in the evening breeze as each silently hoped the silken canopy would be enough protection for their fragile heartstrings.

A few nights before her departure, he drove up for a visit. "Getting excited?" he asked her over dinner. "This is probably the biggest trip you've taken. Other than moving down here."

"I am. And it is by far the biggest trip I've ever taken. I still can't believe I'm going. I think I've wanted to do this for a long time and didn't realize it."

"Go to Alaska, or just anywhere?"

"Good question. I think there are other places I'd like to see, but I'm more curious about Alaska. Garrett and Patrick make the backcountry sound like a mystical place that changes your life. I don't think that'll happen, but who knows." She caught a slight wince and paused. "Never mind. It's all crazy talk. It'll just be good to escape the heat." She took a sip of water and looked away. She didn't want to seem too excited. To give the impression life here was too small.

He watched her settle herself. Sighed. Looked into her eyes. "Just come back, okay?"

"Of course." She reached for his hand. "Of course I'll come back."

Thirty-seven

TRAVEL TO ALASKA MADE FOR A LONG DAY. Charlie had arranged flights from Boston and Miami that met in Dallas. From there they would fly the seven-hour leg to Anchorage together. They hadn't seen each other in a couple of months. Since she'd returned to Massachusetts in April for the Marathon.

"How are you?" she asked him after they'd buckled in.

"I'm good. Work's busy." He pulled the in-flight magazine out of the seat pocket.

"That's not what I'm talking about. I mean since we were in Boston."

~

Maya had flown home for the first anniversary of the bombing. She and Charlie and Karen and her husband and kids drove into Boston.

Charlie had been by the site of his injury two other times since the bombing. The first was in October, six months after the race. He'd started counseling in September. Kept his promise to address the emotional issues, but only after the most grueling of the physical therapy was done. Stoic during the early sessions, eventually he'd surrendered to the tears, the shrieking, moaning. Let his body heave and flail. Eyes red, swollen. Finally, after the hard work, his breathing calmed. Bits and pieces of a life lost for so many years began to return. Childhood memories. January snowball fights with Karen, his face burned from the wind, warmed by his mother's hot chocolate. Little league games, summer nights at Dairy Queen, swatting mosquitoes under the flickering lights of the parking lot. His first kiss with Sierra. First time he held his newborn daughter. Loose strands of joy spinning into a yarn, the soft fibers knitting themselves into a blanket that swaddled his tender heart.

For his first trip to Boston after the bombing, his therapist suggested he take someone with him. A close friend or family member, someone he trusted. He waited for Maya's October return to Seaport, and on Saturday morning she and Karen took him into the city.

"You sure about this?" Karen asked as they climbed into her car.

"Yeah," he said. "It's time." He sat in the passenger's seat, stared out the window, drummed his fingers on the armrest. Karen and Maya snickered as the *Car Talk* brothers offered a Milwaukee mother safe used cars for a teenager, and related to a University of Colorado graduate student the advantages of four-wheel drive. They exchanged glances in the rearview, but each look carried the same message: Stay loose. Let him lead.

They parked on Newbury Street in front of a bakery.

"Maybe we'll come back here afterward and stuff our faces with chocolate cake," Charlie said as he shut the car door. He zipped his jacket, shoved his hands in his pockets, inhaled deeply, and scanned the Prudential Center towering above. They walked up Newbury, rounded the corner, cut up the side street, turned onto Boylston. As they headed toward the library, he nodded at the Pour House. "Or maybe we'll stop there first."

"Dad." Maya shot him a worried look. Karen raised her eyebrows.

"Kidding. Just kidding." He put his arm around his daughter, pulled her close. "Cake, not beer."

As they approached the corner, Charlie slowed. His sister and daughter hesitated, then surrounded him. Each took an arm.

"Okay?" Karen asked.

He paused. "Yeah. But give me a minute alone first. You guys can come up behind me." They nodded and let go. He took a few steps, then put his head down and strode toward the stretch of sidewalk where he'd stood six months before. The moment the sky shattered into a million pieces. The moment his lungs forgot how to breathe.

He leaned against a light pole and looked around. A woman pushing a stroller, chubby-cheeked infant tucked inside under a gauzy white blanket, glided past. A man and woman out for a morning run, sweat spreading across their t-shirts, discussed dinner plans as they jogged by. He turned, looked at the café behind him. The tables half-filled with the ornaments of weekend. Thick slices of French toast covered in powdered sugar. The last few drops of Vermont maple syrup dribbling down the side of the small white pitcher resting next to the matching oval plate. Steam lifting off the coffee cup, newly refilled, the plastic thimbles of half-and-half piled in a bowl by the napkins. *The Boston Globe* folded by the plate. He faced the library. A pair of college students, backpacks at their feet, sat on a bench, phones held under noses, thumbs scrolling, scrolling, scrolling. Life pressed on, propelled itself into normalcy. All these people, bright and in motion. He, invisible and inert. He heard a siren in the distance and jumped, shuddered. Head down, chin on chest, shoulders slumped, he cried.

After a moment, he wiped his eyes, nose, looked back at Karen and Maya, hovering, worried. Motioned to them. They moved slowly toward him, hesitant. He opened his arms and took them in. All of them. All of everything. All that had fled from him, had slumbered inside him, had waited on the end of the couch, watching him. These months. These years. He wrapped his arms around the world, dried his eyes on the downy fabric of a golden Boston Saturday morning. Released the breath he'd held since that Monday afternoon in April. Since her death so many years before.

He pulled away, looked into the watery eyes of his daughter, his sister. Smiled and wiped his own. "Ladies, it's time for cake."

~

A frigid January Saturday, the sun blinding against the newly-fallen crystals from the night before. The streets plowed, sky so fierce a blue Charlie thought the color alone would bring him to tears. He'd woken early, showered and shaved, held his breath a moment whenever the air seemed to flee his chest too quickly. Took his pea coat from its wooden hanger in the hall closet, wrapped his worn, red scarf around his neck, ruffled the dog's fur, pulled the front door closed behind him. Climbed into the cab of his cold truck, rubbed his hands on his jeans as his breath puffed over the steering wheel. "Better I go alone this time," he muttered to the defrosting windshield. "Better they don't know I'm going."

He played with the radio as he traveled the back roads toward Route 1, searched for mindless chatter about the Bruins' win streak. Sipped his Dunkin' light and sweet coffee. "Don't think about it. Just going for a drive."

He turned onto Newbury Street, parked in front of the bakery he and the girls had strolled into three months before. He sat for a moment, stared in the window at the customers picking up croissants, muffins. A man entering held the door for a woman as she carried out a large, white box. Maybe it's someone's birthday today, he thought. Wonder how they're celebrating. If there will be a party with music, balloons. Laughter.

As the door closed, he caught a glimpse of the small table the three shared on his last visit. "Order one of everything," he'd told them. Maya chose a large piece of chocolate cake, rich and moist with thick frosting, a hint of mocha in the cream between each of the four layers. Karen selected a piece of carrot cake, dotted with slivers of carrot and bits of chopped walnuts, nutmeg, cinnamon, lush with cream cheese frosting, covered in coconut, and a wedge of pecan pie, warm and gooey, the pecans spilling onto the plate under a pillow of whipped cream. They huddled around the table, reaching over each other to alternate tastes of coconut, chocolate, buttery piecrust. Chattered about the cooling temperatures to come, family gossip. Anything but what they'd just done, seen. When they'd finished eating, stacked the plates, laid the forks atop, dropped their crumpled napkins on the table, they sat back, looked at each other, smiled.

"I love you, both of you, so much," he told them. They blinked away the bittersweet morning and stumbled out onto the shiny streets of the city they loved.

~

Charlie stashed his keys in his pocket and stepped out into the January cold, his left leg stiff. The weathermen talked of the wind chill, but the sharpness of the air caught him off guard after the heat of the truck. He wrapped his scarf around his nose and mouth, shoved his hands in his coat pockets, lifted his face toward the wind ahead.

Fewer people this time. No mothers pushing strollers down Boylston Street or alfresco diners reveling in the last warm rays of autumn. He walked up to the light pole, looked at the relics of urban life clinging to the peeling black paint. An old sticker from the WAAF rock station. A confession of love scratched on the metal following a night of pitchers and quarters and plastic cups. So much life here, he thought. Ordinary, beautiful life.

He leaned back, rested his head, gazed across the street at the library. The shifting wind hurried an orphaned paper cup along the curb toward Copley Square. A couple, mid-thirties, stood by a tree. The man tall, thin, hair curly and dark, black leather jacket. The woman a few inches shorter, cranberry wool coat and grey hat crocheted with knotty, looped stitches. They bent over his phone, scrolled through screens, surveyed the landscape. She pointed up the street and they set off, heads angled into the wind, bodies together. Ordinary, beautiful life.

Charlie stomped his boots for warmth. Glanced at the pavement. He remembered the day of the race. The young couple, small child. The joy, nostalgia of the before. The chaos, scorching of the after. The tearing away of all that was ordinary. Beautiful. Life could be like that again, he thought. Would be.

He shivered against the cold. Turned to his left, toward the faded blue and yellow paint up the street. Wind at his back, he moved slowly up the sidewalk, until he stood at the edge of the finish line. He stepped into the street, the lanes empty, and walked the last few paces to cross that line. I must leave them here, he thought. The memories, the fear, the pain. He sighed. And more than that. The regret. The sadness. The past. Leave them all here. Begin again.

The drive home, past white lawns fresh with last night's dusting, was bright, pure. He pulled into Karen's driveway behind his parents' car, a few hours early for dinner but happy for the extra time. Couldn't quite get the front door open, so he hit the doorbell with his elbow.

Karen was surprised when she opened the door, understanding now why he rang rather than march in, but confused by the boxes in his arms. "What's all this?"

"I took a drive today." His eyes glistened over the top box. "And I couldn't decide, so I bought all three. Chocolate, carrot, and your favorite. Pecan pie."

As April approached, he didn't feel compelled to be back on the same spot on race day.

"Just in the area, somewhere along Boylston Street," he told his family. "I'm not going to the race to remember the bombing. I'm going to support the city, the people. I was lucky. Luckier than others."

He didn't want recognition or to be part of ceremonies

honoring the victims. He preferred to stand in the shadows. To move on.

"Look, if the Sox want me to throw out the first pitch someday, it's going to be because of my charm and good looks." He smiled, pulled his cap down over his eyes. "In all seriousness, though, I don't feel like I've suffered the way others have. They should focus on the people who lost limbs or family members. The families of that little boy, those women, the police officer."

When they arrived in Boston, they found a spot on Boylston several blocks from the finish line and waited. Karen carried a chair for Charlie. From time to time he sat to rest. As runners passed, he jumped to his feet to yell their numbers. Maya saw him wipe away the occasional tear, but she said nothing. Didn't quite understand the healing process. She looped her arm through his and put her hand in her pocket.

They made their way to the North End after the race. Strolled down Hanover Street and into the family's favorite Italian restaurant. Over pizza, antipasto, and Chianti, Charlie raised his glass.

"I want to thank you all for spending the day with me. I don't think I could've gotten through it without you." He looked at each of them. "It's, um," he lowered his glass and his head. The family waited. "It's difficult." He swallowed. "But I'm glad I came." His face crumpled. Maya leaned over and wrapped her arms around him. She kissed his cheek, let him cry. He excused himself. When he returned he stood at his chair and raised his glass again.

"To the victims and the runners. Boston Strong."

They lifted their glasses. "Boston Strong."

~

Charlie slid the in-flight magazine back in the seat pocket in front of him. He reached over and took his daughter's hand. "I'm okay," he said. He looked past her to confirm the man in the window seat was asleep under his headphones. "My therapist has helped a lot. I think the last piece was going to the race this year. It's not closure. Geez, I hate that word. More like I've come full circle, but I'll probably go around the circle again a few times over the rest of my life.

"I think the bombing will always be with me in some way. I don't dream about it as often anymore. Don't react to loud noises as much. But it's changed my perspective. I feel things more closely now. Spend time thinking about what's important. I didn't tell you because I was a little embarrassed, but she's even got me meditating. Can you believe it? Your old man meditating?"

He smiled and shook his head. Pulled the tray table down and lifted it back up, refastened the clasp. Put his hands in his lap and fidgeted with his seatbelt.

"Can I believe it? To be honest I'm a little surprised, but I'm thrilled. And, please, do not be embarrassed. I mean, if you can't tell me something, who can you tell? Besides, it's totally chill to meditate these days. Maybe I should. Might make me worry less about bookings."

"Why are you worried about bookings? The boat is paid off. You pay your bills. Are you thinking about buying a house?"

"No, nothing like that. I just want to be sure I made the right decision. I guess if my business continues to grow, I'll feel like I have some validation." She smiled, leaned her head against her dad's shoulder. "Guess I still don't know what I want to be when I grow up."

"Does that mean there's a chance you'll come home?"

"Oh, I don't know about that." She laughed, straightened. "I like being away. Like I'm on a permanent Raymond Adventure. But then I think, maybe that's no way to live. Maybe I need to find a reason to stay somewhere, commit to something. I mean, I could sell the boat anytime, pay you back, move to Alaska, or anywhere. There's nothing keeping me in the Keys."

"Not even Chris?"

"Maybe Chris. I could go back to Key West, fish there, marry him. Probably be happy. But something's holding me back.

"I've always had a strong sense of justice. Like the lawyer scales. My gut tells me when they're out of balance. I love Chris, and I know he loves me. I think I love him enough to move where he needs to live. But I'd like to know he loves me enough to do the same."

"Have you ever asked him?"

"In a way, but I've never pushed. Something's been keeping me from committing to him, but I couldn't put my finger on it. I think I'm just figuring it out now as we're talking. I don't need him to move to Islamorada, to actually make such a major sacrifice. But I need to know he would.

"He says he can't leave Key West because of his mom. Maybe she needs the help, maybe it's just a story he's been telling so long he's convinced himself it's true. That she's fragile, even though I know she isn't. If he could find his way out of that story, show me a willingness to move, it would be a big deal. Put us in balance. If he can't do that," she paused, tucked a loose strand of hair behind her right ear, "I'm not sure where we go from there."

"Sounds like you owe him an explanation. See what he says."

"Yeah, maybe. I'll think about it."

"And what about this other little nugget you dropped about moving to Alaska? What's the story with that?"

"I'm just talking. Don't worry. I love the mountains, but I'm not fond of long, dark winters. Now, Hawaii, that's something else." She elbowed her father, shook her head as he shot her a look. "Don't worry about that either. I promise not to leave the time zone without your approval."

They settled in for the flight. Charlie flipped through the in-flight magazine, paused at a photo of a young couple with their daughter on a trail in the woods. He thought about Sierra and how she would've loved this trip.

He remembered a hike they took his last year of high school. A fall day, the height of the foliage. She'd wanted to hike Mount Monadnock all summer, and for whatever reason they'd never made it to New Hampshire. Charlie had football every Saturday in the fall. After his game one afternoon, he told her to be ready the next morning for a surprise. They had to leave early so they'd be back in time to watch the Pats game. Bring a sweatshirt, he told her.

"Where are we going?" Sierra asked as she climbed into the truck, the sun rising over the crisp Sunday morning.

"It's a surprise."

"Come on, just tell me."

"No! Now sit back and enjoy the ride." He popped an Eagles tape into the cassette player. "Belt out a few verses of 'Hotel California' for me. We'll be there in no time."

Sierra sat back and sang along. She didn't have a great voice, but when she heard a favorite, she sang like a rock star. He loved watching her. She seemed so free.

As they made their way west, her singing slowed. She stared out the window at the red maples and golden birch and elm.

She reached a hand out to Charlie. Rested hers on his.

"Thank you," she said quietly.

They were past Nashua before she solved the mystery. "Monadnock? Really?" She leaned over and kissed Charlie's cheek. "Awesome!" She bobbed in her seat with joy.

At the trailhead Charlie threw his knapsack on over his jacket. "Which trail do you want to do?"

"White Dot. The steep one." She grinned as she pulled her Red Sox cap down over her forehead and turned toward the woods.

They set off on the rocky path, the grade increasing as they walked. Halfway up the hike became a scramble, the rocks having tumbled down the mountain ages before and settled in for a long rest. Moving forward meant solving a puzzle. Which crevice could be gripped to pull the body up. Which foothold was wide enough to launch a quivering quadriceps muscle. Sierra determined her way. Charlie found his, a few steps behind. Close enough to keep her safe. To be there if she needed him.

By noon they were approaching the top, the sky opening as they passed the tree line. Sierra stopped on occasion to look out over the valley below. Charlie managed to snap a couple of pictures of her from the side before she saw him and turned away.

"Come on, you have to let me take a few." She smiled at him and rolled her eyes. "Now that's going to be a good one," he said. She grabbed his hand and headed toward the peak.

When they reached the end of the trail, she wandered off to the edge of the mountain. The grey rocks, coarse and windburned, flattened out at the top. She stood with her hands in her pockets, shivered in the thin October air. He came up beside her.

"Pretty cool, huh?" he asked her. He watched her face as she surveyed the horizon, the scarlet reds and daffodil yellows painted among the evergreens. Sometimes she was with him. Other times she was away. "What are you thinking about?"

"That we're up here on top of the world, above all these people down there we can't see. What are they doing? Are they coming home from church? Getting ready for the game? Doing homework? Raking leaves? Then I think, why do I care? They don't care about me. I guess I'm always wondering what's out there. What have I not seen yet? Where should I go? What's beyond Seaport, beyond New England, I'm supposed to see? I love the mountains. I think about them, want to hike to the top. Then I get here, and I think, what else? What's next? There's gotta be more, right?"

She looked at Charlie and put her hands in his jacket pockets. Pulled him closer. "Not that I'd want to go any of those places without you. But don't you wonder? Like your nickname, don't you ever think about going away to school, even to MIT?"

"Nah. It's just a nickname. I may be smarter than a lot of my friends, but I'm not MIT material. And as far as going away, why would I? I think Seaport is cool. I love my home, my family. I'd like to see other places, but I always want to come home. Don't you?"

She took a tissue from her bag and wiped her nose, put balm on her lips. "I don't know. Don't forget, I didn't grow up in Seaport. I love it, and I love my family. But maybe I'd want to end up somewhere else. California, South Dakota, South America. I haven't thought that far ahead, but I can't rule it out.

I guess I'll see what happens when I hear back on my college applications. I can always go away for a while and come back. Doesn't have to be forever."

"But you don't know if you would come back. You might move to Utah and decide they have better skiing. Or San Francisco and figure out you can't live without palm trees. Me, I'm here. I'm the future of Raymond Construction. This is it for me."

He looked out over the valley, the open space. He didn't care about the lives below. Who was grocery shopping or paying bills. Who was playing catch in the yard. He cared about this girl and how to keep from losing her.

She saw his eyes moisten and pulled her hands out of his pockets, hugged him.

"Don't worry, Mit," she said, pulling back to look at him. "I'm not going anywhere. You know I love you. What more could I want?"

~

Charlie looked down at the image in the magazine of the young family. The girl was about twelve or so. She led them along a trail through the woods. The mom followed and dad lagged behind. They were together yet apart. They had each other but weren't afraid to let go. That had been Charlie's mistake. He should have trusted letting go. He looked over at his daughter. She was reading a book on her iPad. How different his life would have been.

Thirty-eight

THAT NIGHT THEY CHECKED INTO THE HOTEL Captain Cook and went out for a walk. The periwinkle of twilight left a glimmer of pale light across the sky as the hour neared ten o'clock. They strolled down the streets of Anchorage, the outline of the Chugach peaks shaded to the east. So much beauty waiting for us, Maya thought, stifling a yawn. A cool breeze blew in off Cook Inlet. She rubbed her forearms and smiled into the wind.

They wandered into a pub and grabbed a small table at the edge of the room. College kids flitted in and out, shouted over the band and pints of beer. Maya watched the groups, the pairings, the laughter and drunken, stolen glances. Shook her head. A sprinkling of the magic wafted out the open door, the fragments scattered into the street. "Same here as anywhere," she said as they left the bar. "Kids drink and flirt."

"Did you think it would be otherwise?"

"I never gave it much thought, but that doesn't mean it's not a surprise. I guess I figured everything would be different here." She shoved her hands in her pockets, hunched her shoulders, tucked away the tiny scraps of disappointment.

"People are people, honey. They all want the same things. Have a little fun, find someone to love, someone they can trust. That doesn't change. Just the scenery in the background. Your mom used to think things could be different in other places. I don't know if I ever convinced her that wasn't the case, but she made her peace with it." He nudged his daughter's arm as they walked toward the hotel. She nodded, a half-smile betraying the frayed edge of sadness.

After a day of wandering the neighborhoods of Anchorage and a full night's rest, Patrick and Garrett picked them up and drove them to the seaplane base. From there they flew into the wilderness for three days of river fishing.

"It's great of you guys to show us around like this," Charlie said as they left the cabin in the morning for the river. "Awfully generous to spend your valuable vacation time with people you barely know. Unless you have designs on my little girl. Then we need to talk."

"Dad, please!" His blushing daughter managed to land an elbow about four ribs from the bottom of the cage, knocking him sideways and eliciting a Cheshire cat grin from her dad. She smirked as he laughed and rubbed his side.

"No, no, sir," Patrick said, laughing. "Maya was a great guide for us. We spent so much time preaching to her about the wonders of Alaska, we had to make sure her trip, your trip, lived up to what we were selling."

"And as far as vacation time, we use any excuse in the summer to take a few days off to fish," Garrett said. "No worries."

Patrick had a friend with a cabin north of Anchorage in an area accessible only by floatplane landing on a nearby lake. The house was a little rustic, but it had electricity and indoor plumbing, which wasn't universal. He'd outfitted the place for fishing and rented it to friends and family. The cabin sat on a short rise, not fifty yards from the edge of a river.

"Your friend knows how to live," Charlie said, climbing into his waders at the edge of the water. A snowcapped peak stood in the distance, puncturing a hole in the sky, the seeping clouds spreading a milky white across the azure blue. Columns of black and white spruce rose with the elevation, a silent choir, huddled in robes of rich green that, after a late evening shower, shimmered under the reflecting light of the morning sun. "Beautiful here."

Maya spent the first day remembering how to fly fish. She didn't use the technique much in Florida, though some of her clients preferred the method. Here the sport was a popular way to catch salmon. She enjoyed the challenge, thought the experience would serve her well back home if she had a few days of practice.

"Use your wrist, keep the line level," Garrett said. "Let me show you. If you don't mind."

"Not at all. It's not my thing, but I want to get better."

By late morning Maya had her first bite but lost the fish. Okay, she thought, it's a start. She watched as the brothers hit on some hefty fish. The salmon would jump and spray, but they were no match for the boys. In the three days they fished together, she never saw either of them lose a fish. Water rushed around her, bubbling, cold. She rubbed droplets off her arm and shivered in the breeze. I'm spoiled, she thought. Our water temperatures are double this back home. She grinned as she cast into the stream. Back home.

The last night at the cabin, they sat around the dinner table reliving their days on the river. The sky darkened toward plum, the hazy light visible out the kitchen window beyond the treetops.

"Tell us about some of your clients," Patrick said. "You must have some great stories."

"Oh, I've got a few, but isn't there like guide-client privilege or something?"

"You've been watching too many *Law & Order* reruns," her father said, laughing.

She smiled, looked out the window. A large moose and her calf had entered the yard. "Look!" she said, pointing. "Wow, I had no idea they were so big!"

"Yeah, they're huge," Garrett said. "And you don't want to mess with them, particularly if a momma has a baby with her. They can be mean. Worse than bears."

Maya watched the animals feed. The mother had long, skinny legs but a powerful torso. The baby had a smaller snout, fuzzy young fur. Awkward and sweet.

"I'll keep my distance. Nothing like that in Florida."

"Enough stalling," Patrick said. "We're waiting for a story."

She sat back in her chair, sipped her second beer, a hoppy pale ale. She remembered one couple who'd chartered Bill's larger boat, the *Wake Up*. They were from Southern California, somewhere coastal. The guy had had a meeting in Miami, and his wife had agreed to join him if they could spend a few days at Cheeca Lodge, a high-end resort in Islamorada.

"For most of the ride out to the reef, all she talked about was Cheeca," Maya said. "That and the boutiques and restaurants in Islamorada. The guy was pretty chatty, too, but mostly about fishing. He kept complaining about Islamorada calling itself the Sport Fishing Capital of the World. Said he'd fished the Pacific for dorado, marlin, and sailfish and didn't see what the big deal was about catching fish in the Keys.

"He just kept going on and on about it. And of course I have to stand there and smile. Bill's in the cockpit, so he's not even dealing with this jackass. I'm nodding and hiding behind my sunglasses thinking I was really earning my keep.

"The wife eventually went into the salon, and then the husband started in about Miami. The traffic, the drivers, the parking. Like the guy had never been to L.A. before.

"We finally get a hit while we're trolling for mahi, and he opens the door to the salon to get his wife. Apparently she didn't fish much with him in California, so he wanted her to take the first one. She comes out, but she has absolutely no interest in catching a fish. Just wants to be left alone to play games on her phone. He starts making a big deal about it, like all she ever wants to do is shop and play games and ignore him, and here he spent all this money on this trip so they could do something together.

"Meanwhile, he sits in the chair to reel in the fish. It was a big dolphin, and it wasn't going down without a fight. You'd think he'd just focus on catching the fish, but he couldn't let it go. Just kept bitching and moaning about her shopping and her phone. Finally, she couldn't take it anymore. Told him to give her the damn rod and shut the hell up already.

"The wife took the rod and sat in the chair. The husband had been working the fish for several minutes, so the end was coming. After a few more minutes, the fish was close to the boat. I grabbed a gaff and stuck it, but the husband took the gaff out of my hands.

"He was sort of rude about it, too, just snatched it from me. I think he wanted to be the big hero to his wife. Such a dick."

Each of the men around the table snickered. Charlie folded his arms. He enjoyed the storytelling skills of his daughter. The memories of Saturday nights flooded him with nostalgia and affection.

"Did you let him bring the fish on the boat by himself?" Garrett asked.

"Oh yeah, I let him. Once he had the gaff, I backed off. So he reaches over the side and pulls the fish up while telling his wife to stand up and bring the rod toward the fish box. The fish is flopping around and blood is flying, but he is determined to finish this himself.

"With the gaff in one hand, he takes the rod from his wife, but the whole time he's going on about how the fish isn't as big as the dorado they catch at home, blah, blah, blah. I'm dying to say something, but I just walk over to the fish box and open the lid. He brings the fish over with him, but he's not quite sure how to do what is normally a two-person job of getting the fish off the gaff while holding the rod. Meanwhile the fish is spraying blood on him and the stern. Some got close to his wife's shoes, too, which was not helping."

"Clearly he hadn't thought this through," Patrick said, grinning.

"Clearly," Maya said. "I take a step toward him to help, but he waves me off. So I just stand there and watch. He tries to dump the fish in the fish box, but he can't get it off the gaff. Finally he shakes it loose, drops the gaff and reaches his hand back to me to hand him pliers, which I do. He bends over the fish box, digs around, and finally gets the hook out. He hands the rod to me, but before he can stand up the fish flops up in his face, smacks him right on the forehead, and he falls back into the boat. In the middle of all of this blood and mess. Which then splatters on his wife. Naturally."

Maya let out a laugh. The other three giggled like schoolchildren.

"I move toward him to help him up, but he waves me off. By this time, I can barely contain myself. He manages to get himself up and then realizes he's got fish blood all over not only himself, but his wife. She's just staring at him like she's going to kill him."

"What did she do?" Patrick asked.

"She calls him a fucking moron and grabs a towel from me, wipes herself off as best she can, leaves her shoes on the deck, and goes into the salon. She's back in ten minutes in a new outfit. Clean as a whistle. He is a fucking moron. But she's a fucking genius."

The men erupted with laughter. Patrick wiped tears from his eyes. Garrett laughed so hard he didn't make a sound. Charlie's Cheshire grin spread as his cheeks flushed to watermelon. Maya chuckled, shook her head.

"He was such an ass. But it shut him up for the rest of the day. He hadn't brought any other clothes, but he was too proud to turn around so we kept fishing. Caught a bunch more dolphin, too, and some tuna. Even had a wahoo steal some of our bait. It was a good day."

"Did Bill know this was going on?" Patrick asked.

"Oh, yeah, he saw the whole thing happen. But this was not Bill's first rodeo. He stayed upstairs and played dumb.

"That guy was something else. He was probably my worst client, though I had others who gave him a run for his money. His wife and him together, hilarious. Any more questions?"

"Only the most important one: Did he tip you?" Garrett asked.

"To his credit, he was a good tipper. But I don't think it was from embarrassment or to apologize. The guy had a huge ego, and with a huge ego sometimes comes a good tip."

"Was it worth it?" Garrett asked.

"I didn't think so at the time. But now that I've been able to entertain you guys, yeah, I think it was totally worth it." She crossed her arms and smiled as she sat back in her chair.

The seaplane pilot was waiting for them the next morning when they closed up the cabin and hiked to the lake. He took off over the water and circled back above the trees. In minutes they were staring at peaks and glaciers. Nothing like this in Florida, Maya thought, like the moose. Wonder if I could get used to it?

They landed in Anchorage and the boys packed their gear in Garrett's car. He drove them downtown to their hotel.

"You guys leave in the morning?" he asked.

"Yeah, we get a train up to Denali," Charlie said. "Can we buy you dinner?"

"I think we each need to report back," Patrick said, looking at his brother. "Right?"

"Bring your girlfriends, too. It's no trouble," Charlie said.

"We would, but they are in a bit of a tiff," Garrett said. "Until we work that out, we're keeping them apart. But listen, you guys have a great night and a blast up in Denali. Maya, send us an email, tell us all about it. We want to hear how much you love it. And send pictures." He winked at her and climbed out of the car to hug her goodbye and shake Charlie's hand.

"I don't know how to you thank you guys," she said. "It was great."

"Just make sure you pass some of that salmon around to Chris and your roommates," Garrett said. "And to your family at home, too, Charlie. We want more converts coming to Alaska. The right kind. People who want to get off the big ships and see the land."

"Text me when you're coming back to Florida. We'll get on some good fish. Maybe some tarpon next time?"

"We'll take you up on that," Patrick said. He hugged her goodbye. "Safe trip. Pack your bear spray."

Thirty-nine

FATHER AND DAUGHTER boarded a train in the morning for Talkeetna, a funky little town about a three-hour ride through the wilderness. Maya opened a book, but she couldn't take her eyes off the scenery. So beautiful, she thought. Vast. Amazing we haven't ruined it yet.

After checking into the lodge, they walked over to the ranger station and looked at the board of climbers who'd attempted to summit Denali so far that summer. Impressive, she thought. We're not so ambitious.

In the morning she grabbed a couple of raspberry cinnamon rolls from the Roadhouse and they headed for their tour. A floatplane would fly them with a few others into the park and land on a glacial lake. Guides would meet the plane and lead the small group on a hike.

"This is about the best thing I have ever eaten," she said, wiping glaze from the corner of her mouth. "Plus it's as big as your head. You have to try one."

Charlie lifted the dense pastry from the paper bag and bit into the doughy goodness. "Damn, I may never go home. We better be careful. We've already been weighed for the trip."

On these smaller planes, the airline weighed the passengers and their gear before letting them on board. The pilot would arrange the seating accordingly. He sat Charlie up front and placed Maya in the third row next to a photographer from Germany.

They were airborne in minutes. The pilot banked to the left and circled back toward the park. They passed forest and open fields strewn with pine. Maya looked down into the glacier as the plane flew through the mountains. The moraine made the ice look grey and tired, reminding her of Seaport's narrow, slushy streets on a February morning. Piles of peppered snow, dreary and waiting for the balminess of March to melt away the winter's dirt and sorrow.

The pilot banked again. Maya had a clear view of the side wall of Ruth Glacier. The crags and shadows gave way to blue waters hiding underneath. She knew the ice was cold and hostile, but the blue drew her in. Reminded her of Florida Bay, where the shallow green turned to topaz as the depth changed. Funny, she thought. Reminds me of home.

They landed on a lake in the middle of the park. The passengers deplaned and stared at the vertical walls of ice. Peaks of snow and moraine surrounded the narrow, green fields of tundra. Maya pictured a giant hand squeezing the earth until mountains squirted toward the sky. No place to go but up. She marveled at the enormity as they hiked the slope.

"I can't get over the size of everything," she told her dad. "I felt small before, but this is almost incomprehensible. In Florida I take up space. Here, I'm a speck of dirt."

"Reminds you how big the world is," he said. "And how beautiful it would be without us. Makes you wonder why we're here at all."

On the flight back the pilot circled the mountain. The sky clear, snow blowing off Denali made the mountain seem colder, distant, unattainable. More than twenty thousand feet above the ocean. She shook her head, bewildered by the number. I can't fathom it, she thought, then smiled to herself. Of course I can't. In my world, I think in depths, not heights.

The following day they boarded a train to the park's main entrance. She sat glued to the endless landscape passing by the window, her iPad tucked away in her bag. An eagle flew above the train, raced the locomotive to a stand of trees in the distance. They passed a creek, a moose wading through the icy water. Deep forest stretched so far away, the wood seemed to swallow the horizon whole.

The next morning they boarded a bus into the park. Denali had one road in and out, and private vehicles weren't allowed past the fifteen-mile mark without a permit. Maya had signed them up for a tour that would travel about halfway through the park in hopes of seeing wildlife and views of Denali. Neither was guaranteed. The bus might turn a corner and come upon a moose crossing the road, or the vehicle could be puttering along, the passengers unaware as a bear passed quietly behind.

Chances of viewing Denali were similar. On a cloudy day the peak could be outside the bus's windows and remain invisible beyond the clouds and fog. Tour bus drivers warned their clients they would be lucky to see the mountain at all.

Maya was cautiously optimistic, having learned to accept the moods of Mother Nature. Maybe they'd see a grizzly or snap a few photos of the mountain if it was "out" that day. She was ready with her phone. Her dad had a camera.

The tour started with the guide providing a short history of the park. "Most important," she said to her group, "is this video camera connected to the system on the bus, the drop-down screens above the seats. The camera can zoom in a good ways, so if you see something moving, yell and I'll try to get it on camera."

Charlie was skeptical about spending eight hours on a school bus, but within a half hour he was transfixed. Plodding along the dusty, winding road, they watched Dall sheep feed along the grassy hillside. A moose and her two young wandered down into the valley. Later in the morning the driver stopped the bus and turned to face the crowd.

"See those specks on the side of that slope? Wait 'til I zoom in. Might be a grizzly and her cubs." She focused the camera and the mother bear came into view. Two babies waited up the slope. "*Whoa*, hang on. The cubs are running uphill now."

The lore of a momma bear protecting her young unfolded on the screens above. The mother bear faced downhill as a male grizzly headed toward her.

"He's going after those cubs, and she's not having it," the driver said. "Watch her run him off."

The mother stood and roared at the brown male grizzly. He took a few more steps toward her and stopped for a moment before retreating downhill. She waited, then followed her cubs up the hill, looking back every few yards to keep the male away.

"Wow," Maya said. "Hope you got some pictures. I was too bug-eyed."

"Oh, I got some, don't worry," Charlie said.

Mid-morning the bus rounded a corner to find a moose standing beside a lake. The driver stopped to let people take photos and then started up again. As the bus headed down the road, a passenger shouted to the driver.

"Look! The moose just took off."

She stopped the bus again. "It's being chased," she said. She pointed the camera toward the scene. "See those three coyotes following the moose? Now look up there." She moved the camera up the hill. "Two more circling around the front. They're surrounding it."

The two approaching from the top of the hill closed in and forced the moose back toward the lake. The pack had their prey trapped. The moose scrambled and fell into the water. A back leg shot up in the air. Two coyotes pounced. The driver turned the camera away.

"That's nature for you, right there," Charlie said. "Doesn't get any more real than that."

More sightings followed into the afternoon. Sheep and moose. Caribou grazing on the high grass. A fox hiding beneath a bush. Sunlight and shadows at Polychrome Pass. An eagle flying across the valley floor. The mountain itself, out for the day. Rugged, snowy crests poking through wispy clouds into the wide open sky.

As the driver wrapped up her last story before the tour ended, a man near the front asked if she'd ever had a better outing given all the wildlife and views of the mountain they'd seen. "Well," she said, "you guys had a great day. Usually at the end of a tour I tell people, 'Don't feel bad you didn't see much. The animals are fickle. The mountain's sometimes covered in fog. Come back again. You'll see more next time.'

"You people," she said, stopping the bus and turning to look at her passengers, "should never come back to Denali." The travelers laughed and nodded. "You'll never have another day like you had today."

Charlie and Maya weren't ready for the afternoon to end. Since they had about another seven hours of daylight, they decided to hike a trail they'd been saving for the next day. The sun was out, and weather could be unpredictable. Better to make the attempt today. They were ready for some movement after so many hours on the bus.

The trail left from the main road and began with minimal change in elevation. Maya was still picturing the coyotes surrounding the moose, though her mind wandered to her own wild life back home. Her father broke the silence.

"What do you think so far? Enjoying the trip?"

"Oh, yeah. It's amazing, especially this morning. You?"

"Same." He noticed her serious expression. "You seem deep in thought."

"Chris emailed me this morning. Guess he had too much to say to send a long text. He asked about the trip, how you're doing. Then he said there's a job opening at a firehouse in Islamorada. A friend of his told him about it. One of the guy's buddies is moving to Miami."

"Is he telling you this because he's applying?"

"Better. He's asking if I want him to apply. Says he'd like to, but wants to make sure it's okay with me first." She looked at her father, smiled.

"I guess that's a 'yes' then, hmm?" He put his arm around her.

"Definitely a 'yes' with bonus points for asking first. Feels different this time. I think this is good."

They hiked in silence. She thinking of Chris, of the plans they would make, of life beside this gentle man. Charlie sneaking glances at his daughter. Reflecting on the passage of time, on reckonings, revelations. On the consequences of confession. Of the pain sowed by muted utterances, words blown across open valleys, sharp truth slicing through the low, green tundra scrub. The wind casting forth regret until all the lovely leaves tumbled away.

By the time they hit the switchbacks, their lungs were laboring. At the top they stopped and surveyed the view. Craggy peaks stretched across the expanse before them. Until the jagged edges faded into the chalky sky. Until the mind curved, bent, renounced belief that the land would ever end. That anything else, anywhere else, was possible.

"Unreal," he said. He drank some water and handed her the bottle. "Finish this one. I have two more." She drank the rest and wiped her mouth with the back of her hand, stuffed the empty bottle in her pack.

They took some photos and sat on a rock to rest, backs to the wind. Maya shivered when the clouds covered the sun. She pulled her cap down and tugged her sleeves over her hands.

"Cold? You want to head back?"

"Not yet. I'd rather sit awhile."

Charlie nodded, set his pack at his feet. Looked at the miles of wilderness stretched out before him. The mountain ranges faded from snowy white to pale blue to silvery grey before disappearing beyond the edge of the world. He stole a glance at his daughter, hesitated. It's time, he thought. Long past time for a lot of things.

"There's something I've been wanting to tell you. About your mother and me." He opened another bottle and took a long drink, offered it to her.

She shook her head, looked up at him. "What is it?"

He drew a deep breath, released. Readied his mind, his will, for the words he'd waited so long to say. "Her pregnancy with you wasn't a surprise to me. I sort of planned it."

Maya sat quietly for a moment. She stared at him until he met her gape.

"What do you mean, 'sort of planned it?' " Her breathing sped. "Either you did or you didn't. And why would you do that to her?"

"Because I loved her so much."

After their hike up Mount Monadnock his senior year, Charlie began to tune into Sierra in a different way. If she bought a magazine, he watched to see if she looked at the clothes or the travel articles. When she talked to her friends about colleges, he listened for clues that she might be thinking of leaving New England.

The summer after he graduated from high school was close to perfect. He was working full-time and hadn't started classes yet. Sierra had a job, but they were together most nights for at least a few hours, either alone or with friends. Saturdays were beach days. Sundays he made sure to take her somewhere, anywhere, out of town. A walk along the Marginal Way in Ogunquit. An afternoon at the New England Aquarium. Miles along the back roads of Massachusetts for an ice cream cone. He felt if he kept her moving, she'd be more likely to stay put.

When fall came he immersed himself in school and work. His limited time with her made him more attentive to what she might do. He held his breath as she collected brochures from all over the country. UCLA. Arizona State. Michigan. Miami. When packages arrived from UMass and Boston College and Maine, he breathed again.

She started applying in the fall. Northeastern had rolling admissions. Her acceptance arrived quickly. She was happy, but more were coming. Then UCLA offered a scholarship.

He couldn't remember when the idea came to him. Maybe sitting at the kitchen table together, Sierra reading through brochures while he worked on calculus problems. Maybe when they were in bed together, when he felt closest to her. Maybe when they were apart, when the fear of losing her was profound.

One night before their date, he took out a box of condoms and poked pin holes through each one. He knew it wasn't likely to work, but knowing only lessened the guilt. Wasn't enough to dissuade him. A couple of months passed without success. Finally, he changed tactics.

"Uh-oh," he said. He rolled off the bed. "It came off."

"What do you mean it came off?" Sierra threw off the sheet and ran to the bathroom. "Did you not put it on right?"

Charlie sat on the edge of the bed, stared at the carpet. Thoughts ricocheted around him, bounced off walls. What was I thinking? What if she's pregnant? He moved over when she returned, sat beside him. "Hey, it's going to be okay," he told her. He brushed her hair out of her face. She turned toward him, face drawn. He watched her fears race his for the nearest surface, skidding off the closet door, leaping toward the ceiling, circling the light fixture. College. Telling her parents. Raising a child. All their anxieties collided until they enveloped each other, choked off the air. Until the muddled mess strangled itself, collapsing on the carpet into a pile of worry, panting under the heat of the close room.

He put his arm around her, rubbed her neck. The weight of his actions flattened his shoulders. God, please don't let her be pregnant, he thought. I'm such a fucking idiot. If I love her so much, how could I do this to her?

Maya stared at her father. "I can't believe this. I, I need a minute." She stood, jammed her hands in her jacket pockets, strode across the broken rocks to the back side of the mountain as her mind whirled. How could he? And what am I supposed to do? She looked back at him, huddled against the cold. She thought of Chris and what she'd do in that situation. I'd leave him, she thought. But we're older.

Her dad had been young, desperate. Chris was mature enough to know a relationship had little chance of surviving such deception. If not for that, she realized, Chris might go to any lengths to keep them together. In love at eighteen, he may have done the same thing. She winced, kicked a stone down the path. I might've loved him anyway, she thought. She walked back across the windy plateau and sat beside her father. Looked out at the horizon, shook her head.

"Say something, Maya. At least tell me if you're mad." He pursed his lips, twisted the water bottle in his hands.

"I don't know what to say. Yeah, I'm mad you'd do that to Mom, or to any woman. Jesus, Dad! It's a total violation of her body, her rights, her trust. It's just wrong!"

"I know, I know. I knew the moment it happened. I was young and stupid. But I loved your mother so much. I couldn't bear the thought of her going to California. Plus I knew she liked some of the New England schools, so it wouldn't be such a sacrifice for her if she stayed close. But I know it wasn't up to me."

"Did you really think she'd go to college if she got pregnant? That she wouldn't do exactly what she did? Give up her dreams?"

"No, I didn't think that far ahead. I figured we'd make it work. She could commute to Boston or somewhere close and we'd raise a kid together. It was a selfish thing to do." He fidgeted with the bottle. "I've been wanting to tell you this for a long time. I wanted you to know who your father really is and who your mother really was. It's not that she didn't want you. The moment she saw your face it was over. She wouldn't have cared if she'd been accepted to college on Mars. It was like she grew an extra heart that day. She'd already given me one. She gave the other one to you.

"But there's another part of who your mother was, and as you get older I'm starting to realize you're just like her in that way. You know me. I'm a homebody. Give me a couch and a dog and I'm happy. Your mother was an explorer. She wanted to take you everywhere. Show you everything.

"I started all these Raymond Adventure stories when you were little so you'd remember your mom. I thought it would create memories that would keep us closer as a family somehow. What I didn't realize is those magical places we went on Saturday nights, had she lived we would have gone there anyway. Your mom would have packed us up and led us there.

"The irony is that by making up those adventures and trying to make you remember who she was, I completely forgot myself.

I should have known all along. I should have told you more real stories about your mother."

Maya thought of the bunnies in the backyard, of the small creatures running from her, of what her mother said. That we run from those we love. Maybe we're scared. Maybe we don't know why. She thought if her mother hadn't become pregnant, she would have left Seaport after high school. Gone to college somewhere far away. Run from the one who loved her. She and Charlie would have grown apart like most young couples.

Charlie remembered an afternoon in high school when Sierra had a dentist appointment. He drove her to the dentist's office. They sat together in the waiting room. He picked up a *Sports Illustrated*. She grabbed *Time*. As he flipped the pages to see the latest baseball news, he looked over to see her reading an article about the California coast.

Charlie was smart like Sierra, but in that moment he realized he wasn't curious like she was. She wanted to know random facts about places and the people that lived there. Saw lives in colors that Charlie didn't know existed. He was a black and white, primary color kind of guy. Sierra's world had eight shades of orange and a dozen shades of green.

Maya looked over at her father, his head in his hands, cheeks damp. She touched his arm, sighed. "I know you meant well."

"I did," he said, sniffling. "But it's not enough to mean well. You have to do what's right. I've never forgiven myself for what I did to your mother, and I'm not asking you to either. I just wanted you to know the truth."

She nodded. "I appreciate that. I have this feeling I need to forgive you, which is weird because if you hadn't done it I wouldn't even be here. Maybe not for me. Maybe for Mom."

"I understand." He patted her knee and took his hand away.

"So, did you tell anyone else? Did you ever tell her?"

"I did, kind of. I mean, yes, I did. I just don't know if she heard me. And I told Mikey."

Charlie explained that as Sierra weakened and the doctors could only give her medicine for the pain, he realized he needed to make his peace. One afternoon he and Mike were sitting on the front steps while a nurse checked on Sierra. Mike came around a lot in those final days.

"How are you doing?" he asked Charlie.

"Shitty, but so is everyone. Sierra's folks are a mess. I'm trying to figure out how to say goodbye. And some other stuff, too." He picked up a leaf from the walkway and tore off little pieces, let them blow away in the breeze. "There's something I never told her. Never told anyone. Feel like I should."

"Can you tell me? Or is it too personal?"

Charlie brushed the last bits of leaf from his hands. He thought telling his buddy might help, might make it easier to tell his wife.

"When Sierra got pregnant, it wasn't an accident. Not on my part." He looked at his friend and looked away. "I messed with the condom. I wanted her to get pregnant. So she wouldn't go to California."

Mike opened his mouth to speak but shut it. So much he wanted to say, but the guy was suffering. Wasn't his place to make him feel worse. He sighed.

"Geez, man. You never told her?"

"I was never able to. But I'm going to tell her today. She deserves to know."

"Are you kidding me?" Mike asked, no longer able to restrain himself. "She's your wife, the mother of your child, and she's in that house dying," he said, pointing behind him. "You think now is the time to tell her? You want that to be her last memory of you?

"For God's sake, Charlie, man up. If you're looking for forgiveness, go talk to Father Joe. This isn't about you anymore or your guilt or your relationship. You did something bad. Lucky for you, it turned out great. You guys have been happy together, and you have a great kid. It's not like that's what made her sick. The doctor told you her pregnancy had nothing to do with the cancer. Just let it go. Let her go."

He's right, Charlie thought. I feel guilty. But this isn't about making myself feel better. It's about Sierra knowing the person she married, what that person is capable of. She can decide how to remember me.

Later that afternoon, he sat beside her bed. She'd been dozing, drifting in and out. Over the last few days there were moments when she was with him and others when she was off in a dream. When she asked about Maya, he told her about the new words in their child's vocabulary. Cantaloupe was the latest. She said it over and over as her grandmother handed her chunks of melon, the juice dribbling down her chin. Sierra smiled at the image.

In the next breath he told her about a new family moving in down the street. Maya had already played with their young daughter. Sierra's eyes flitted back and forth as she stared at the wall, her mouth a flat line. He couldn't tell if she'd heard a word.

So that afternoon, he didn't know what to expect. Sierra had been sleeping, but when she woke she reached over toward him. Her eyes were closed.

"Sierra," he whispered. "There's something I want to tell you."

"Mmmm?"

He pulled his chair closer to the bed, held her hand. "Before you got pregnant, I was hoping you would."

She smiled, opened her eyes into slits.

"Then I did more than hope. I started poking holes in condoms. And that time it slid off, it didn't slide. I did it on purpose. I wanted you to stay home. Not go to California or Siberia or anywhere else. I wanted to be with you. I'm sorry. I should have told you then, but I didn't know how. I just thought you should know."

Her smile remained while he spoke. She looked at him with the same sleepy expression. He wasn't sure she'd heard him or understood what he'd said.

"I love you," she whispered. "I always will."

"I told her," Charlie said to Maya, "but I'm not sure she heard me."

Maya looked at her father, at his long gaze out across the horizon. She noticed the grey seeping into his hair. Saw the wrinkles undulating across his skin, the rise and fall of waves left by years of regret. No, she thought. Waves wash away our sins. His brow, his eyes, his jaw, those creases are not the remnants of water washing gently across a smooth surface. They're the niches left within rock from the chipping away of joy, peace. Her father had made a choice, and the consequences of his choice had sculpted the contours of his face, his soul, his life.

They sat quietly for a moment. His actions had kept her mother home, she thought. That was why he'd never moved on. He'd stolen her freedom and never forgiven himself. She tilted her head and looked at her dad. He'd been sad for more than twenty-five years. Spent his whole life trying to fix things, people. Time for someone to fix him.

"She heard you, Dad. She loved you anyway. Maybe she loved you more." She paused. "To be honest, I think if she hadn't gotten pregnant, Mom would have wanted to go away to college. She had the same wanderlust I have. It's in our DNA. But I also believe it would have been a much harder decision than you realize. I think she loved you as much as she loved the idea of leaving." She sat a moment, looked at her father.

"She heard you. Who knows, maybe she knew all along. Maybe she thought what you did allowed her to avoid making the hardest decision she'd ever have to make. In the end, I think she believed it was meant to be.

"I don't have to forgive you for Mom. Mom already did."

Charlie put his arm around his daughter, pulled her close. He wiped his eyes and looked out over the mountain ranges disappearing before him, the outer edges of his pain beginning to dissolve into the thin air.

He took a bag of trail mix out of his pocket and poured some into his palm before passing the bag to his daughter. She chewed on a peanut and raisin and thought about her mother and what it must have been like to be pregnant so young. She tried to imagine what she would have done. Would she have been willing to give up her freedom to raise a child?

Maybe I wouldn't have been able to go through with it, she thought. Would have ended the pregnancy and run away. I'm good at that. Maybe it's not wanderlust that keeps me from staying in one place. But the fear that whatever I'm running from will catch me.

She gazed at the expanse of land and sky before her. Such a

beautiful part of the world. I'm glad I came. But it's time to go home.

Charlie looked at the next peak and the one behind that and a third off in the distance. He thought about Sierra and how her face changed when she stood on the top of a mountain. He wondered if Monadnock would have been enough for her, or whether there always would have been another mountain to climb.

That night Charlie and Maya sat across from each other, nursing pints of Alaskan Amber.

"What do you think?" he asked. "Salmon, salmon, or something with salmon?"

"Salmon burrito for me. Haven't tried that yet."

"Sounds good." He closed his menu. "Tell me what's going on. You were quiet on the hike down. And when I woke up from my nap, I spotted you sitting outside sketching. Haven't seen you do that in a while. What's up?"

She hadn't drawn anything in some time. Life at home was busy. Since she was a kid, she'd only been moved to draw when she was relaxed and thoughtful.

When they'd finished the hike, she'd felt the urge. She found some stationery in the desk in the room and grabbed a pen and phone book to lean on. Sat outside and put the book and paper in her lap, rubbed the skin of the sheet between her fingers. Not mountains this time, she thought. She drew a horizontal line and some small waves. A structure grew out of the water. Alligator Light. Seagulls flew in the distance.

"I was thinking about the trip and how great Alaska is. And also that I don't want to move here. It's awesome and I may want to come back someday, but it's not home."

"So what is home? Do you know?"

"Might just be Islamorada." She sipped her beer. "Maybe I needed some time away to have some perspective. Or I needed to come to a place like this, somewhere I've always wanted to see with all this beautiful country open in front of me." She reached her arms out to the side. "It's like the whole world is here in Alaska, and I love it. But when our time here is over, I want to go home. And by home, I think I mean Islamorada.

"It seems weird to finally be sorting this out, but also really good. I've been wondering for the last few years if I was ever going to find a home anywhere, or if I'd constantly have the urge to pull up stakes and leave. Not anymore. I feel like I belong there."

Charlie sat back in his chair and folded his arms. This was good news, he told himself. She wasn't running to some far-flung river to guide fishing trips under the midnight sun. She wouldn't be in Boston, but she'd be close enough. He smiled at her.

"Does Chris have something to do with that?"

She shifted in her seat. "If you had asked me a week ago, I would have said no, or I don't know. But now that he's trying, yeah, that's part of it. Maybe I feel more permanent about the place because I can see him there with me now.

"When I was in Key West, something was holding me back. Maybe subconsciously I thought we needed to get a little separation from his family. When I moved to Islamorada, I felt like I was starting to find my groove. My work was more challenging. I went out on Bill's boat by myself. Then I got my own boat. My boat. My business. But something was missing. At first I thought it was the place, that I might need to move again. I was starting to worry I would never feel settled, that a breeze would blow and I'd pack my stuff and move somewhere new. Now that Chris is offering to leave Key West, I'm pretty sure that's what was missing.

"It's not that I need to move whenever the wind blows. I just had to find reasons to stay." She smiled, blushed. That old familiar chill ran up her spine. Maybe Mom agreed.

She climbed into bed that night and pulled out her phone. She hadn't responded to Chris. They had a busy schedule, cell service was spotty. She read his email again.

She pictured him sitting at his kitchen table, typing the email and trying to come across as excited but not pushy. He wouldn't want to pressure her. To offer to move was a big step. He would have agonized over the decision, discussed it with his mother and sister and uncle, made sure they would bless this change. She came to the end of his message and read the last sentence. "Do you want me to apply for the job?" She saw him scrolling back through the email, checking that the autocorrect hadn't changed any of his words. This is important, he'd be thinking. She imagined him leaning his elbows on the table, reading through the message again. Hitting send.

She saw him put the phone down, clear his plate, move to the sink. Wash his dishes, push in his chair, wipe down the table. That's what I want, she thought. That's what's missing. Having someone you know so well you can predict every movement. You see the smile before the cheek dimples. Feel the rough skin before the hand grabs yours. You walk into the bathroom after he's showered, and you smell the soap mingling with the steam. It smells different from when you shower. It's his scent. Warm and familiar. Chris.

Maya read his email again. I do, she typed. She hit send, sat back, wiped her cheek. I do.

Forty

FATHER AND DAUGHTER PARTED WITH A PLAN for Maya to come home for her birthday in September. Charlie returned to Seaport and hit work full stride. He'd managed emails and texts while away, but his cousin Todd had looked after Charlie's jobs along with his own projects. Charlie needed to check that his guys were on track, get back into the feeling of work. Of building something.

He spent the summer moving through the rooms of his house with presence and purpose. The TV ran, Archie tapped across the floor, but the air was different. He opened the windows and kitchen door when he returned at night. The screen door pattered soft refrains in the breeze as the stress of the day drifted out. He watched the Sox play with the sound off, rubbing Archie's back in long, slow movements that calmed both man and dog. He slept at depths new and dark and quiet.

One morning he woke from a dream. Sierra had been there,

in the room. She kissed his cheek and backed away, let his hand drop from hers as she waved goodbye. Wait, he told her, I'm still here. She tilted her head and smiled, blew him a kiss and stepped into the dark. He lifted his hand to tell her to stop, then blew her a kiss and waved. Goodbye, he thought. Goodbye, Sierra.

As he turned away from her he found himself sitting in Fenway Park. Bottom of the fifth, Sox up 4-2 over the Orioles. A batter approached the plate. Two outs, two men on. The crowd cheering, whistling, laughing. Charlie looked up as a woman sat down beside him. She was turned away, but her hand brushed his arm. The batter took the first pitch, a called strike. Charlie looked down at his arm. He watched the hair rise, the skin sensing something, someone. On the second pitch the bat smashed the ball, launched it over the Green Monster. Spectators jumped up, hands in the air, screamed and clapped. The woman stood and looked at him. Charlie rose and raised his hand. She high-fived him and smiled. He couldn't see her face.

The eastern sky lightened as Charlie drove to the office. He met with Todd, asked his cousin to check on a couple of his jobs. Charlie had an appointment and would be gone for the day. He drove west, the windows down, air cool. The dew was still drying on the lawns of Massachusetts when he crossed into New Hampshire. He pulled into the lot, grabbed his pack, and headed for the trailhead. Took the steep trail.

He remembered the hike up Monadnock with Sierra. She was a fast hiker, happy to pass people on the trail on her way to the top. He kept up but let her lead. This was her thing, her love, to be climbing, moving forward, upward. For him, motion hadn't mattered. Standing still hadn't mattered. What mattered was having her with him.

Time to find the joy in movement again, he thought. One foot in front of the other. Go somewhere. Look out across a valley. Think about what other people are doing. Who's mowing their lawn? Who's taking their kids to the beach? Wonder about something.

He followed the trail, watched his footfalls, a tree swaying in the breeze, the shadow of a boulder on the side of the path. Stopped, sat on a rock, took out a bottle, wiped his forehead. The water was cold, clean. He picked up a small stone, grey and beige with a streak of rust running through the middle. He turned it over and over, rubbed the rugged granite under his thumb. Squeezed the stone and set it on the ground. A small part of the world, he thought.

At the summit he walked around the top, looked out over the towns below. He thought about his family, Sierra and Maya. What they could have had, what they did have. He wondered how many people out there were as lucky as he. He laughed to himself. None.

Two women came up beside him to look out over the vista.

"That view is something else," one said to the other.

"Yup," the second replied. "I loved coming here as a kid. Seemed so much grander then. The mountain, the view. Now everything seems smaller, but more beautiful. I don't think I appreciated this place enough."

She backed up to put her bag down and stumbled, knocked into Charlie and grabbed his arm. "Oh, I'm so sorry!" she said.

"Don't worry about it," he laughed. "Happens to me all the time. Here, let me get that." He handed her the cap that had fallen from her head. He noticed the red B on the front. Nice touch, Sierra, he thought, and smiled again. He winked at the woman, tipped his cap. The hair on his arm rose. He headed down the trail.

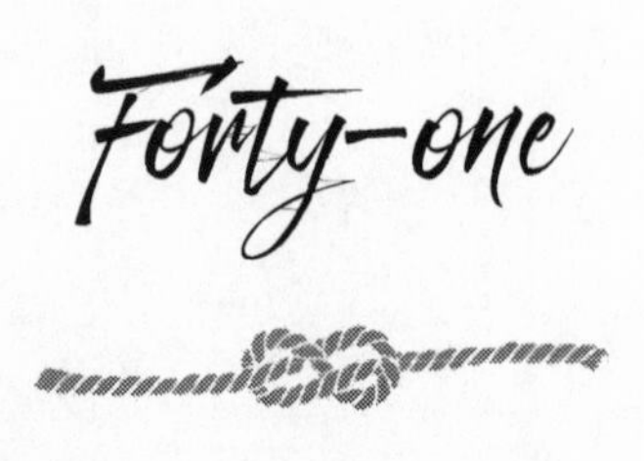

Forty-one

MAYA'S RETURN FROM ALASKA was similar to Charlie's. She had a full summer of bookings scheduled. The moment the airport shuttle pulled away, she focused on fishing. She spent the next day preparing for the stream of clients. Checked the engine, cleaned the hull, organized her tackle, collected bait. After a few days, she felt like she'd never left.

Chris applied for the position in Islamorada. They discussed what would happen if he landed the job, what would happen if he didn't. If he moved to Islamorada, they'd live together. If he didn't, they'd have to have a different conversation. In soft moments, poling through the shallows, or late at night, whispering into the phone on her pillow, Maya considered moving back to Key West. She held her breath while they waited.

He got the job, and life changed quickly. For the first couple of weeks they stayed in Maya's room at Mark's house. Then they found a place to rent and began the complicated dance of combining lives. Things each took for granted as personal decisions were negotiated, sometimes without discussion, as they merged their solitary pasts. Grocery lists. Laundry folding. Where the mail collected at the end of the day. Heavy sighs. The biting of tongues. In the quiet moments of compromise and contrition, they built bookshelves, hung photos. The words not said turned the tango into a waltz and finally a close, slow dance.

As Maya adjusted to a life with fewer closed doors, she found comfort in the solitude of longer runs. She frequented the bike path along U.S. 1 and explored the neighborhoods off the main highway. When she wasn't rushed, she drove south to Long Key State Park, where a loop trail of just over a mile wound through shady hammock, the packed sand leading to open views of the ocean as the path dipped close to the water. She ran laps as she cleared her mind.

One morning she awoke without a plan. She'd had a half-day trip the day before, and the boat was clean and healthy and resting in its slip. No clients scheduled. The wind blowing just enough to keep a last minute day-tripper from looking for a backcountry outing. Chris was working. What to do, she thought. First, a run.

She threw on a shirt and running shorts, jumped in the truck, headed south. She passed the ranger station, turned into the parking area, and prayed to the running gods she'd have the trail to herself. She smiled as she rounded the corner. No cars in the lot.

She laced up and set her watch, shook out her legs to see what kind of run this would be. Two laps if she was tight. Four if an average day. If she felt loose and relaxed, six or eight. She drew a deep breath and hoped for seven.

Maya entered the hammock and curled through the trail, skipped over roots and around the trunk of a poisonwood tree. She emerged in a clearing. Tiny crabs raced across her path, the small creatures diving into holes as she hopped over them. The tide was out, the trail dry. She drifted off into her runner's daydream, keeping one eye out for a slow-moving hermit crab or startled black snake.

The morning was warm, the sun already singeing the air. An occasional wind gust blew in from a roving storm cloud, teasing the cooler temperatures of the coming fall. More moons passing doesn't matter as much anymore, she thought. The waxing and waning, the movement of time. I don't fear the turning pages of the calendar any longer. Maybe that means something. About me, my dad. About this place.

She looked up at the sky as a cloud moved in to block the sun. Nice of God to provide me a break from the glare. Then she thought better. No, that's not it for me, at least not now. Maybe for some, brings them comfort. For me, it's my mother. She's up in the heavens, gazing out over the world, looking for me and my dad. Sun so bright she shields her eyes while she finds us. Her hand provides the respite. That's the image I conjure.

The sun glinted off the rippling waves as the cloud rolled away.

Maya settled into a rhythm after a couple of laps. More focused in the rooted hammock sections, a bit faster on the open sand, with an occasional nod to the Atlantic as she rounded the curve toward the trailhead. With each breath she drifted into memory. The night before when she'd come home from the marina, she'd left her bag in the kitchen and headed to shower. Chris had just finished. He stood at the sink with a towel around his waist, combing his hair and smiling as she entered. She leaned in and kissed him, and he reached out and touched her waist. He let his hand linger a moment and told her he would start dinner.

She showered and pulled back the curtain, stepped onto the rug to dry her hair. Moved to the sink and grinned at the beer he'd left by her hairbrush. That's my guy, she thought.

Maya remembered that moment as she finished her last lap. She walked for a few minutes to cool down, paused by the beach. Looked out to the east, to the fine line where green met blue. I'm always looking out, she thought. Never seem to look in, look back. She turned and faced the mangroves behind her. A cardinal fluttered from the ground to a low tree branch. She searched past its wings. Saw the gnarled roots and fading leaves, the damp sand and rocks. The front yards of Ocean Drive in Seaport, the back alleys of Key West. She thought back through the places of her life. Maybe finding home isn't about finding where you'll be, she thought. Maybe it's finding where you are. Maybe that's where contentment waits.

She considered the way life is sliced into moments. How some moments last for seconds, others for hours, and still others endure for years. How some intersect over the course of a lifetime, sometimes traveling in parallel. Some run like a current under the ocean before a wave breaks at the shore and folds back underneath itself. Or in fury, one moment pierces another at the heart, the blade plunging until life seeps away. Until the soul of the broken moment passes on. And how some moments cling to the life of another. Perhaps desperate, parasitic. Or merely in love.

I try so hard to grasp these moments, she thought. To line them up single file so I can take inventory and shine them with a soft cloth. If only life were so simple. If only I could control the moments of my life, hold them to my chest, struggling, until they surrender to my embrace. No, what good would that be? I should hold them close, but only when they're young, when they're growing, the tufts of their newness still soft on their infant heads. I should cradle them, rock them to sleep, and when they wake, let them take flight. I should hope all the moments of my life learn to soar.

She turned and walked toward the trailhead. Crossed the bridge that led back to the parking lot and stopped to watch an egret stepping through the shallows of low tide. She smelled the ocean meeting the earth, the decay of fallen leaves. Another season past.

That night she came home to candles and flowers and a missing piece of her life waiting on bended knee. Another season to come. A home. A life.

"PLEASE APOLOGIZE TO YOUR DAD FOR ME," Chris said days later when he dropped Maya at the airport. "I feel so bad I can't come."

"Will you stop worrying? He knows you just started a new job. He'll see you when he comes down for Thanksgiving." She kissed him goodbye.

"I'm just sorry we won't spend your birthday together. But we'll celebrate again when you get back. Promise." He pulled her in for a long hug.

Maya stowed her bag and climbed into the window seat. Tuesday morning, flight half full. A man slept in the aisle seat. The middle was empty.

She pulled a sketch pad out of her bag. Since Alaska she'd

been drawing when she had a few minutes. It relaxed her, took her mind away from bookings and the cost of fuel.

First she sketched Tennessee Reef Light. Smaller than Alligator Light, less dramatic. She'd had clients in from Knoxville the week before who'd asked for a ride by the lighthouse. The image had stayed with her.

She flipped the page and considered what to draw next. She looked out at the clouds. One had a white and jagged peak. Reminded her of Denali. She rested her pencil tip against the pad. Nah, she thought. Not feeling the mountains today.

She gazed out the window and wondered what mesmerized people. Mountains were majestic, mysterious. Lighthouses, too, captivated. Was it size? Shape? The abrupt height against the sky? There was romance in conquering a mountain, reaching the summit. Also romance in life alone at sea. She glanced at the cloud again. The peak faded.

Maybe they both represent something away, something other than where we stand. They show us possibilities. We can rise, search for more. She shook the thought from her head.

She thought of George and Linda and the boys. They had a small home. Money was tight. But George never wanted more than he had.

Gladys, Thomas. When Maya told Thomas about the rainbow flag, the news seemed bittersweet. Thomas felt closer to his mother, savored their relationship. But he regretted not knowing his father better. Maya never had a relationship with her mother, but the cause was out of her hands. She couldn't imagine having the opportunity to be close to someone she loved and letting that chance slip away.

Moments like these made her wonder what her mother would have been like. Maybe they would have fought. Maybe she would have driven Maya farther than Florida. Or maybe they would have been close, best friends, and Maya would have stayed home. Maybe there would have been a brother or sister.

Maybe her father would have told her mother the truth, and she would have left. Screw you. I'll make my own Raymond Adventure. Maya doubted that but had no way of knowing. Since that's the case, she thought, I prefer my fantasy of what she was like, what we would have been like together. She was air, sunlight, beauty, love. That's the photograph I'll keep of her.

She tapped her pencil against the pad. Drew a straight line. The horizon. Flat, unknown. In front she drew two chairs on a beach. Sunset. She looked at the simple drawing. I can hike to the peak of every mountain, climb to the lantern room of every lighthouse, she thought. Or I can sit on the beach with the person I love and feel the hourglass sand flow through my fingers.

"HEY, SWEETHEART," CHARLIE SAID. He reached out for a hug. "Good flight?"

"Yeah, good." She kissed his cheek. "Chris said to tell you again he's sorry he can't be here."

"I know, he texted me as soon as he dropped you off. He's a good guy." Charlie glanced sideways at his daughter.

She smiled, a broad smile, deep. "Yeah, he sure is."

Maya spent much of the week visiting people and places. She reconnected with high school friends she hadn't seen since graduation. Stopped by the marina to see the fishermen who'd first taken her out on the water. She told them about her business. They exchanged fish stories. Coming back to Seaport felt different now. Her return felt conclusive, like she was closing a loop she hadn't known she'd left open.

On her twenty-ninth birthday the family gathered at Karen's house. Her uncle worked the grill. Her cousins came for dinner. They lived between Seaport and Boston, away but close. Maya loved watching them together. One teased another and the third jumped in. Two on one for a moment, until one made a joke and a second switched sides. It was a constant tussle of energy, drawing their parents in with laughter and knowing looks from years of first days of school and Christmases, ski trips and bad dreams. They were different from her and her dad in how they expressed affection. She and Charlie chopped vegetables and told stories. Karen's family wrestled and raced and watched Bruins games. In the end they all parted the same way, holding fast and true.

After dinner Karen took out a chocolate cake with a two and a nine stuck in the icing. The family sang. Maya cut pieces and passed plates.

"Your first 'last' birthday," Karen said. "How does it feel?"

Maya laughed. "Feels weird. Like it got here too quickly."

Charlie smiled. "They all feel that way. Quicker every year."

On Maya's last night in town, Charlie had a special evening planned. They drove up to Portsmouth. He led his daughter into an Italian restaurant where he'd reserved a table.

"I'm not going to drink, but if you want something, feel free," he told her.

"No, I'm good, thanks." She looked around the room. "This is great. The old brick walls and beams on the ceiling. Neat old building."

"I've always loved this place. I took your mother here once for Valentine's Day. I'd earned a bonus from Grampa and wanted to do something special. Was I surprised. Right after the cannoli she told me she was pregnant with you. Blew my doors off. I'd been holding my breath for weeks hoping my plan had failed and thought maybe I was safe. But she'd taken a pregnancy test and it was positive. She couldn't believe it. Said she didn't know how to tell me. Then there it was, right there on the table between us. I didn't know how to tell her."

"What did you do? You must have freaked out. Even after everything you'd planned."

He sipped his water. "I did freak out, initially. Couldn't speak. But I rallied. Figured it was meant to be. I loved your mother so much, I told myself fate was giving me the way to keep her. I couldn't bring myself to tell her then. Was afraid I'd lose her. So I played like the hero.

"I've been thinking about it lately, how I waited so long to tell her, when she was already dying. I know what you said, that she heard me, and maybe she did. But I think by that time, it didn't matter anymore. She loved me and you so much, I could have told her anything. Your mother, the saint she was, would have forgiven me, would've said it was meant to be. That God helped us along so we'd have you. So when she was gone, I wouldn't be alone." Charlie looked around the room, swallowed, cleared his throat.

"I haven't been back here since that night with your mom. But this is a special place, because in my mind, when I let myself off the hook, it's where my life with you began. That's why I wanted to take you here. Plus the chicken parm will knock your socks off."

He winked at his daughter. Hoped she didn't notice his watery eyes. She did.

The server came and set plates on the table in front of them with the warning they were hot from the oven. Maya cut a piece of the chicken, twirled the melting mozzarella around her fork, dunked it in the thick sauce, blew on the end before biting.

"Oh, man, you weren't kidding." She sat back in the booth,

wiped her mouth, smiled at her father. "If you love this place so much, why haven't we come here before?"

Charlie took a slice of garlic bread from the basket and dipped it in the marinara. Bits of crunchy crust fell to his plate as he chewed on the buttery middle, the garlic and tomato sauce settling on his taste buds.

"Because of what this place meant. Because I should have told your mother the truth sooner. I thought if I brought you here, you'd sense I was hiding something. And I wasn't ready to tell you yet. I was afraid. I needed to get over my fear, tell you the truth, before I could share this place with you." He paused. "But I'm glad I did. I've always wanted to take you here."

"Then this is a great place for us to have an in-person Raymond Adventure story," she said. "How does Italy sound?"

"Sounds great."

Together they wove a tale of Tuscany. A gondola ride through Venice. Pasta at a café in Rome and pizza in Naples. Then they planned a trip for the following summer with Chris. The Yucatán Peninsula awaited the three of them in the fall.

"Dad," Maya said when they'd returned from their journey, "do you still feel like Mom's with you?"

Charlie wiped his mouth on his napkin and sat back in his seat. "Sometimes, though I'm starting to see it's time for me to get out and meet more people. Maybe go on a date. Experience something outside my little world of Seaport and work and family. I've never had the courage to explore like your mother had, and I think I've used her memory as a crutch as well as an excuse to avoid venturing out in the world. Because I didn't want to leave her behind."

"Is it hard still having her around?"

"Yes and no. It's hard because I want to touch her. But

there's comfort in having her near me." He sipped his water, paused.

"I have to stop living with her ghost. I used to want things. Or not things, but the feel of things. Archie's coat. My old Sox blanket. Over the years I've drifted through my days, not feeling much of anything. But the other night, Archie jumped up on the couch and I stroked his head. I felt his fur on my skin. He licked me, and I rubbed the dampness from my hand. I was feeling it in that moment. Then I felt this warmth. Like a breath coming back into my body. Weird, right?"

"Not weird. Letting go, moving forward. That's what we all talk about, moving on, finding your place. I mean, I love Chris, and I'm thrilled we're taking this next step. But I still have no idea what I'm doing. I figure as long as I keep feeling, it'll come to me at some point, or just happen." She paused.

"I had this guy on the boat a few weeks ago with his son. The kid was about eight or nine, and he loved fishing. He would watch his dad bait a hook with this incredible focus. And the dad clearly loved fishing, too, but he was completely dialed in to his kid having fun. Like he had a sense this would be an important day in their lives.

"As he was leaving at the end of the day, he thanked me almost with tears in his eyes. His son was out of earshot, and he told me it was the first real outing they'd had since his wife died a few months before. He said it was great being out on the water with me, because he felt like I didn't just take them fishing, that I guided them through this special moment. What he said to me was really beautiful."

She looked out the restaurant window. A car stopped to let a couple cross the street. They waved a thank-you to the driver and jogged to the curb. She turned back to her father.

"Some days I reach over the side of the boat and feel the salt water. It's soft like the fleece inside mom's old sweatshirt. Sometimes when I run I sprint the last quarter mile until I can't breathe. When I'm done, I'm doubled over, panting, sweat's dripping off my back. I love those moments because they remind me I'm alive and doing something, feeling something. Getting somewhere. It's all out there, and I just have to keep trying to find it. Even if I have no clue what 'it' is.

"Then sometimes I have a day like the one with the guy and his son, and I remember what you told me a few years ago, that what I'm doing matters. And I think I may already be where 'it' is. Maybe it found me. Maybe I finally let it."

The next day Charlie drove Maya to the airport. He pulled up to the curb for departures and jumped out of the truck, set her bag on the sidewalk. She put her head on her father's chest. He wrapped his arms around his daughter.

"You be good. Wear a hat and lots of sunscreen." He laughed, pulled away, wiped his eyes. "Give my best to Chris. And call me when you get home. Okay?"

"I will. And thanks for a great birthday." She looked at her father's face. The wrinkles didn't seem so deep. Didn't seem to be chiseled into rock. More like they were ebbing with the waves. Like she could watch them drift out to sea. She tilted her head, smiled. "We'll be okay. I can feel it." She kissed his cheek, took the handle of her bag, and headed for the terminal.

Charlie rested his hand on the side of the truck. The metal was warm.

Epilogue

MAYA PULLS THE CAST NET AND EMPTIES THE LAST of the pinfish into the live well. She stows the net and starts the engine, points the boat away from the mangroves and into open water. She crosses the channel, speeds under the bridge, heads east. Away from the setting sun.

She lowers the throttle as she approaches the lighthouse, lets the boat drift with the current in the shadow of late afternoon. A breeze ruffles her ponytail. She turns off the engine, settles back in her seat. "Hi, Mom," she whispers. Squints into the last rays of the day.

So much going on now, she thinks. I should come here more often. Get away from the tourists and the wedding plans and whatever else makes the days flee before I can stop and savor them. Be a part of them. She looks up at Alligator Light, breathes in the salt cascading off the blowing wind. Glances out at the horizon, back to shore. To her home. Her life.

She reaches under her collar and pulls a chain out from under her shirt, opens the clasp and places the chain and ring in her hand. Rubs the tarnished gold. "Charlie and Sierra" still legible on the inside of the band. "I wish you were here," she says to the wind. "Just for one day. I wish we had just one day together. I wish I knew you." She pauses, turns her face to the wind. "I hope you know me." She reclasps the chain around her neck and tucks the ring under her shirt. Sits for a moment. The boat rocks with the waves. The wind draws a few briny tears from the corners of her eyes.

Maya starts the engine and heads back to the marina. She pulls into the slip, empties the pinfish into the bait pen, sets her gear on the dock. She hoses down the boat, wipes the seats dry. Starts toward the truck, stops to take a last look at the skiff. "Night, Duke," she says, smirking at the pet name she's kept to herself. No need to share him with the world. Let them have the other name. She smiles at the words painted on side of the boat, turns to walk down the dock.

Squish the Fish.

Author's Note

HURRICANE IRMA

I wrote the first draft of this book in December 2015 and January 2016, well before Hurricane Irma came ashore in the Florida Keys and tore so much natural beauty into bits and pieces. Many people in the Keys remain devastated by the storm. I hope anyone still feeling the effects of the wind and water finds peace and strength with each passing day of sunshine.

One sad remnant of the storm was the destruction at Long Key State Park. The loop trail Maya runs, the Golden Orb Trail, is one my husband and I have run for years. That small dirt path holds a special place in my heart. When we were able to return to the trail months after Irma, we were devastated by the damage. Mangroves stripped bare. The trail unrecognizable in many places, some areas completely blown open. The main bridge that closes our little loop wiped out. A gut punch.

We're fortunate that the hardworking women and men of the Florida State Parks and the Friends of Islamorada Area State Parks are assisting Mother Nature with the slow rebuilding process. It will be decades before the mangroves return to their stature before the storm, but we're already seeing the results of the labor and love of these folks. I'll be passing along some of the proceeds from the sale of this book to the Friends. If you love nature, please consider doing the same. Or giving to any state, national, or local park in your area affected by storms, wildfires, or other natural disasters.

Acknowledgments

I'm thankful for a lot of people in my life, more than I can mention here. So many of you asked about the book along the way, encouraged me. Thank you all for that love and support. A few were part of the process.

Lisa Carman gave me a copy of Stephen King's *On Writing* as I started this project. King's lessons helped me focus my time and set reasonable goals for completion. Thank you, Lisa, for the book and the encouragement you sent with it.

Caren and Blain Brinson read the sections involving fishing and provided valuable comments. Many of the technical points in the story are based on lessons I learned on their boat. Thanks for the information and all the mahi and tuna Bob and I have enjoyed over the years. Captain Camp Walker answered my questions about life as a guide in the Keys and fishing for particular species. I'm grateful for his willingness to share his time and knowledge with me. Christine and Rich Fogel provided valuable commentary on the medical scenes, both Gladys's heart attack and the effects of the bombing. Thank you both for sharing your expertise and support in this process. Any inaccuracies in the book, whether regarding fishing, medical descriptions, or otherwise, are entirely mine.

Jenn and Bob Sampson read my first few pages and convinced me I had a story to tell. Jenn was also the first reader of the first full draft. I'm thankful that her ability to read so quickly made waiting for that initial review short and painless. I'm also thankful for Kathryn Ortega and Paula Pagnini, who followed soon after. All three of these women provided constructive, thoughtful, and loving support as I worked from the first draft to the ones that would follow.

Oscar Rivera also read an early draft. He wasn't happy that the story failed to include car chases and flying bullets, but his visceral response to the truth about Charlie made me realize I could reach different people with the flaws of my characters. Thanks for always being there for me.

Richard Miller and Shari Lauer read drafts during the doldrums, when I was trying to figure out how to move the project forward. They helped me realize I had something, but something that needed more work. Kathy Shearin provided a boost as I entered the final stages of editing. Thanks to all of you for your thoughts and encouragement.

The Gainesville Poets & Writers group was invaluable to the final crafting of this novel. I knew I had a good story. They helped me make it a better book. Thanks to all the wonderful folks who attend those Tuesday night sessions. Special thanks to Cassie Selleck and Jani Sherrard for the additional reading and guidance. I would have been proud to have published a novel. But without your help, I wouldn't be nearly as proud of this one.

Finally, thanks to my greatest love and fan, my husband, Bob. I had many moments of doubt during this process. You never did. For that and so many other reasons, I'm forever grateful to and for you.

I love you all.

Fern

Made in the USA
Middletown, DE
13 December 2019